BLOOD & BONES: TRIP

Blood Fury MC, Book 1

JEANNE ST. JAMES

Jeanne ST. JAMES

Acknowledgements:

Photographer: Dante Dellamore

Cover Artist: Golden Czermak at FuriousFotog

Cover Model: Robert Kelly

Editor: Proofreading by the Page

Beta readers: Whitley Cox, Andi Babcock, Sharon Abrams & Alexandra Swab

Blood Fury MC Logo: Jennifer Edwards

Warning: This book contains explicit scenes, some possible triggers and adult language which may be considered offensive to some readers. This book is for sale to adults ONLY, as defined by the laws of the country in which you made your purchase. Please store your files wisely, where they cannot be accessed by under-aged readers.

Keep an eye on her website at http://www.jeannestjames.com/ or sign up for her newsletter to learn about her upcoming releases: http://www.jeannestjames.com/newslettersignup

Join her FB readers' group for all the inside scoop here: https://www.facebook.com/groups/JeannesReviewCrew/

Author's Note

Welcome back to Manning Grove, PA...

This is where my Brothers in Blue series was based. If you haven't met the Brysons yet, it's recommended to read that series before this one, but not necessary. The Bryson brothers, Teddy and their family will be making appearances throughout the Blood Fury MC series. I hope you enjoy this new MC world. Not necessarily new to Trip, but new to us. Come along for the ride... But hang on tight.

"Be the leader who will carry another's chains that they can't carry themselves."
~ Robert Kelly
(Cover model for Blood & Bones: Trip)

Prologue

TURN THE KEY

"Sometimes you have to burn yourself to the ground before you can rise like a phoenix from the ashes."
~ Jens Lekman

TRIP STOOD in the middle of the deserted building, shaking his head, wondering if it was worth the fucking hassle to start the club back up. To reclaim its territory.

But what other fucking choice did he have?

He'd already had it set in his mind, not only to do it, but to do it right this time.

He wouldn't let his father's club, which died a violent death, just remain a memory. And a bad one at that.

But now that he had done his time in the Marines, done his time in prison, he needed something.

Because he had nothing.

Except his granddaddy's run-down farm, a barn full of farm equipment he had no clue how to use and didn't want to, and the abandoned warehouse he was currently standing in on the outskirts of town.

While he was in prison, his lawyer had shown up and read him his granddaddy's will.

Yeah. He got everything.

Sig got nothing.

Trip was sure his brother wasn't happy about that, if he even knew.

But most likely Granddaddy had made up the will when Trip was still doing time in the service and not doing it behind bars. Unlike Sig who had been in and out of county jail, or the state pen, off and on since he turned eighteen.

But now here he stood. In an empty building, feeling fucking overwhelmed. But still, it was something.

And something was better than nothing.

He also had new ink on his back and an old cut in his hand.

The leather was worn, the rockers and patches on it dirty. All except one.

One rectangular patch on the front had been torn off by his own fingers after using the point of his buck knife to loosen the threads. The patch that used to say "Buck" was now replaced with one that said "Trip." But above it, the patch that had deemed Buck as president remained. That now belonged to Trip.

He'd also used that same knife to remove the 1% diamond patch off the back. He wouldn't need that one anymore.

The club used to be outlaw. But Trip was determined to keep it above board. For the most part.

He'd spent many a night down in Shadow Valley talking with the members of the Dirty Angels MC, soaking up everything their prez named Z told him. Learning how to rebuild Blood Fury stronger than ever. How to keep the money flowing into the club's coffers.

One way to do that was to keep the members out of prison and, even better, keep them breathing.

Dead or incarcerated members weren't any good to a club.

And there had been too many of those in the Blood Fury MC in the past. It had been its downfall.

Trip didn't want that mistake to happen again.

So, they had to play the game. Keep shit on the up and up as best as they could. Become a powerful force, strong enough to withstand the occasional bump in the road.

He had no fucking clue how he was going to pull it off, but he would take the advice he was given and do his fucking best.

He scrubbed a hand through his long hair before tucking it up under his baseball cap, blowing out a loud breath and shrugging on his cut.

His cut.

It wasn't his father's any longer.

This club was no longer his father's, either.

This world, even as broken as it was, now belonged to Trip.

It was his and he wouldn't let anyone destroy it again.

The Fury was about to rise once more. This time stronger and smarter.

Chapter One

6 Months Later

THE RUMBLE of his straight pipes died as he turned the key and shut off his sled.

Instead of the roar of his exhaust, he now heard the drilling and hammering of a whole crew of local Amish folk.

The "Plain People" knew how to get shit done fast, get it done right and get it done cheap. Thank fuck they were available. Luckily, they were hungry for the work, since the economy had been slow in the area lately. Which meant they'd cut him an extra sweet deal, which he appreciated since with all the construction he was getting done, his money was starting to run low.

They also appreciated the extra work Trip had been throwing their way, too. Because they all had a bunch of mouths to feed and families to raise.

Hell, they even had the women and children out here on Trip's farm working, too. The kids were scurrying around getting whatever was asked for. Nails, tools, water, whatever. The women would show up at lunchtime in black vans driven by Mennonites, feed their men and boys, socialize for a bit and then disappear.

Most of the younger women eyeballed Trip when he was around. He'd tipped his head to a couple of them and they'd run off giggling and whispering.

But none of them were for him since he was one of the "English." And if they knew he'd spent six years in prison, they'd run away and never come back.

Or maybe if they knew, they'd lift their dresses, bend over and let him give it to them good. They probably fantasized about a man like him. One that smelled like exhaust and cigarettes instead of cow pies and horse shit. Maybe some of those women had a fantasy bucket list of doing it with an ex-con with tattoos.

Trip snorted. His own imagination was getting the fuck out of control. He needed to get laid. It had been a few months since he'd sank himself balls deep in some hot tail. Not since he came back to Manning Grove permanently and began to work on restoring the farm. Not since that last trip to Shadow Valley when he went to pick up his father's Harley, now restored and customized by Jag Jamison at Shadow Valley Body Works.

But since he'd been back, he'd been keeping on the DL around town. Not looking for pussy. Not recruiting. Not asking around for some of the old BFMC members. Keeping low mostly because he didn't want to raise any flags to Manning Grove PD. Didn't want them trying to put out the fire before Trip could get it burning.

Back in the day, the police and the original Blood Fury members constantly clashed. So, he needed to handle everything carefully. The club needed to be a force to be reckoned with before the pigs came along trying to squash it.

He also needed to show them they could be good neighbors and not terrify the local folk. That when they rolled through town on their sleds wearing their cuts, the women and children wouldn't have a reason to run screaming.

One corner of his mouth tipped up as he dismounted and left his sled parked at the house. As he strode down the rutted stone and dirt lane toward the barn—something else that needed repaired on that long list of his—he pulled a tin out of the inner pocket of his cut. He'd had one of the Amish teens hand roll a shitload of cigarettes from the tobacco they grew. He tucked one between his lips, dug his pop's Harley Zippo lighter from his front pocket and lit the tip. He paused as he sucked the smoke deep into his lungs, held it, then slowly released it.

Now *that* shit was good. Not like the shit he'd been paying a left nut for at the store. He might have to make a deal with the Amish to buy rolled cigs in bulk, then turn around and sell them...

No. Fuck no.

No more prison time for him.

Selling illegal smokes would catch him a federal charge and he was done with that shit. He'd already spent too much time playing prison politics and trying not to take a shank between his ribs. Or a dick up his ass.

Or being forced to toss another man's salad.

Fuck that shit.

He made it through almost six years without doing shit like that. And he didn't feel like taking that risk again.

He took one more long drag, pinched the end to extinguish it and tucked it back in his tin.

It took a few seconds for his eyes to adjust as he walked through the barn's new front entrance. His step stuttered and he put his boots in reverse until he was back outside. He looked up.

And smiled.

A new sign hung above the door.

No, it was the old sign he'd brought back from the warehouse. The day he rented a box van, took a few of the stronger Amish men with him and loaded everything that wasn't complete shit into that van and brought it back to what he was dubbing "The Barn."

But the wood sign above the door didn't say "The Barn." No.

It read...

For one, For all
For our brothers
WE LIVE AND DIE!

Yeah, it sucked. He wished it was better. But it was what it fucking was.

He could change it. A club reborn might need a new motto. But Trip could remember as a kid hearing his father yell, "For one, for all, for our brothers..." And as one, the rest of the members would yell out, "WE LIVE AND DIE!"

Just thinking about it sent chills sliding down his spine.

It was supposed to represent how strong their brotherhood was. But in the end, those words, that battle cry, meant nothing since they all turned on each other. Or at least, most of them. The ones that weren't shot dead, anyway.

He took a walk around the inside of the barn, running a hand over the custom- made wood bar, checking to make sure all exterior walls were reinforced with steel between the original wood exterior and the new interior drywall, something that was highly recommended by the president of the Dirty Angels. The Fury didn't have any enemies at this point, but that didn't mean they never would.

He peeked out the rear door into the new section attached to the original barn—what Trip was calling the bunkhouse—where the construction crew was still working. The concrete floors were already poured and set, exterior walls up, the roof finished, and they were quickly framing the inside to create one bunk room to hold six prospects, a common bathroom for them to share, and then seven private rooms with their own small bathrooms. Bathrooms just big enough to shit, shower and shave. Only members in good standing would be offered those.

He heard a few of the men working upstairs on the second level of the bunkhouse. He was having two apartments built up there. If he didn't need them for BFMC members, he'd rent them out and put some extra scratch in his pocket. He made sure the stairs leading up to their entrances were on the outside, just in case that happened.

He wouldn't need one of the apartments for himself since the farmhouse was in good enough shape to live in at this point. It could use a bit more work, but it would do for now until he was more flush and the club's coffers weren't in the negative.

The house had to wait, since the barn and the bunkhouse were priority because no club existed without members.

No club existed without a church.

No club existed without an executive committee.

Right now, it was a club of one.

Him.

A president who presided over no one.

That shit had to change.

His fucking gut churned at the thought maybe he was doing this all for nothing. Nobody would want to patch in. No one would want to be a lower than dog shit prospect.

Then he'd have a really nice fucking building on a farm he had no plans on farming that he could jerk off in.

Maybe throw himself a couple pity parties.

And drink himself half to death.

Fuck.

He needed to talk to some people in town. Dutch being one of them. Crazy Pete another. And from there, maybe he could dig up some other former members, or even some blood of former members.

If not, then again, he'd have a huge fucking building where he could whack his dick by himself.

And that would suck.

He also needed to find his half-brother, Sig, even though he had no clue where to even begin looking. Besides checking prisons and jails online for his name.

At least that'd be a start.

Trip wasn't even sure if Sig would talk to him.

Not just because of Trip inheriting the mess their grandfather left behind but because of their father.

He gave the head Amish guy, the one with the longest salt and pepper beard, a nod, and ducked back into the barn, which now had an open floor plan, with wide plank floors and a large center fireplace to help heat the building.

Almost like a goddamn ski lodge.

Not that he ever saw one in person. There was no way he was strapping long, flexible blades to his feet and then heading down a mountain like some crazy motherfucker with a death wish. That was what snowmobiles were for. But, anyway, the barn was as nice as some of the photos he'd seen of those high-priced ski resorts. Only much more fucking badass. And definitely better than that rusted-out, drafty, rat-infested warehouse.

The new BFMC church would be *the shit.*

He jogged up the thick, rough-cut wood stairs to what used to be the hayloft and once he hit the second floor of the barn, he stopped and inhaled the scent of oak. Wouldn't be long before that fresh cut lumber smell was gone and was quickly replaced by smoke, weed, booze and pussy.

The first three would be easy. That last one, though...

He didn't even want to think about where his future brothers would find snatch to scratch their itches. The town wasn't tiny, but it also wasn't any kind of metropolis where females who weren't jailbait were plentiful. So, they might be on their own for a while just fisting it. Though, he didn't want any sweet butts, or patch whores, or cum-bucket hang-arounds staying in the bunkhouse.

It wouldn't be like military barracks, but it also wasn't going to turn into some whorehouse.

Fuck that.

The second floor had been sectioned in half. One portion had been closed off and turned into storage. For booze, supplies, whatever. But the other... He stepped farther into the finished loft, which was now where the executive committee would meet. He walked around the old, worn, wood table that sat in the center of the large open area. The long table that used to sit in a back room at the warehouse.

The table where his father used to sit. The table that needed a good cleaning and polish.

He ran his fingers over the carved center—the insignia of the Blood Fury MC, the same as his center patch—which was covered in dust and dirt.

Pretty fucking fitting.

The dust needed to be blown off and the dirt scrubbed away, and it would be as good as new, just like the MC. Or at least, he hoped.

He moved down to the far end to the chair with the highest seat back and traced the initials that had been crudely carved into the armrest. Probably with a knife similar to what Trip carried.

B.F.D.

Yeah, his old man thought he was a *big fucking deal*. Probably a lot of Buck's club brothers didn't know what those letters actually stood for. Burchell Fletcher Davis.

He pulled the heavy chair away from the table and settled himself in it, putting his elbows on the armrests and trying it on for size.

He flatted his palms out on the tabletop, spread his

fingers wide and closed his eyes, imaging what it was like back then to sit at the head of the table. To hold that power. To be the one with the final word on all the decisions.

To hold the fucking gavel. The one that sat inches from his fingertips. The one which had BFMC engraved in the dull metal band circling it.

His goal was to build an empire. Just like the Jamisons and the Doughertys did with the Dirty Angels MC.

The memory of Zak Jamison jerking his chin toward the diamond-shaped 1% patch on Buck's cut, along with the man's words, were fresh in his mind. "Sure you wanna deal with that fuckin' headache? That right there'll cause you to fail in your attempt to build somethin' strong. Havin' fuckin' brothers constantly fightin' the law, livin' in a concrete box, or dyin' for no good reason, won't help you build shit. It'll just tear everythin' down."

Those words had him ripping that patch off his cut right then and there in the DAMC's courtyard and tossing it into the roaring bonfire.

It was one of the times he'd headed down to In the Shadows Ink. And on every trip, he had Crow add more ink, not just to the Fury's colors on his back—to make sure they were dark and deep and wouldn't fade—but to the full sleeve he'd always wanted and refused to let a prison hack start.

He wasn't anywhere near done yet, either. Those tats were just the beginning. Part of this journey.

And now, after spending all that time down there and with his Marine brother, Slade, a DAMC member, he had cemented their club as an ally. And, *thank fuck*, since they were the strongest MC in the state, maybe even the region. So, it would be good to have the DAMC at their backs, if needed.

But Trip hoped the Fury could rise without them by building a solid foundation and growing it from there.

Now all he needed was some members and a committee to sit around that table.

He picked up the gavel, the very one his father held, tested the weight of its handle in his palm, and then sharply pounded the table once before tossing it with a clatter into the center.

"Meeting fuckin' adjourned."

TRIP TUCKED his sunglasses into the collar of his T-shirt and squinted until his eyes adjusted after entering the dark and dingy interior of Crazy Pete's bar in town.

He jerked his ball cap lower on his head in an attempt to be somewhat anonymous even though he was wearing his cut, which clearly stated what and who he was. And he had ridden through town on his loud as fuck sled, which wasn't very subtle.

He'd caught a few folks' heads turning but hadn't seen any sign of the brothers in blue. Though, he was pretty fucking sure if he was seen around town enough, someone would run to the pigs and rat him out.

Maybe he should rethink wearing his colors while in town until the club had more than one fucking member.

That might be good.

Trip remembered the bar since he'd been in there several times with his pop when he was a kid. Crazy Pete was one of the original members and one of the few who survived the MC's fall-out.

And was one of the members, who was not only left breathing, but who decided to stay in town.

Pete would probably be in his mid-to-late sixties now, but that didn't mean Trip wouldn't want him on board. The man would have knowledge and, from what Trip could remember, wasn't a complete motherfucking asshole. At least when he wasn't pissed.

Back in the day, the bar had been under the club's thumb, which meant a constant flow of cash into the coffers by taking a healthy cut. Especially since it was the only actual bar in town. The other liquor licenses were held, and still were, by the hotel in the town square, which had a lobby bar, and one of the fancier restaurants, The Carriage House.

That was it. Anyone who wanted to drink cheap, drank at Crazy Pete's.

But he hadn't seen Pete in over twenty years, which was one reason he was wearing his cut. So the man would take him seriously.

"Yo! You can't wear colors in here."

His eyes scanned the mostly empty bar until he found the woman who had yelled at him.

It wasn't just any woman. It was a *woman*. One hard to miss.

And now seen, he had a feeling would be hard to forget.

She was standing by one of the pool tables, putting away cue sticks and organizing worn-down cubes of blue chalk.

That reminded him. He needed to find some used pool tables and all the shit that went with them.

Fuck. One more thing to add to the never-ending list.

He needed prospects, and soon, to do some of the dirty work on that list.

He focused his attention back on the woman now moving between the *seen-their-better-days* pool tables. "Says who?"

"Says me."

Trip pursed his lips and tilted his head as he watched her leave the area sectioned off by a half wall from the rest of the bar where the tables, chairs and ancient jukebox were set up.

"And who the fuck are you?"

She shot him a smile—a nowhere near friendly one—as she passed him and made her way behind the bar.

So, she was a server. Or a bartender.

Or just a plain ol' bitch.

But bitch or not, she had caught his dick's interest, which surprised him.

Couldn't be the long, shiny black hair with the dark blue streaks that fell in soft waves around her slender shoulders.

Probably not.

Couldn't be the eyes that had narrowed on him like ice blue laser beams trying to burn a hole between his eyes.

Nope.

Couldn't be the full sleeve of colorful tattoos that covered her left arm or the small gold hoop in her right nostril. Or even the wide black leather cuff that circled her right wrist.

Fuck no.

Maybe it was the worn black jeans which fit her long, slender legs. Or the heeled black leather boots that climbed up her calves.

Or the loose white tank top advertising Crazy Pete's, that she had a portion tucked into the front waistband of those jeans. A thick black leather belt also cinched her waist snugly, emphasizing just how narrow it was.

Also couldn't be the black bra straps that played peek-a-boo from the back of her tank, along with a portion of another tattoo that spanned her upper back. A tree of some sort.

No. It wasn't one of those things at all.

It was all of them combined.

It also could have something to do with the attitude that rolled off her in thick waves. Just like her hair.

Thick, silky waves he could lose his fingers in, rip her head back and take her fucking bossy mouth.

Yeah.

Fuck.

Now he needed to fuck someone, and he doubted she would voluntarily be that someone.

Though, if she did volunteer, he'd make an exception to his normal taste of thick women with thighs and tits which could smother him to death while he busted a nut.

Yeah, that's what he normally liked. Not chicks who looked like they should be standing on a stage as the coked-up and wired lead singer of an all-female rock band.

While she looked like a badass, it was probably just an act. A way to piss off mommy and daddy.

He could see it now. Her parents set up a really fat college fund, and when she turned eighteen, she probably gave them the finger, threw all of her belongings into a black Hefty bag over her shoulder and hauled ass out of her upper-class two-story home to make her "own way in the world."

She was thumbing her nose at society.

"Take off the cut and order a drink, or get the fuck out."

Normally he'd choose the "get the fuck out" option but he was there to talk to Crazy Pete and that was what he was determined to do. Whether he had to deal with the black-haired ballbuster first or not.

He approached her—since she now stood behind the bar with her hands on her narrow hips—shrugged off his cut and tossed it on top of the bar inside out to conceal his colors. Then he settled his ass on one of the stools and rapped on the shellacked, but severely scratched and chipped, wood top with his knuckles. "Jack."

She lifted one dark brow sharply. "With Coke?"

"It look like I got a pussy?"

She quickly spun around and Trip barely caught her shoulders jerk. After grabbing the bottle of Jack Daniels on a shelf above the bar, along with a shot glass, she turned around, her face not showing a hint of amusement.

Damn.

She slapped the shot glass in front of him and gave him a generous pour.

He tipped his chin up at her in thanks and downed it in one swallow. He let the burn subside before pulling out his tin and a half-smoked hand-rolled.

"Can't smoke in here."

"It's a fuckin' bar."

"Yeah and you can't smoke in here. It's the law. I don't have an exemption."

"You mean Pete don't." He reluctantly tucked the cigarette away.

She stared at him for a minute, then leaned back against the back counter, crossing her bare arms over her chest. That pushed what little cleavage she had higher and gave him a taste of what she had hidden behind the loose top.

She wasn't top heavy, but her tits were just right for how trim she was. Trim and lots of fucking leg, bringing her up to about his shoulder. But at least she wasn't overly skinny with arms and legs like sticks. Where he didn't have to worry about breaking bones when he pounded pussy.

When he raised his empty shot glass, she pushed off the counter and grabbed the Jack, once again giving him a long pour. This time it was almost to the very top.

"Not gonna make money over pourin' like that."

"Who said I'm not charging you double?"

Fuck. She could sear the hair right off his nut sac. Trip grinned.

He quickly lost that grin when she touched his cut. She flipped it inside out until the colors were showing and put it back on the bar, spreading it out in full display. Her long, delicate fingers, circled with a few silver rings, traced the top rocker that said "BLOOD FURY" and then the bottom rocker that said "PENNSYLVANIA" before hesitating on the part of the leather that was darker and cleaner because it had been hidden behind the 1% patch.

Her nostrils flared slightly, and one finger slowly traced the outline where the diamond used to be.

"Why are you wearing this? Colors for a club that has been dead and buried for the last twenty years?"

Trip's back snapped straight and his chest tightened. He grabbed the shot glass and downed the whiskey, wiping a hand over his mouth before allowing himself to breathe.

"What do you know about it? Pete talk about it?" Was Pete getting senile in his old age and rambling about the past to his employees?

Those light blue, almost gray, eyes studied him behind thick, black lashes. "Why are you here?"

"Why do you care?"

She shrugged. "It's my bar."

"How is it your bar?"

"Pete was my father."

Trip frowned.

Before he could say anything, she cut him off, pointing to the large center patch on his leather cut. "Out of the ashes of ruin rises the Phoenix?"

What the fuck was going on? "What?"

"You heard me. There's a reason you came in wearing that cut. There's a reason you're in this bar. And I can figure out why. But I don't think it's smart. Let the club lie where it landed, which is six feet under. Too many families were ruined in the process of that painful, violent death. Including mine."

"It's not gonna be like that anymore." And he hoped to fuck he was right.

"So you say. How are you going to make it, besides doing illegal shit?"

"Build up club run businesses. Recruit fresh blood and collect dues."

"Fresh blood." She snorted softly and shook her head. "But you're in here looking for old blood hoping to build a new, more progressive club? You know MC's aren't the Boy Scouts, right? Bikers don't want to sit around and work on earning their damn badges."

Trip set his jaw. Why the fuck did he care what she thought? "Think it's a joke." He stood and pulled out his wallet.

"Maybe I do."

Right. He didn't need this shit. He pulled out a twenty and threw it on the bar. "Anyway, lookin' for your pop."

She snagged the twenty, lifted it to the light and inspected it. "You're not going to find him here."

He tucked his chained wallet into his back pocket. "Then where can I find him?"

She folded the twenty neatly and tucked it into her front pocket instead of the register. "In the cemetery, because he's dead."

He sat back down, yanked his hat off his head and raked his fingers through his hair. Her eyes followed every one of his movements. He purposely scrubbed at his beard to see if she'd focus on that, too.

She did.

Trip found that interesting. He tugged his hat back on and tucked his hair back under it again. He needed to get a new skull cap to keep his hair from being knotted while he rode. Only pussies who rode crotch rockets wore baseball caps backwards.

He certainly wasn't a pussy. But he was interested in the one in front of him. The one with the translucent eyes that held a few deep secrets. "What's your name?"

"What's yours?"

He jerked his chin toward his cut. "Already know it."

As she brushed her finger over his name patch, his dick twitched in his jeans. There was something too goddamn intimate about her touching it like that. It was like the patch was attached directly to his cock.

"And you already know mine, too, Trip."

He blinked in confusion, then kept his face neutral as he raked his gaze over her once more. At least the parts of her that weren't hidden behind the bar.

Fuck. He now remembered Pete having a girl. He'd seen her more than a time or two before her mother took her and left town in a hurry when the club began to fall apart. Back then, she had long hair, but it was a light brown, not black. And, of course, no tattoos or piercings. Plus, no attitude to boot.

She'd been sort of sweet on him from what he could remember. Followed him and Sig around like a fly on shit. She always wanted to hang with them, but they had chased her away since they hadn't been at the age yet where girls were important. Back then they had been just a nuisance.

He couldn't remember her name, though. *If* the woman standing before him was even her. Pete could've had other kids with someone else after his ol' lady hit the bricks.

Though, this one looked about the right age.

"Remember me, Trip?"

"No," he lied.

"I remember you."

I remember you.

The hair on his arms and neck stood.

Fuck. Did he do something bad to her? Did he hurt her in some way?

He *might* have pushed her down once in his haste to get away from her. To get her away from him and Sig. To get her to stop bothering them. He closed his eyes for a second and the cries of a little girl came back to him. In pain. In rejection.

He did that. He caused that.

He reached out and snagged the large letter "S" that hung from a long black leather cord around her neck before she could stop him. He studied the silver pendant in his palm and wracked his brain trying to remember her name. But it slipped from his hand as she quickly stepped back out of reach, putting not only the width of the bar between them but an invisible wall.

"Stella," he whispered, lifting his gaze to hers.

She didn't answer, but he could see it in her face he was right.

Stella, the one that used to chase him around the warehouse and the courtyard insisting she was going to marry him. And he'd yell back right in her face, "Get lost, you crazy bitch."

Memories began to crash around him. Taking him back to that time he thought he'd forgotten.

It started when he was about ten and she was probably six. And ended that last time when he was about fifteen and she was eleven when he finally snapped. She tried to kiss him, and he shoved her away so hard, she stumbled back and cracked her head against a concrete block wall.

He didn't mean to make her bleed like that. His intent wasn't to hurt her. He just wanted her to stop bothering him. But it had pissed off her old man, which in turn pissed off Trip's when he heard what happened. And Trip got his ass kicked so hard by both Pete and Buck that he couldn't move for two days afterward.

He learned his lesson that day to never put his hands on a female in anger. The painful bruises were also a good reminder for weeks afterward.

It wasn't long after he hurt her that the club imploded, so he never saw her again. Her mother split, taking Stella, and so did Trip's, taking him along with her.

A twelve-year-old Sig was left behind because Trip's

mother didn't want anything to do with him. Not surprising, but still...

It was the last time he saw Stella. The last time he saw who he discovered later was his brother.

And the last time he was in Manning Grove until recently. Until the day after he walked out of SCI Huntingdon. The day after he earned his freedom ten months ago and vowed to never be caged like a fucking animal again.

"I'm thinking you remember now," she said softly.

Trip pushed from the stool, grabbed his cut and muttered, "Sorry your pop's dead."

With that, he turned and shoved his sunglasses on, not just to protect his eyes from a late April's bright afternoon sun, but also to hide his regret from her.

He walked out of Crazy Pete's, shrugged on his cut, mounted his bike and rode the fuck out of town.

Chapter Two

As he turned the key to cut the engine of the old Ford, the exhaust backfiring sounded like a gunshot, causing Trip to jump out of his skin and his heart to seize.

Fuck. That had brought him back to his fucked-up time in the Marines when his unit was being targeted by *not-so-friendly* fire.

He sat stiffly in the seat waiting for his heart to stop racing and his narrowed vision and arrested breathing to return to normal. Once it did, he glanced out of the windshield to see he'd drawn some attention.

No shit.

Speaking of shit, he needed to check his fucking pants after that.

Four men stood in one of the open bays of Dutch's Garage, staring at him. The oldest one had his greasy hands planted on his hips over his just as greasy gray coveralls and was shaking his salt and pepper head, heavy on the salt.

The driver's door on the old rusty 1948 Ford wrecker squealed like a stuck pig as he opened it and climbed down. A little WD-40 would fix that right up. It would have to since he didn't want to spend the dough right now to restore the tow truck.

"That '48 looks familiar," the old man shouted across the parking lot. His grin quickly disappeared as his gaze dropped to Trip's cut. He had removed it, flipped it right-side out and shrugged it back on as soon as he'd stepped onto the concrete. "Fuck. That looks way too familiar, too."

Trip eyed up the foursome cautiously, not sure which way this encounter would turn yet. "It should, old man."

"Who you callin' an old man, boy?"

"One whose face has deeper cracks in it than my ass."

The old man stepped forward, breaking out of the line of thoroughly confused men. "Recognize that truck, recognize the colors, tryin' to recognize your ugly mug. Strugglin' though, must be my old, addled brain."

"Or inhalin' too many gas fumes."

Trip approached him and they met halfway between the old Ford and the garage. Dutch's eyes dropped to Trip's name patch and his dull brown eyes widened.

"Fuck," Dutch muttered under his breath. Trip's own shoulders dropped a bit when he saw the old man relax. "Sorry 'bout your granddad. Good man. But what the fuck you doin' here? Thought you were off fightin' for my freedom to drink beer and eat pussy."

Trip guessed word hadn't gotten back to Manning Grove that he'd been fighting for his own freedom. Maybe his granddaddy kept it quiet, since his own son had ended up dead over stupid shit and then both his grandsons ended up in prison over doing stupid shit, too.

Like father, like sons. Clyde Davis had probably been far from proud of the rotten fruit that fell from the family tree.

"I inherited the farm."

Dutch yanked his grimy baseball cap off his head and slapped it back on with a jerk. "No shit. Gonna sell it?"

He guessed Dutch hadn't heard Trip had been back in

town permanently for the past couple of months, either. Trip must have done a good job keeping low. Plus, he'd bought the motel under a business name and sold the warehouse quietly to a developer who was going to rip it down. It probably also helped that the Amish certainly weren't hanging out in town gossiping. "No."

His thick salt and pepper bushy eyebrows rose. "Gonna farm it?"

"Fuck no."

"What're you gonna do?"

"Bring back the Fury."

Dutch scowled and sputtered, "Well, that's just plain fuckin' stupid, boy."

Trip ground his molars. He figured he'd get some resistance. But so far, he was two for two.

"What's the point of that?"

"Wanna rebuild my father's club."

Dutch jabbed a crooked finger in his direction. "See? That there's a fuckin' big problem. The Fury wasn't your father's fuckin' club. It was *our* fuckin' club. All of ours. That was one mistake Buck made. It was supposed to be a brotherhood. He was not the goddamn king." Dutch shook his head, muttered a curse under his breath and said, "Need a goddamn beer." As he strode away, he waved his arms at the three men still standing there listening to everything that had been said. "Get the fuck back to work. I ain't payin' you to stand around and scratch your fuckin' nuts."

The three guys grinned and disappeared back inside. Then Trip heard, "You fuckin' comin', boy?" from the open garage door.

Trip guessed he was having a *goddamn beer*.

Not ten minutes later, after two *goddamn beers* and at least a dozen loud belches between them, Dutch was still shaking his head with his grimy boots kicked up on a desk that probably hadn't been cleaned off in at least ten years.

Trip was slouched in another chair on the opposite side of the desk in a cluttered hole of an office. He had a can of generic piss water hanging from between his fingers and held between his spread knees. Because men with big balls like him needed to give his sac some room. Or at least Dutch had told him he had big balls by resurrecting the MC. Trip took it as a compliment. Dutch probably didn't mean it as one.

"Where you gettin' the scratch to do all this, boy? Clyde's life insurance couldn't have been that much."

Trip took a long drag on his hand-rolled, then let the smoke roll out of his mouth toward the ceiling in rings. "It wasn't. Only twenty grand. But it gave me a down payment for The Grove Inn."

Dutch choked on his mouthful of beer. He coughed a few more times before asking, "You bought that fuckin' dump?"

"Yeah. Gonna fix it up when I get more scratch and use it for a steady stream of income."

The old man shook his head and made a noise that Trip could interpret as "stupid fuck." But the actual words that came out of Dutch's mouth were, "Good luck with that."

"Also sold all the farm equipment in the barn and shed. Got a nice chunk of change for all that. Turned around and used what I got from the sale of the warehouse to restore the barn and add on to it."

"You sold that rusty ol' tin can? What are you gonna do for a chapel?"

"Just said I invested it in the barn. Makin' that the Fury's new church."

Dutch didn't say anything for the longest time, he just studied Trip. But he could see Dutch was taking a short trip down memory lane. And probably not a good one.

"Prolly for the best. That warehouse don't have any good memories left."

"And it's at the edge of town near the pig pen."

"Yeah, twenty years ago the pigs were in the old township buildin' on the other side of town. They weren't clear up our asses. Good call on that." His rheumy brown eyes hit Trip's. "Still don't know why you wanna unbury what's dead."

"Got nothing else. Only got what Granddaddy left me. That's it."

"You've been gone twenty years, boy. Gotta have more than that."

Trip shook his head. "Everything I had, what I worked for was taken away from me."

"Why?"

"Fucked up. It cost me. Still payin'."

Dutch pursed his lips making the wiry hair on his upper lip and chin stand out like a black and white porcupine. Then he dragged his hand over his beard. "Not my business," he finally grumbled.

"Needed a place to land, needed a place to start fresh, and my grandfather handed me that opportunity." At the right fucking time, too. Not that he wanted his grandfather to die. He'd been the only family he'd had left beside Sig.

Dutch squinted one eye at him. "Ain't startin' fresh. Startin' with rotten ground beef and tryin' to make it a strip steak."

Just like Stella, Dutch thought what Trip was trying to do was a fucking joke.

Well, he wasn't laughing. "Got a motel that needs a little work to start helpin' fill the coffers, got the barn restored, gettin' a bunkhouse set up for prospects or members who need a place to crash. The farm's got plenty of space for the club to grow. Also gonna build a big-ass pavilion and have plenty of parkin'. And best part is the fuckin' farm is outta town so it's private. Pigs won't be breathin' down our fuckin' necks. Townsfolk won't be nosey, either. It's perfect. Want the chance to fix what my father fucked up."

"He wasn't the only one who fucked up, boy."

Maybe so.

Dutch jerked his chin up. "Who you got?"

"You." And Trip hoped like fuck he did.

Dutch shook his head, ripped off his cap and threw it on the desk. He scratched the sweaty mess of gray hair that had been hidden underneath it. "Don't fit in my cut no more. Put that away twenty years ago and haven't looked at it since."

"Time to dust it off, Dutch. You're one of the Originals. Need you."

"Need to leave all that shit to the younger generation. The men who still got piss and vinegar in their blood."

"No, Dutch, need you."

"Without me, who else you got?"

"Just me."

"Fuck," Dutch dropped his head and shook it. After a few moments he lifted it and looked out of the open office door toward one of the men who was leaning against a fender of a car, not even bothering to pretend not to eavesdrop. "That boy's got a sled."

"Yeah?"

"He'd fit in my cut."

"You'd still need your cut, Dutch."

"Damn, if you ain't a persistent fuck. Just like your pop."

Trip smiled. "Tell you what, when you get a chance, stop out at the farm, look at what I'm doin'. Decide then." He tilted his head toward Dutch's mechanic. "Bring him. And whoever else is still around. Spread the word."

"None of the Originals are around. Even Pete's gone."

"Know it. Went to Crazy Pete's yesterday lookin' for him."

"Yeah. Real fuckin' shame. The cancer got 'im about a

year ago. His daughter's runnin' the joint. Or tryin' to. In the last few years, Pete let it go to shit, he was so sick."

"Saw that. Ran into her, too. She's a piece of fuckin' work."

Dutch grinned and took another swig of beer. "Just like Crazy Pete."

Right. "Gonna be recruitin', too, so if you think of anyone..."

"Yeah, 'bout that..." With a groan, he dropped his feet to the floor and pushed himself out of his office chair. "Get-tin' old sucks." He jerked his head toward the door. "Let's get you a couple bodies." Dutch lumbered out to the garage bays with Trip on his boot heels. "Heard all that?" he asked the guy, who looked about in his late twenties.

"Heard it." He was studying Trip.

"Whadya think?" Dutch asked the guy.

Even with his tattooed arms crossed across his chest, the man shrugged. "Maybe. I gotta prospect?"

Trip spoke up. "Been thinkin' about that."

Dutch turned toward him. "What you been thinkin'?"

Trip had given this a lot of thought. Especially since he was tired of being a club of one already. "Any Originals are welcome as long as they don't hold any grudges. Long as they're willin' to start fresh. For now, any blood of Originals will be patched in, too. Anyone without any ties, gotta prospect first. Maybe do six months. Once the coffers are full and we got enough members, they gotta prospect for a year. But for now? Gonna be a little lenient."

"There you go, then. Got your first member. Prolly don't remember this one," Dutch said pointing to the guy. "Younger than you. Ol' lady kept my boys away from the warehouse as much as possible."

Trip's eyes slid from the guy to Dutch. "He's your son?"

"Yeah."

Trip turned to the guy who still hadn't straightened

away from the car. He had his ankles crossed, too, like he was comfy right where he was at. He was also wearing a smirk Trip wasn't sure he liked.

"Got a sled?"

"Dutch told you I did."

Trip smiled, but it wasn't a friendly one. "Yeah, he did. But since you're a man, you need to speak for yourself just like a real man would."

That got the guy on his feet and his smirk wiped away. He dropped his arms and planted his hands on his hips covered in greasy jeans. "Got a '75 FLHF Shovelhead."

If it was in good shape, it was probably a sweet bike. "In good workin' order?"

"Fuck yeah."

"Want in?"

"Depends..."

"You want in, you're patched in since your Dutch's blood. Only offer you're gettin'. Don't accept it now, then you'll need to prospect." And Trip would make sure to have fun running him through the damn gauntlet.

"I'm in."

Trip dropped his head, stared at his boots and once he could wipe away the grin, he lifted it again. "Thought so. Got a road name?"

"Cage."

"Cage? How the fuck d'ya get that?"

"I gave it to him. Taught the boy to work on sleds. Prefers to work on cages," Dutch grumbled.

"Pop thinks there's an endless supply of bikes to work on. The garage would go outta business if we only worked on sleds. This ain't the old days."

"Hopefully that will change," Trip murmured. "I'll get you your colors. Get your mommy to buy you a cut and sew them on for you."

Cage's jaw went tight. "Don't got a mommy, but there's

a fuckin' tailor in town. Get me my colors and I'll get 'er done."

Trip gave him a nod. "Good."

Cage gave him an answering nod, then sauntered away.

Before he had gone too far, Trip called out, "Cage... One more thing..." He waited until Cage stopped and turned his head to look at him over his shoulder. "Gonna be your president." He met the man's narrowed blue eyes. "Might not want to forget that."

"Know how it works," Cage grumbled, then continued on his way.

"Doubt you do," Trip muttered under his breath.

Trip turned back to Dutch, who was grinning. "Not sure where he got his attitude, musta been from his momma." Dutch shook his head. "Was great at suckin' and fuckin' my cock, but the rest of the time, the bitch was impossible to live with."

"His mother wasn't Bebe?" Trip remembered Dutch's ol' lady. In fact, he remembered Dutch having a son around Sig's age.

"Yeah."

"She split when the rest of 'em did?"

"Yeah, but left the boys behind. Never wanted to be a mother. And the club fallin' apart was the perfect excuse for the bitch to escape. Left me raisin' the two hellions all by my fuckin' lonesome. And tryin' to run this damn shop."

"How old's Cage?"

Dutch squinted as if he was thinking hard. "Don't fuckin' know. Lost track... Old enough to drink, not old enough to have a lick of fuckin' sense. But then his older brother don't have any, either. That's my fault for tryin' to raise those boys myself."

It wasn't Cage he remembered from back then, it was Dutch's older son. Rook, if Trip remembered right. "Wasn't Rook around Sig's age?"

Dutch's brown eyes landed on him. "Yeah, 'bout there. And Cage was born 'bout five years later."

Trip did some figuring in his head. That meant Rook was about thirty-two now and Cage about twenty-eight. "Where's Rook?"

"Somewhere where the sun don't shine."

"Fuck. Sorry to hear that."

"Yeah, But he's a short-timer. Just got a month or so to go yet."

Huh? "He ain't dead?"

"Fuck no, boy. He's in County."

"Where?"

"Lycoming."

"What'd he do?"

"Bought weed from an undercover pig, then fled."

"That's it?"

"And then took the pig to the ground."

"And?"

"And knocked 'im the fuck out."

Damn. "Out soon, huh?"

"Yeah."

"Where's he goin' after he's out?"

"No fuckin' clue. Rook does what Rook wants to do." Dutch shook his head. "Though he's a damn good mechanic."

Trip might have to make a trip to Williamsport and offer Rook a place to land when he gets out.

"Anyway, got your first member. Now you got a club of two."

"And you. That's three."

Dutch ignored that. "Need your executive committee."

"What spot you want?" Trip asked, hoping he'd bite.

"None. Leave that shit to you young fucks."

"How 'bout interim VP? 'Til I get who I want."

"Who do you want?"

"Sig."

"Fuck, boy," Dutch groaned.

"Know where he's at?"

Dutch's bushy eyebrows shot up. "Makin' his ass VP already and you don't?"

"Nope. It's on my list." That never-ending fucking list. But Dutch was right, he needed to fill the committee so decisions could be made and set in stone. The whole "live free, ride free" shit was a myth. All MC's had rules that the members and prospects had to follow. And they all had someone to enforce them. One more thing added to the list. Finding someone to fill those boots. Someone *willing* to fill those boots.

Damn, he needed to start crossing some of those things off. No time like the present.

"Yo, Cage!" Trip yelled across the garage.

Cage's head popped out from under the hood of an old Chevy sedan.

"My first order of business is makin' you Road Captain. Can you handle it?"

"Can handle anything you fuckin' throw at me."

Right. The only question would be if Cage would throw that shit right back. Like a goddamn monkey throwing its own shit at people standing outside its cage.

Trip's lips twitched until he heard, "What about me?" from behind him.

"What about you, Mouse?" Dutch grumbled at one of his mechanics.

"Got a bike."

Trip turned and checked out the twenty-something guy. "Name's Mouse?"

"Mickey. Dutch just likes bein' a dick."

Dutch snorted but didn't deny it.

"What kind of sled you got?" Trip asked.

"An Indian."

If you didn't own a Harley, an Indian was the second-best bike out there. "What kind?"

"Dark Horse."

A Dark Horse was a badass bike. And while Harleys were the norm and sometimes required in an MC, he needed to decide if an Indian was good enough.

Another executive decision he needed to make on the fly. Or needed to delegate to his new Road Captain.

"Yo, Cage!"

Dutch's son lifted his head again, appearing annoyed.

"His sled bad enough to ride in your lineup?"

Cage's eyes slid to Mouse and back to Trip. "Yeah." He ducked his head back down.

"There you go, Mouse. You're in."

"Name's Mickey."

"Name's Mouse. If you survive six months of being a prospect and earn your rockers, then, and only fuckin' then, I'll let you change your road name. Got it?"

Mouse nodded. "Yeah. Got it."

Now he had a prospect, a Road Captain and a reluctant temporary VP. He was getting somewhere.

"How 'bout the other one?" Trip asked about the other twenty-something guy in the corner. Watching and listening but keeping quiet.

"Sparky there?" Dutch barked out a laugh. "You that desperate?"

Trip didn't want to admit he was. "What's wrong with 'im?"

Trip was pretty sure the mechanic could hear him and Dutch quite clearly. Especially since Dutch had a booming voice. On a volume scale of one to ten, the old man talked at a fucking twelve.

"Don't ever think his balls dropped. Still livin' with his momma over in Liberty. Might even still be sucking on her tit, too." Dutch raised his arthritic hands, palms out. "Just like the military, don't ask, don't tell."

Trip shook his head. "He good with bikes?"

"The best with bikes. One of those idiotic savages."

Trip bit back a laugh. "Idiot savants?"

"Yeah, one of those. Why I hired him. Told 'im I wouldn't change his diapers for 'im, though."

"He got a bike?"

"Yeah, a Huffy. With a ding-a-ling and streamers."

Damn.

Trip called out, "Sparky." He jerked his head, indicating the guy should come over.

Sparky didn't even hesitate.

"That all true?" Trip asked him.

"Like to suck on tits, but not my momma's. Don't have a sled but have been savin' up for a brand new one. Livin' with my momma so I can do that."

"Your momma need you there? Or can you leave?"

Sparky shrugged. "I can leave. Dutch don't pay me enough to pay a lot of rent."

"No rent. Got a place for you if you wanna prospect. Give you a bunk, roof over your head, showers, and a kitchen. Everything you'd need, just gotta share it with others. Need a sled, though."

"My uncle used to be in a club. I can get his old bike fixed up for now. Been sittin' in my aunt's shed."

"Harley?"

"Yeah."

Well, hot fucking damn. "That'll do. What's your name?"

"Whip."

"Whip?"

"Yeah, started out as a joke when my great granddad used to call me a young whippersnapper and Whip stuck."

"You like it?"

Whip lifted one shoulder. "Yeah."

"Then you're Sparky. You can change it once you earn it."

"Fuck," Whip—now Sparky—muttered.

Trip smothered his grin. "You in?"

"Fuck yeah."

"Welcome to the Fury." Trip held out his hand. They clasped palms and bumped shoulders. "Don't change diapers, though. Just a warnin'."

Dutch snorted next to him. And they stood silently as Sparky went back to work.

"Truth is. He's a good one. I give him and Mouse a lot of shit to build their character. Can't get any better prospects than them."

"That's only two and still need to fill the table first, Dutch. Beggin' for you to take the VP spot 'til I can get Sig."

"Lemme think about it. I'll stop out at the farm tomorrow, bring these knuckleheads and check shit out."

"Sounds like a plan." Trip turned and looked out of the open bay door. "Got a favor."

"Damn, boy, askin' for a lot today."

"No more runnin' guns, no more peddlin' drugs, no more prostitution, no more shakedowns and everything else the club used to be involved in. Doin' it right this time."

"Didn't hear a favor in there."

"Need you to work on the '48. Get it in tiptop runnin' condition. Maybe Bondo the rust spots 'til I can get the bodywork done right."

Dutch's eyes narrowed. "For what?"

Trip was sure Dutch already knew that answer, but he said it anyway. "Gettin' the repo business back up and runnin'."

"Gonna need a bond, a license, a—"

"Know what's involved. Gonna do it right."

Dutch's eyes were focused on the wrecker when he asked, "When you want it done?"

"Soon as possible. Gettin' all the paperwork together and submittin' it later this week."

"When we stop out at the farm tomorrow, I'll get one of 'em to bring it back."

Trip nodded, grateful. "Keep an ear out for a decent but cheap rollback, too, will ya?"

"Got one," Dutch grumbled.

"One you wanna part with?"

"No."

Trip rolled his eyes. "Then I'm lookin' for one. I'll start with the wrecker and a rollback and go from there."

"How much repo-in' you think you're gonna do 'round here?"

"Not gonna limit it around here, but I remember Buck keepin' pretty busy in the wrecker."

"Buck was busy fuckin' women. Tellin' Tammy he got a repo job, then he'd land in some other bitch's bed. Also stole cars with that wrecker. You know that?"

Great. "No."

"Now you do. Also gonna need secure storage for the vehicles you snag. Otherwise, won't get your license."

"Yeah, know that. Gonna put some thought into it."

Another damn thing he needed to cross off that endless list.

Chapter Three

HER OLD CHEROKEE rattled like it was about to leave Jeep parts strewn along the long, rutted half-dirt, half-stone driveway leading up to the Davis's farmhouse.

At least the thirty-year-old vehicle still started. Though, she wasn't sure for how much longer, since it had over two hundred thousand miles on it. She still owed Dutch for the new exhaust he installed after the old one rusted off and dragged, creating sparks the entire trip from the bar to the garage across town.

Luckily, it had made it without lighting the whole town on fire and her managing not to get a ticket. It now had a shiny new exhaust system on it, even though the rest of the vehicle looked like dog shit.

Whatever.

She couldn't buy a new-to-her SUV until she turned the bar around and it stopped hemorrhaging money. *Hell*, it wasn't even hemorrhaging money anymore because there *was* no money, it was now falling into a pit of debt. Which was getting deeper by the day.

Crazy Pete's was the only real bar in town. For that reason alone, it should be packed every night. She needed to get it turned around and soon. Problem was, to make it more inviting cost money and she didn't have it.

She might never have it.

But she needed that bar. She needed to make it a success, because it was the only thing she had left.

The *only* thing and she wasn't letting the damn thing go. Not until there was a sheriff's sale and she was dragged out of there against her will when it was sold from underneath her.

But she couldn't let that happen. She just couldn't.

She released her held breath when her Jeep made it to the house in one piece and she shoved it into Park.

Stella had never been out to Clyde's old farm. She never had a reason to be out there. The old two-story house wasn't completely visible from the road and she wasn't surprised to find it had a really cool wraparound porch. Or *would* be really cool if it was in better shape. It needed some work on both the railings and the steps from what she could see. In fact, the whole house needed a good scraping and the wood siding repainted. The brick chimney also needed to be repointed. The windows looked original which meant they caused drafts. And the back door...

Was beautiful with two long panes of etched glass panels in it. The antique wood door just needed a little TLC. Like the overgrown flower beds and shrubbery surrounding the house. The lawn was patchy, if you could even call it a lawn. It had been mowed but was due again for a cut. It looked more like weeds than grass.

An old brown wrecker, needing just as much work, was parked next to the house. Sitting beside it, an older Harley.

However, the bike didn't need any work. It was striking and in perfect condition, which meant someone had dumped a lot of money into it to restore it.

Trip. Because a true biker would make sure his sled was top notch before anything else. He could live in the biggest shithole, have no other transportation and could even be starving, but he'd forgo the rest of life's comforts to have a great bike.

Stella shook her head. Fucked up priorities.

Well, she had no room to judge. The bar, the apartment above it and her vehicle all needed a lot of work, too. Her father had run the bar into the ground during the last year or so he was alive. Stella had told him he should sell it and live out his remaining days burden-free, but he refused, stating the bar was his life and he was going to die in it.

Which he did.

A regular of Crazy Pete's had called the police to do a welfare check on him when the front door remained locked during normal business hours. One of the officers found Pete sitting on one of the stools, slumped over the bar. A half-drunk beer sat in front of him and a burned-out Marlboro was found in the ashtray near his cold, life-less hand.

He died doing what he liked, she guessed. Problem was, he died alone.

He wasn't supposed to be smoking or drinking but Pete had been a stubborn old fuck and hadn't listened to the doctors.

By the time they caught his lung cancer, he was stage four and it had already spread.

So, in the end, not smoking and drinking wouldn't change the outcome. Max Bryson, the Chief of Police, had called her to give her the bad news, saying he believed Pete knew it was his time and wanted to leave the Earth on his own terms.

She hadn't had the best relationship with her father. Actually, not much of one at all. On a rare occasion they'd talk after her mother dragged her out of Manning Grove along with the rest of the ol' ladies when everyone scattered.

All the kids she knew from the MC disappeared in

different directions. All her friends in Manning Grove, not part of the MC, were left behind, too.

She and her mom started fresh.

Stella turned her head to look at the barn about two football field lengths away from the house.

She had to start fresh one too many times than she would've liked.

And now Trip was back.

In Manning Grove.

Making his own fresh start. But she wasn't sure if he was doing it the right way.

When everything went down with the club twenty years ago, it destroyed a lot of families. Members ended up dead, as enemies, or in prison, and most never saw their families again.

Now the former president's son wanted to take those broken pieces and attempt to patch them back together. The son of the man who had been the main cause of the Fury exploding like an M-80 in a mailbox.

She got out of her Jeep, grabbed what was sitting on her passenger seat—her excuse to go out to the farm—and heard what sounded like construction noises. Saws, hammers, voices of men in the distance.

But she saw no one out front. All the noise seemed to be coming from behind the barn.

As she took long strides in that direction, she wondered if Trip was even up yet. Maybe he was still in the house and it was just the construction crew working this early in the morning.

It was early for her, too. She usually closed the bar around two a.m. every morning and getting up at the ass crack of dawn was not something she enjoyed doing. But once the bar opened at eleven, she wouldn't be able to get away since she *was* the only employee. She couldn't afford to pay anyone else right now and there wasn't enough business to get anyone to help out for only tips.

As she walked the length of the old barn, it was obvious where the new section started, which more than doubled the size of the original structure. The BFMC clubhouse was going to be pretty fucking epic. But she wondered if Trip was setting his sights too high.

Her own sight landed on a few men at the very rear of the building. The Amish could be seen working on the second floor, both from the open doorway at the top of the exterior steps and in the large picture windows that faced the field and woods behind the building.

Bet that was a nice view. Especially during sunset. Or a fresh snow.

A solid steel door on the lower level was also propped open and lights were on inside. Stella found it curious that the only windows in the barn and the new addition were on the second floor, all along the front, the sides and in the back. But the first floor? Nothing. The walls and doors also appeared solid.

Kind of like Crazy Pete's, where there wasn't a window downstairs, but the apartment upstairs had a few in the back, luckily. Mostly because people wanted to drink in peace and not have people gawking in the windows and also because windows were a lot less likely to get broken by drunks if they didn't exist in the first place.

Maybe Trip had the same idea.

She stepped inside and let her eyes adjust from the bright natural light of the April morning to the artificial one.

Tilting her head, she heard music and decided to follow it. She walked down a very short, narrow hall from the back door into what looked like a bunch of rooms. Or at least, from what she could see, a wide corridor with a bunch of doors.

She peeked into the first one on her left. The room itself was pretty large and included the metal frames of three double bunkbeds and a wall of closets. That was it. No one was in there and certainly no one was living there yet. The first room to her right looked like a locker room. Showers, toilets, sinks. Sparse and utilitarian, reminding her of a dorm. As she moved through the center area, she peeked into each room as she passed. Small bedrooms with what looked like tiny bathrooms attached. No furniture. The walls hadn't even been painted yet. The drywall had been taped and spackled, the concrete floors painted with some kind of brown-colored sealer. Most likely for easy clean-up.

She counted as she went. Seven bedrooms with bathrooms, plus the larger room with the bunkbeds. Eight bedrooms in total.

Which proved that Trip was pretty confident that the Fury would rise once more. Otherwise, he'd have to use that space to house farmhands and get his grandfather's farm working again.

Or open a winery.

Stella snorted softly. If Trip were smart, he'd abandon the idea of restarting the club and do just that. Grow grapes and make wine. He might be more successful at it since wineries were really popular.

Hell, maybe she should take her own advice. But at least he had the land, the buildings and the money to do it.

At the end of the hall and right before the entrance to the original barn, in which the door was also propped open, was another room. It had a single gray swinging door like you'd see in a diner, only those were usually double doors to avoid head-on collisions with busy staff rushing in and out.

She paused to listen as the song coming from that room changed to *Carry On Wayward Son* by Kansas. The volume was cranked up and someone was singing along.

She dropped her head, closed her eyes and listened for a few more bars.

Oh yeah, he knew the words.

She slowly pushed the door open, the music now hitting her full force. She held the door open as she scanned the room.

A kitchen. Not like one found in a home, but more like a commercial kitchen on a smaller scale. The counters, the microwave, the large gas stove, the built-in oven, the oversized commercial refrigerator and what looked like a large chest freezer were all stainless steel so they would be easy to clean. Nothing was fancy, but everything was basic. They weren't going to be serving food to the public, but definitely feeding themselves. Again, like the rest of the rooms, very utilitarian.

Trip thought of everything. The old warehouse had been nothing like this. It had been a shithole of epic proportions. And, if she remembered correctly, at the time no one cared.

For the Originals it had been all about partying, fucking and raising hell. No one gave a shit if you went hungry, were cold, had a bed to sleep in or a toilet to shit in. Or even if you'd showered.

Stella placed what she was carrying on top of a stack of boxes—which she assumed were full of kitchen supplies—and stepped around them, trying to find exactly where the deep voice was coming from. That rough masculine voice singing a song that fit him more than he might be aware of. Or maybe he was.

She took a few more steps and spotted black boots planted on the floor, knees encased in dirty denim cocked, all attached to a man whose shirtless body disappeared under a cabinet. Or part of him, at least. Trip was so muscular and his chest so broad, he was jammed—what looked like uncomfortably—through one side of the cabinet doors.

His distinct abs, covered in a fine sheen of sweat, lifted and fell with each line of the song he belted out.

She leaned back against the center island counter, crossed her arms and enjoyed the show.

Kansas faded away and Deep Purple's *Smoke on the Water* began to fill the room. Unfortunately, the singing stopped, but one boot began to tap with the beat, as well as what sounded like a drum solo was heard on a metal pipe from under the sink.

With as loud as it was, she could stand there all day watching those abs ripple in tune with the music and he'd never know.

That was dangerous for him. Not because she was watching, but because he was unaware she only stood a couple feet away from him and could've killed him easily before he could react.

She kicked his boot with hers, causing a chain reaction of him jerking, a loud clunk, an even louder "Fuck!" and Trip scrambling from under the sink, wielding a plumber's wrench like a club.

His brown eyes widened when he saw her, and he quickly climbed to his feet.

Fuck, he was tall. A lot taller than when he was fifteen. And he hadn't been small then. At least to an eleven-year-old Stella.

"What're you doin' here?" he asked as he rubbed at a red spot on his forehead.

She ignored his question while she let her gaze roam his bare upper body. The distinct muscles, his black and gray inked sleeve that went all the way up his right arm and over his pec, his broad shoulders. Tats on both of his sides along his ribs. The beard. The trail of dark hair from his navel and led to the unknown.

The hair on his head...

His light brown hair was pulled back in a ponytail. She hadn't realized it was that long since he'd been wearing a hat at the bar and must have hidden the length underneath. It wasn't super long but enough to be able to tie it back. It might hit his shoulders if she pulled the band from his hair and let it loose.

As tempting as it was, she wasn't going to do that.

She cleared her throat. "Working up a sweat?"

Still gripping the adjustable wrench, he wiped away the beads on his brow with his forearm. However, that didn't erase the frown he wore as he turned down the music from the old portable stereo on a shelf above the sink. At least now she could hear herself think.

"No fuckin' air in here, yet."

Yet. Which meant there would be eventually.

"Going to spoil your future brothers with all these modern technologies, like running water, electricity and cold beer."

He put the wrench down next to the sink and then jerked his chin to somewhere behind her. "Hand me my shirt."

She peered over her shoulder at where his discarded cut and T-shirt laid, then turned back to him. "Why? Kinda like what I'm seeing."

"Yeah?"

"Yeah," she murmured. She probably shouldn't have admitted that, but it was too late to take it back now. "Bikers usually aren't that built. They work on their beer guts, not their obliques."

He sucked at his teeth for a second and let his gaze roam over her from top to toe. She couldn't fault him for it. She'd done it to him and was still ogling him without any shame. It was only fair he returned the gesture.

"Had lots of time while in prison. Keepin' the body healthy keeps the mind sane."

She hadn't heard that he'd done time. But then, she hadn't heard shit about him since the day they all beat feet out of Manning Grove. Not until he walked into her bar and back into her life a few days ago.

She sighed, grabbed his tee and tossed it to him. He used it to wipe his face and chest, then threw it over his shoulder.

"Not going to put it on?"

He cocked an eyebrow. "Do I need to?"

"I think you're safe without it. For the most part, I can control myself around half naked men."

She swore she heard him say, "Pity," under his breath.

Huh. "What were you in for?"

"To learn a trade, apparently."

Like most occupants of the federal, state or county system, he probably insisted he was innocent and was wrongly housed by the taxpayers. "Is that where you learned plumbing?"

"Among other things."

When he reached up to jerk the band from his ponytail, Stella swore the whole Earth stopped spinning and everything went into slow motion. The way his abs clenched, the way his biceps bulged as he reached up and let his hair fall around his face, the way he raked his fingers through the damp strands before gathering them back up again and securing the black elastic tie around it.

Damn.

At eleven, and even before, she wanted to marry that boy. Now at thirty-one, her thoughts had nothing to do with wedding vows.

Nothing at all.

She bit her bottom lip and forced herself to remain leaning back against the counter, with her palms planted firmly on the edge. Otherwise, they might end up planted on his chest with her bottom lip between *his* teeth instead.

She shook herself mentally.

He was the last fucking thing she needed in her life.

The very last fucking thing.

She was done with "bad boys." Her father had been one. And so had her husband. Bad boys were great to look at, great for fantasies, but hell to live with.

Complete utter hell.

She foolishly wanted him when she was young. She wasn't so young or foolish now.

"Why you here, Stella?"

Her nipples pebbled at him saying her name. The same way they had when he'd picked up her "S" pendant and held it in his palm. When he'd done that, she swore an electric current had run from his hand through the leather cord and right into her chest. Like being struck by lightning.

She needed to mentally break free of the hold he held her in, the one quickly resurfacing from twenty years ago.

She needed to remember the last time she saw him. The day he shoved her away and cracked her head open on the wall. Her fingers automatically went to the back of her scalp where she could still feel the raised scar from where she had to get stitches. While it was hidden in her hair, she'd never forget it was there.

Oh yeah, that was a good reminder of how he was bad news. "Dutch stopped in for a beer last night and gave me the complete low-down on the latest town gossip. Couldn't stop talking about you. The club. And your new repo business. Got my curiosity piqued."

"Sounds like he was there for more than one beer."

She shrugged. "Yeah. It took about four beers to tell me everything." Four beers and three shots of whiskey. She kept telling Dutch she really didn't care about any of it, but he kept talking and there wasn't a lot of business at the bar to warrant escaping him.

She also loved Dutch like a grandfather, so she hadn't wanted to be rude.

"So now you're out here bein' nosy."

She tilted her head and studied the man before her. He didn't look away when her eyes hit his. In fact, he held them for so long it almost felt like a challenge.

One she knew how to win. "He told me Cage is your new Road Captain."

His brown eyes narrowed. "Know him?"

"Of course. How could I not? He's Dutch's son."

"How well you know him?"

Ah, there it was. He was a typical man, wondering if she and Cage had sex. "Well enough."

His jaw worked a couple of times. "Seems to be a dick."

"He can be. Which means he'll be a perfect addition to the Fury."

"So, you came out here to tell me that Dutch was out runnin' his mouth. That it?"

"No."

"Then why else are you here, Stella?"

Right. Why else was she there? She could've given Dutch the item she wanted to give Trip and not come out here at all. She could've stayed away and minded her own fucking business.

She needed to concentrate on the bar, forget the past and ignore whatever Trip was trying to do with it. But for some reason she couldn't.

For some reason she couldn't leave well enough alone.

He jerked slightly when she finally pushed off the counter and moved toward the stack of boxes.

She didn't ask him to follow her, but he did. She snagged the item as she passed the boxes and kept moving, out of the swinging door, into the barn and then stopped.

It was fucking *awesome.*

Completely awesome. And would make a great tasting room for a winery.

She could see it now. Blood Fury Red.

Red wine would be better than spilled blood.

She took a few more steps deeper into the barn and then spun on her heels causing him to almost run into her. She shoved her father's BFMC cut into his stomach and he grabbed it out of instinct, but she didn't let go.

Their fingers brushed and his thumb slid over her knuckles. Probably by accident...

She quickly released the leather vest and stepped back. "Figured you can hang it on the wall. Or give it to someone who might need one. Not doing me any good where it was."

It took forever for him to drop his eyes from hers to the cut in his hands. His nostrils flared just slightly as he checked out the back and then the four rectangular patches on the front. Crazy Pete. Treasurer. Manning Grove. Original.

His jaw worked and an emotion she couldn't identify crossed his stoic features, but quickly disappeared. He was still staring at the worn cut when he asked, "Don't wanna keep it for sentimental value?"

"No." Just one more reminder she didn't need. When she donated all her father's clothes after she moved in and cleaned out the apartment, it was one thing she couldn't rid herself of. She knew how much pride was in those colors. She also knew the cut needed to be handled properly.

Now she could leave that to Trip.

"He shoulda been buried in it."

His rough whisper raced through her, causing her to shiver. "Yes. He should've. But he wasn't wearing it when he died, and I wasn't here when he was buried. Plus, he hadn't been a member for twenty years."

"Colors never die."

That whisper seared her. It made her regret not arriving

in Manning Grove in time to find it and give it to the funeral director. It had been her responsibility and she failed. "The Fury's colors did, Trip. They died and now you're trying to dig them up again."

His fingers curled hard enough to fist the old leather as he cleared his throat. "Colors never die," he repeated, louder this time.

The unexpected, raw emotion pulling at him was beginning to suck her in, too. She needed to shut that shit down. Otherwise, she might tumble back into that deep, dark pit of loss. She took a mental step back from the crumbling edge. "Anyway, do with it what you'd like. Pass it on. Display it. It's yours now to do what you want."

He nodded and moved to the full-length bar on his left, laying the cut carefully over it.

She followed him, impressed with what she saw. She concentrated on the bar, which was amazing. It looked like it was hand-crafted out of solid oak, sanded and stained to bring out the natural wood grain, then shellacked to a high shine. She ran her fingers over the glossy, glass-like top, noticing under the thick clear coating, the club colors had been burned into the wood.

She was jealous Crazy Pete's didn't have such a beautiful bar. Hers was original and some of the wood had split and the shellac had cracked, chipped and patrons had carved words into the top.

"You make this?"

"No. Learned a few trades inside but woodworkin' wasn't one of them."

It was her turn to mumble, "Pity," under her breath.

"One of the Amish guys, Samuel, made it. Built the back bar, too."

Her eyes scanned the noticeably empty back bar. Not a bottle of booze to be seen, but she was jealous of the craftsmanship there, too. If she only had the money...

"Might need to hire them to fix up Crazy Pete's." Though at this point, that was more like a pipe dream than reality.

She needed to start doing promotions and adding entertainment to bring back the customers. Maybe even book a few of those traveling revue shows. Male and female alike. Whatever was needed to make some quick cash, turn around and dump it back into the bar.

"You got the scratch?"

She wondered how much she should reveal to the man whose chocolate brown eyes were focused on her.

She schooled her face too late when he said, "Don't got shit, do you?"

She glanced around the new BFMC church. "This is everything you have, right? This land, the house, the buildings. This is it. You've got nothing else, right?" When he didn't answer her, she continued. "Like you, I've got nothing else." Though, he had a lot more than her.

"Whataya mean?"

"I've got nothing else. The bar is it. It's everything I own. Everything I have. The only thing left that belongs to me."

"Sell it. Take the cash and go get somethin' else."

"Why didn't you sell the farm?"

"Already know why."

"Right, you wanted to make something from nothing." Again, she didn't get an answer. "It's not a choice for me. I also need to make something from nothing."

"Got a choice to sell it."

"And then what?"

"Then you start fresh."

"This is my fresh start," she whispered. "I can't fail."

"Then don't."

Then don't.

Pete's life insurance had been very small. Enough to

cover his burial expenses and allow her to restock some liquor and beer. But it had been gone in a flash.

Unfortunately, property taxes would be due again in a couple of months.

Shit was becoming overwhelming. Maybe Trip was right. She should just sell it, take whatever she could get and cut her losses. She couldn't shake the feeling of drowning.

A grumbled, "Need booze," pulled her out of her self-pity.

"What?"

She must have been so deep in her own wallowing, she missed him pulling on his T-shirt. It was old and worn with thin spots and stains. And it fit him like a glove. A shirt which should be used as a rag did not distract from the man. At all.

She gathered her wandering thoughts. "If you haven't noticed, there's a liquor store on Main Street."

"Know it."

"Well, there you go."

"Need more than that."

"You need more booze than what the liquor store holds?"

"Need a continuous supply at a good price."

It hit her then what he was saying. She shook her head. "No."

"Need scratch, right?"

She raised her palms up and took a step back. "No fucking way. Getting booze from me isn't legal. Private club or not. Last thing I need is to have the Liquor Control Board shutting me the fuck down. I'm not risking that. If you're that desperate, there are some crazy fucks that live up on the mountain who make moonshine and other shit. Get it from them."

"Might do that, too."

She shook her head again. "I don't want any part of that. I just told you the bar is all I have left."

"It's not makin' you any money, Stella. Dutch said Pete ran it into the ground, unable to keep up with it."

"His cancer—"

"If it was too much, he shoulda fuckin' sold it or asked for help."

"He was stubborn."

"Aren't we all?" he muttered.

"Get a private club license and deal directly with PLCB yourself."

Trip shook his head. "We can help each other, Stella."

She wasn't sure she liked the sound of that. "How? By getting me thrown in jail? Or losing a liquor license which is just about impossible to get?"

"You just said it. They're hard to get. No fuckin' way are they givin' me a license for this place."

"You can buy your booze retail."

"Or we can make a deal that'll benefit us both."

She *definitely* didn't like the sound of that. "I'm not liking this deal, Trip. In fact, you can go fuck yourself." As she spun on her heels, ready to get the hell out of there, he grabbed her wrist and jerked her toward him.

He pulled her so close they were only a few inches apart. His eyes were intense as he dropped his head to stare into hers. "Stella. You fuckin' need help."

"Not the kind of help that fucks me. And not in a good way." She'd had too much of that already.

"It doesn't have to be that way," he growled.

Oh, was he getting pissed? Well, she was already there. "No? Then tell me how it would be."

"Thinkin' the Blood Fury invested some money in the bar back in the day. Pete probably wouldn't have had his bar if it wasn't for our club."

Her blood ran cold at his words. "Our? You mean your."

"Wanna make a deal. This way it's legal. You need help and so do I."

"I don't need that kind of help. And what your proposing might not be legal."

"Make me a partner, then you won't be sellin' me shit. I'll be buyin' the booze all legal like."

What? He wanted to be a partner? Was he fucking crazy? "And taking that booze off the premises."

"For special events."

"Special events," Stella spit out, air-quoting those words. "Right. And what the hell do I get out of all this? The bar isn't even making a fucking profit."

"It will. If you let me help."

"Oh, yeah, because you can run the bar so much better than me, right? Like you don't have enough shit on your plate."

"Can get you cheap labor. Help pay for upgrades. Afford to buy better booze. It's the only bar in town, Stella. You fix it up right, there's nowhere else the townsfolk should wanna get drunk."

She couldn't deny he was right about the last part, but the rest? She was not going to be indebted to him. No fucking way. She was not selling her soul to the devil. "You scratch my back, I'll scratch yours?"

"Babe, you can scratch my back any fuckin' time."

Babe. "You're not talking about an itch, are you, *babe*?" This was a bad, bad, very bad idea to come out here. To meet with Trip. She could've mailed Pete's cut. She should've stayed away. Far, far away.

"I've got an itch."

"They carry rash cream for that at the Old Towne Pharmacy."

He ignored that. "How far you in the hole?"

"It doesn't matter."

"Yeah, it does. In my eyes, the club owns a part of that bar."

Fuck. Fuck. Fuck. "Maybe you need glasses, then. The club's name isn't on that fucking deed. Yours isn't, either."

"But mine could be."

Her heart pounded in her throat. She had no doubt that the club helped fund her father's bar. It helped fund Dutch's garage. It helped fund all the rest of the businesses, too, legal and illegal. And in turn, those business paid a percentage of the profits to the club.

She knew all of that because of Dutch. She knew most of the BFMC history because of him. He liked to talk when he was drinking, which meant he talked a lot.

Normally MC members didn't talk club business with anyone outside of the club. It was strictly forbidden. But because Pete had been an Original and Stella was his daughter, Dutch felt it was okay. Plus, the club was gone so there was no one left to answer to.

She was not telling Trip any of that. No fucking way.

However, if he insisted she pay a percentage of the profits to the club, then that could very well be the last nail in the coffin. And he would be holding the hammer.

She would have to walk away, and he could buy the bar from under her, pennies on the dollar. And, once again, she'd be left with nothing but lint in her pockets.

"I gotta go," she mumbled, giving her wrist a yank.

Instead of releasing her, he pulled her even closer and dropped his head until their lips were inches apart.

If he kissed her, she was kneeing him in the nuts. She could not let that happen; she would not let him break her.

But he didn't. Instead he said, "A partnership could benefit us both. Think about it."

She didn't need to think about it. She knew a partnership between the two of them could be dangerous.

For her business.

And for her.

She tugged her arm from his grasp, and he released her, letting his fingers drag along her skin as he did so. She turned and instead of leaving the way she came in, she headed out the front door of the barn.

She did her best to walk calmly until she got outside, then she power-walked to her Jeep.

She shouldn't let him shake her. She was no longer eleven. She was no longer a foolish, love-struck girl. She needed to remember that, no matter if being around him took her back to that time. She needed to remain strong and resist that invisible pull she'd always felt with him.

As her Cherokee rattled back down the driveway, she realized he had shaken her enough she had forgotten to tell him the other reason she had stopped out.

She had forgotten to tell him about Judge.

But she wasn't turning back to fix her mistake.

Despite what he thought, she didn't owe him anything. So fuck him, he could find out about Judge on his own.

Chapter Four

TRIP STEPPED out of the afternoon sun and through the darkly tinted glass door into Justice Bail Bonds. The buzzer notifying the occupants of his arrival caused a whole bunch of growling and barking.

Snarling, more like it.

The hair on the back of Trip's neck rose and he froze in place, expecting ferocious dogs to come charging at him and tear him to pieces.

They didn't, but two dogs with huge blocky heads and *not-so-friendly* faces slammed their big-ass paws onto the half-door that barely kept them contained behind the counter at the back of the retail space.

The bail bonds business was in the strip mall attached to the Walmart on the far end of town, where most of the commercial businesses not owned locally were allowed. The town's council wanted to keep Main Street as "quaint" as possible with small family-friendly, locally-owned shops, restaurants and the like.

Justice Bail Bonds did not fit their definition of "quaint."

But down on the east side of Manning Grove, anything went. Except for strip clubs or adult stores and that sort of shit. For that kind of entertainment, one had to head south. Far south. The council wasn't having any of that in a town that held—what they thought—some historical significance.

He was surprised there was even a bail bondsman around here and wondered if it even got enough business. If it didn't, it might work in Trip's favor.

Both dogs, which looked similar in structure and coloring of white with large patches of brindle, had become quiet as soon as he had stood still.

But no one had come out to greet him from the back. And until they did, he wasn't taking one fucking step further. He didn't feel like becoming their afternoon snack.

He had nothing against dogs. Normally. But these two had wide black leather collars around their thick, muscular necks, big teeth and watchful eyes.

He respected dogs who respected him.

"Yo!" Trip yelled, causing the dogs to react again. Their barking was hopefully a lot worse than their bites. With the size of them, he was pretty sure they could jump the painted plywood half-door if they wanted to. Or bust through the shitty latch that held it closed.

What the fuck. The buzzer, the dogs going ballistic and him calling out "Yo!" wasn't good enough to catch someone's attention? What kind of fucking place was this?

He grimaced when a beast of a man with a beard way too fucking long, a bunch of ink and a mean expression stepped behind the counter from the narrow hallway in the back. An answering, "Yo," was his deep greeting.

Holy fuck. Trip almost didn't recognize him. The man was huge. The teenager he remembered hadn't been. In fact, he'd been sort of gangly.

Had things fucking changed.

Judd Scott, aka "Judge," shouted at the dogs, "Stand down," and they both shut up instantly with a tail wag.

Trip jerked his chin toward the two dogs, now staring at him quietly. "They yours?"

"One of 'em."

And then didn't he unlatch the fucking door and let the dogs surge in Trip's direction?

Not only did Trip's asshole pucker at warp speed, but his balls retreated deep within his body cavity as one of the dogs shoved a nose into his crotch. And not gently, either.

Usually he liked an introduction before he got his nuts nuzzled. "They eat today?"

"Yeah, you're safe. Jury, stop molestin' the fuckin' guy." Judge's dark eyes hit Trip's. "Unless you like it?"

"Gonna say I like my women a bit less hairy."

"Yeah. Me, too." Judge snapped his fingers at the two dogs. "Jury. Justice. Knock it off. Go settle."

With one last sniff from each of them, the two dogs turned and with long tails held high and wagging at a leisurely pace, circled a few times and settled on the floor nearby with wide yawns.

"Good guard dogs," Trip muttered.

"The best. Got good instincts when it comes to people."

"Guess I passed their inspection."

"Just gotta pass mine next."

With a quick glance at the dogs, both now licking their own junk, he discovered Jury was a female and Justice a male. Information Trip didn't really need or care about. Though, at least he wasn't molested by the one with balls.

He cautiously approached Judge who now stood in front of the counter, leaning back against it, thick, muscular arms crossed in front of his chest. His lips were pressed tight as his dark eyes tracked Trip.

When Trip held out his hand, Judge stared at it for a long fucking time. But Trip refused to drop it. He was there to make amends and wouldn't leave until he was successful. Even if he ended up being dog food.

"Look like your old man," Trip finally said to break the uncomfortable silence.

"Yeah, so do you. Not sure why you're here."

"Bullshit. You know why I'm here." Trip was sure Dutch gave him the heads up because it was Dutch who told him where to find Judge.

"Drop the fuckin' hand. Not acceptin' it 'til I'm ready."

"Will you ever be ready?"

"Depends on what shit comes out of your fuckin' mouth."

Fuck. Trip reluctantly dropped his hand and nodded. "I'm not responsible for the shit my pop did."

"Yeah. But you're back diggin' in unhealed wounds. Pickin' off the scab and expectin' it not to sting."

"Time to heal those wounds and move past 'em."

"Not by doin' what you're doin'."

Trip heard the silent "asshole" Judge tacked onto that. "Was hopin' you'd join us. Would like you to take your pop's old spot."

Even with the thick beard, Trip spotted a muscle popping in Judge's cheek.

"You mean his old spot in fuckin' prison? Or the one six feet under 'cause he was ambushed in his cell while doin' life without parole because of the Fury? Which one, Trip? 'Cause I'm not lookin' to fill his boots in either of 'em."

Trip had no clue Ox, one of the Originals and, at the time, the club's enforcer, was dead. When Razor had shot Buck, Ox had no choice but to do the same to Razor for killing the club's president. Then Razor's brother shot at Ox, and that Original ended up dead, too. Ox went to Greene, a max security prison near Pittsburgh, for being convicted on two charges of first-degree murder and a shit-load of other charges.

He wasn't the only Original that had gone down at that

time. When members start taking sides and having hard feelings, shit tends to go sideways quickly.

"Need a Sergeant at Arms."

Judge tilted his head as he looked down at Trip. Yes, down. Judge had to be six foot three or so. Trip was just over six foot. He wasn't small, but sure felt like it next to Judge. The man's whole presence just felt larger than life.

"You hear any of what I just fuckin' said?"

"Heard you loud and fuckin' clear, Judge. Need to make the Fury strong, solid. Need you to help make that happen."

"So, you snag the president's spot like you own it and then make all the fuckin' decisions, that right?"

"The committee will make the decisions. But need a committee first."

Judge shook his head. "And you appointed yourself as the one who should sit at the head of the table."

"Once the club's reestablished, if I don't deserve it, vote me out. You know how it works."

"Yeah, know how it fuckin' works," Judge muttered.

"Dutch said you got your pop's sled."

Judge grunted.

"And you kept your pop's cut."

Another grunt.

"Shoulda been buried with Ox."

No answering grunt that time. But the man's jaw was now as hard as concrete.

"There's a fuckin' reason you didn't bury it, Judge."

More silence.

"Don't need the fuckin' hassle," the man finally said. "Don't need the pigs breathin' down my neck. Not in this business. Gotta keep shit above board. Gotta keep my record clean, 'specially for my concealed carry permit. Bein' a heavy for an MC can fuck up everything I built."

"Then don't take your pop's spot, just wear the colors.

We all grew up together, we were all brothers once. We can be that again."

The buzzer sounded as the front door opened and a man maybe a couple years younger than Trip walked in. He wore dark sunglasses and his long hair was braided from his forehead all the way down to the top of his back. Since the sides of his head were shaved, it reminded Trip of a mohawk or, *hell*, a damn Viking. He wore a light-weight black leather coat, even though it was way too warm for that.

Both large dogs jumped to their feet and ran to him. Not snarling like they had greeted Trip but wagging their tails and whining. Keeping his eyes on Trip, the man leaned over and ruffled their coats and heads.

"There's my babies," he murmured to them. Both dogs circled his legs as he straightened and did a chin lift to Judge, who returned it.

"Any luck?" Judge asked.

"Fuck no," the man answered and shrugged out of his coat, hanging it by the door.

Trip now realized why he wore the coat. The man was packing. He wore a leather double shoulder holster, with both holsters filled.

"Trip," Trip introduced himself as the man's dark eyes landed on him again.

Those dark eyes slid to Judge, then back to Trip.

He pursed his lips, patted both dogs on the head one more time and then said, "Deacon."

Trip didn't think Judge had a brother, but he kind of remembered hearing Judge had a younger sister. In fact, a lot younger, if he remembered correctly.

Deacon eyeballed Trip's cut, then his gaze sliced back to Judge. "He here for a bond?"

"No," Judge grunted.

"What's he here for?"

"You a cop?" Trip asked.

"I look like a cop?"

No, he didn't. Not with the hair, the beard, and both arms heavily tattooed. Not to mention, the gold ring piercing his left nostril. "Wonderin' why you're packin'. Could be undercover."

Deacon's grin was tight. "Packin' 'cause I work here."

"Didn't think this was a bad part of town."

"It ain't. Carry 'cause I'm a bounty hunter. I work for my cousin."

Cousin.

Right. There were a few similarities between the two, but they weren't enough to be twins, that was for damn sure.

"This the guy Dutch was yappin' about?" Deacon asked Judge.

"Yeah, that's him."

"Dutch has been doin' a lot of yappin' lately," Trip grumbled.

"Not every day someone comes into town wantin' to raise the dead. Gives folks somethin' to yap about," Deacon said.

"Not wantin' to raise the dead. Wantin' to start fresh. Also, have a proposition."

"Ah, fuck," Deacon groaned, moving behind the counter and removing his shoulder holster. "What's the proposition?" he asked Judge.

Judge shrugged, his eyes still on Trip. "Haven't heard that part yet."

"What part did you hear?"

"The part about me steppin' into Ox's boots."

"Fuck," Deacon groaned again. "Gonna guess the answer to that one." He twisted his head toward Trip. "Let's hear the rest."

"Besides the Fury, also gettin' the repo business up and

goin'. Thinkin' since you have skip tracin' experience, you could provide that service for me when I need it."

Deacon snorted. Judge remained silent.

"But probably already knew that since Dutch has been runnin' his mouth."

Judge finally spoke. "State gonna give you a repo license since you're a felon?"

That snag was another reason why he was there. "Probably not."

"Then you might just wanna tow for Dutch."

"Dutch has his own rollback."

"Then you're shit outta luck."

"License doesn't have to be in my name."

"Askin' for a fuck of a lot, Trip. Not only to wear the Fury's colors, but to be Sergeant at Arms. A risk to my business. Then you're hintin' at me puttin' your repo license in my name. Another fuckin' risk. Haven't seen you in twenty fuckin' years. You walk the fuck in here and want to do nothin' but take. What the fuck do I get outta all of this besides your dick up my ass? Anal ain't my thing unless I'm the one givin' it."

"I'll fuckin' do it," Deacon announced, shocking the shit out of Trip.

"Do what?" Judge barked, glancing behind him at his cousin.

"Put the repo license in my name. If they're just lookin' for felonies and misdemeanors, I'll be good."

"What do you want in exchange?" Trip asked him. He might be Judge's cousin, but he didn't know Deacon. And the man jumped at the chance way too quickly.

"A cut."

Of course. "A cut of the business?"

"Want a cut. Wanna wear the Fury's colors."

"That it?"

"And a cut of the business."

And there it was.

"Ten percent and I'll do all your skip tracin'. Since I'm a bounty hunter I can help you find people. I won't do any of the towin', though. Got too much shit to keep me busy here."

Ten percent. Trip had been ready to offer anyone who stepped up to get the repo license some sort of cut, but he wasn't sure about ten percent. That was a nice chunk of change. However, if Deacon was good at hunting people, he'd also be good at finding vehicles and their deadbeat loan holders. Plus, it didn't hurt that Deacon could pack legally, unlike Trip. If he needed help in a tight spot, Deacon might be able to step in.

Even at ten percent, it was a good deal. He'd get the repo business rolling, he'd get another Fury member, and... "You good with scratch?"

"Fuckin' great with snatch *and* scratch. Do most of the bookkeepin' here. Why?"

"Need a Treasurer. You in?"

Deacon grinned. "Yeah, I'm fuckin' in."

"You got a sled?"

"Got a decent one. But once I start gettin' that ten percent, buyin' me a new 1250 Custom. Seen those fuckers? Shit's badass as fuck. It'll keep me rollin' in pussy."

Judge grunted. "Maybe that's your damn problem. Not supposed to be rollin' in it like a dog rollin' in shit. Supposed to be fuckin' it with that tiny dick of yours."

Deacon's hand dropped below the counter and Trip could imagine he was grabbing his crotch. "Big enough to choke you."

"You gonna do this?" Judge asked Deacon, not looking any kind of happy.

Deacon shrugged. "Yeah, why not? Extra scratch will help me get my dream bike. Don't gotta do much extra work for it. Plus, I get to wear the Fury's colors."

"You weren't around when all the shit went down," Judge warned him.

"Yeah, but I know about it and he's," Deacon jerked his chin at Trip. "gonna make it all work, right?"

"Right," Trip muttered. He was going to do his fucking best.

Deacon reached over the counter and punched Judge in the arm. "C'mon, asshole, let's do this."

"This ain't like some rec club, Deke. An MC's a goddamn brotherhood. You live and die for it. Live and die for each other."

"Yeah, I get it. And I woulda prospected years ago if one of 'em was around." Deacon glanced at Trip. "I gotta prospect?"

"You're Ox's blood, right?"

"Yeah, my mother's Ox's sister."

"Then, you got Fury blood. You get a cut and also sit at the table as Treasurer."

Deacon smiled. "Can handle that."

"Good," Trip said. "Can you handle talkin' Judge into wearin' his pop's cut and sittin' next to you at the table?"

"Whataya think, Judge?" Deacon asked him. "We'll no longer be cousins, but brothers. Always wanted a brother," he teased.

"Then your pop shoulda stopped fuckin' your mother up the ass. Normally babies aren't born like that, you just happened to be a fuckin' miracle."

Trip dropped his head to hide his grin.

"Who else you got?"

He lifted his head at Judge's question. "Cage as Road Captain."

"That fuckin' dick," the big man grumbled.

"Dutch as VP 'til I can get the spot filled. Mouse and Sparky as prospects." He didn't get a reaction from Judge from any of those names. Only Cage's, which made Trip wonder if he made a mistake making the man Road Captain before he got to know him.

"That it?"

"Yeah, that's it for now. Lookin' for more prospects, also lookin' for more blood. Know any, send 'em my way. The bunkhouse is almost finished. Got a place for someone to live if needed."

"Rent free?" Deacon asked.

Trip hesitated. He was planning on letting the prospects stay for free in their bunk room. They'd have to pay for their own personal shit. But the rest of the rooms... "Not free, cheap. Maybe a C-note over the monthly dues." At least that would cover some of the expenses.

"Ain't bad. Cheaper than my shithole. Might have to take you up on one of those rooms."

"Also got two apartments. One is spoken for, though. The other, gotta figure out what kinda scratch I want for it."

"Got pussy?" Deacon asked.

"Not yet."

"Booze?"

"Workin' on that."

"Don't sound like much of a club," Judge grumbled.

"Gotta start somewhere. With you as the enforcer, just need a Secretary and we can have our first meetin'."

"Didn't say I was takin' it or even joinin'."

"At your granddaddy's old farm, right?" Deacon asked, ignoring his cousin.

"Yeah."

"We'll both be out to scope it out. I know anyone interested, they gotta prospect?"

"Yeah, right now six months. Unless they're blood of one of the Originals. Like you." He turned to meet Judge's dark eyes. "Like Judge."

"Ain't gonna get an opportunity like that anywhere else and maybe never again." Deacon came through the half-door and approached Trip. He held out his hand. They clasped palms and bumped shoulders.

"Brother," Trip mumbled.

"Brother," Deacon mumbled back. "Always wanted a brother," he said again, this time not in a teasing tone.

"Now you got one," Trip answered, his eyes slid to Judge. "More than one."

"How you gonna pay for all this shit?" came from the tall man with the *less-than-happy* expression.

"Bought The Grove Inn. The repo business. Dues. Workin' on some other shit."

One of Judge's dark eyebrows lifted. "All legal shit?"

"Yeah. Gonna do my best to keep shit above board. Keep my ass and everyone else's out of concrete boxes, whether it has bars or goes six feet under. No more bloodshed between brothers."

"Just brotherly love," Deacon said in a sing-song voice and then made kissy-faces at Judge, who returned the gesture with a middle finger salute and a scowl.

"Who's gonna run these businesses? Prospects?" With each question Judge asked, Trip could see his interest slightly increase. Though, he was trying hard to hide it.

"Yeah, hopefully. Patched members who need a job. Ol' ladies." Trip shrugged. "If I gotta hire people, I hire people."

"Who's gonna help you repo?"

Trip hesitated. Here was where he hoped Judge's flicker of interest didn't burn out. "Hopin' Sig."

Judge's head tipped back, and his jaw got tight again. "Sig."

"Yeah."

"Think that's a good idea?"

"Guess I'll find out when I find him."

"He wanna be found?"

"Don't know," Trip answered Judge.

"You might want good things for the Fury, not so sure Sig will. And not so sure that 'brotherly love' Deke was rippin' on will exist between you two."

It sounded like it hadn't been twenty years since Judge saw Sig, which surprised Trip. "You know where the fuck he's at?"

"Nope."

"You willin' to find him for me?"

Judge turned to Deacon. "Man must got a fuckin' monster set hangin' between his legs."

"Takin' that as a compliment," Trip told him.

"Don't. Havin' a set like that only makes 'em a bigger target. And it hurts a fuck of a lot more when you get kicked in 'em."

"True. But I'm tryin' to not only rebuild but repair the past. Willin' to take the hits if I need to."

"No reason to. Could let it all lie where it was."

"I could. But it's all I got and I'm gonna take what I got and make it into something." He paused, then added, "With or without you, Judge. Though, I hope you join us."

"Don't sound invitin'. No pussy, no booze, and a bunch of assholes."

Trip grinned at Judge. "Means you'll fit right in."

Deacon snorted, whacked Trip on the back and said, "Leave lookin' for Sig to me. I'll see what I can do."

"If Deke can't find 'im, no one can," Judge said. "Hope you don't fuckin' regret it when he does."

Trip hoped he didn't, either.

Chapter Five

STELLA SAT at a table in the back by the old jukebox. She had slipped enough quarters in it to play a few of her favorite songs while she paid bills.

Or attempted to pay bills.

She looked at the mountain of torn open envelopes sitting in front of her. She had divided them up into past due, due now, due soon and *you're-fucked-if-you-don't-pay-these* piles. The last one included a couple of her utility bills and liquor invoices.

Without electricity and booze, she might as well board up Crazy Pete's. But the collection of unpaid bills in front of her was a lot larger than the balance in her checkbook.

She scrubbed her hands down her face and sighed loudly so she wouldn't scream instead.

She couldn't afford to pay her expenses without customers. It was only a little after midnight, closing time wasn't until two, and she hadn't seen a customer since ten. Even then, it was only the guy who lived down the street and regularly walked in to buy a six-pack.

Thank fuck for him.

As Joan Jett's rendition of *Crimson and Clover* wailed from the speakers, Stella also wanted to wail.

She wanted to kick, scream, cry and stomp her foot. But she knew it wouldn't do any good. Instead, she dropped her head into her folded arms and breathed deeply in and out of her nose.

A few minutes later she was back at Trip's barn, seeing him shirtless and working hard. Determined to do everything he could to bring the Fury back better than ever.

Her memory began to shift... Instead of releasing her wrist when they were standing toe to toe, he refused to let her go. And when he dropped his head, he did it until his lips were right above hers.

She didn't want him to kiss her then, but she wanted him to kiss her now. She wanted to feel his lips against hers.

And then he did. Firm lips taking control, his tongue sweeping through her mouth, tangling with hers.

She didn't fight back. She didn't shove him away. She allowed herself that moment in time to simply let go. To forget her worries, forget everything else except for him.

Nothing else existed but them. In that moment.

No past. No future. Just the now.

Deepening the kiss, he lifted her hand and put it on his chest over his heart, so she could feel the strong *thump, thump, thump*. Her palm absorbed the warmth of his skin and her fingertips pressed into his rock-hard muscles.

He pinned her hand there, his so much larger than hers. So much stronger than hers.

His kiss became desperate, like he couldn't get enough of her. He released her hand and dug his fingers into her hair, holding her where he wanted her. Forcing her face up, her lips to open wider.

Her own heart beat as quickly as his. A longing shot through her, making her clench in places that hadn't been touched in ages, because she'd been too exhausted and too distracted to even take care of her own needs.

Her mind had been occupied solely with surviving.

Her breasts ached for his touch, and so did everything else.

She had wanted to marry that boy. But what she wanted from him now had nothing to do with love, commitment, or even "forever."

Nothing at all.

She groaned into his mouth, encouraging him, begging him to touch her.

She needed his touch to remind her she was very much alive. How she wasn't dead inside and to stop going through life like a zombie.

Every day was a struggle. Not just one, but many.

She wanted to accept his help, but she couldn't. She needed to do this herself. Needed to prove she could succeed on her own and didn't need to depend on anyone again.

She desperately needed his help and it would lighten her load, but her pride...

Her damn pride...

She didn't need him. She had to find another way.

She broke the kiss, jerked away from him and opened her eyes.

She wasn't in the barn. She was still in the bar.

She had no idea how long she was out, but she must have fallen asleep and her memory had turned into a dream. She lifted her head from her arms and her heart skipped a beat, then began to race.

Trip stood in front of the table, his hands on his hips, watching her with his brown eyes, darker than normal. "Must've been a good dream."

"Part of it," she murmured, because she couldn't deny her panties were damp from their kiss. The deep rumble of his voice might be a factor, too. "How'd you get in here?"

"Had the fuckin' door unlocked."

His pissed off growl cleared the remaining cobwebs from her brain, and she glanced at the time on her cell phone.

Damn. The bar was technically still open since it was only shy of one a.m. She still had an hour to go.

Fuck it. She would close early.

She began to gather the piles of envelopes and bills into one. "What are you doing here?"

His eyes watched her every move. "Checkin' up on you."

Her hands stilled, then she started gathering everything even faster. "I don't need checked on."

"Wanted to see if you thought about my offer."

SHE DROPPED her eyes from his. "Thought about it." Trip and his offer was all she'd thought about the last few days.

"And?"

"And the answer is still no."

The song on the jukebox changed from its current song to *Do You Wanna Touch Me.*

She groaned silently. Why had she been on a Joan Jett kick tonight?

She surged from her chair and he stopped her by grabbing her wrist.

Just like at the barn. Like in her dream.

Why did he think he had the right to touch her? Or, *hell,* restrain her. "Let me go, Trip."

He jerked his chin toward the table. At the bills, at her anemic checkbook, at her puddle of tears of frustration. "Will you fuckin' admit you need help?"

"I don't need your help."

His head jerked back. "See how you said that? Don't need *my* help, but you need help. Fuckin' let me help you, Stella."

Boy, he was stretching her words. "Why do you care? Why do you want to help me?"

"'Cause... 'cause this bar was part of the club and I don't wanna see it fail. Don't wanna see you fail."

Bullshit.

The bar maybe, because he thought he had a vested interest in it. But her? No. Her failure would only be beneficial to him by giving him a chance to swoop in and steal it from her.

She pulled free of him, relieved when he let her go without a fight, and she went over to the jukebox to change the song. Of course, the next song was *Love Hurts* by Nazareth.

If that wasn't her fucking life's theme song...

Jesus. She reached behind the jukebox and pulled the plug from the outlet, killing both the power and the music.

Suddenly, the bar was way too fucking silent.

He didn't look even remotely happy. Well, good, she wasn't, either. She did not need him barging into her life and trying to take over.

And she certainly didn't want to owe him shit.

She was not going to be indebted to some badass wannabe, who felt the need to dig into a past that had turned out shitty for just about everyone involved.

Just no.

She slammed the cover of the checkbook binder closed before he got a good look at the balance, grabbed all the bills, shoved them into the binder, and strode across the bar.

Away from him.

She walked faster when she heard his footsteps behind her.

As she stepped behind the bar, she came to an abrupt halt, blocking his path. "You can't come back here."

He ignored her and bumped her from behind with his chest to move her out of the way. "Watch me."

She shoved the over-stuffed binder under the bar to deal with tomorrow and watched as Trip grabbed a bottle of Jack off the shelf, a glass from the rack, and poured himself a double. No, a triple.

She couldn't afford for him to drink for free, especially top shelf shit. Whether the club "owned" a part of Pete's or not. "You need to pay for that."

He downed the whiskey, grimaced and slammed the glass onto the bar. He pulled his large leather wallet from his back pocket and dug out a twenty. When he held it out and she reached for it, he jerked it away.

What an asshole. "Throw it on the bar and I'll get you your change," she said as she moved toward the cash register.

Unfortunately, she had to pass him to get to it. As she did, he fucking grabbed her *again*!

This time by the back of her neck and as she brought her hands up to break free, he snagged her wrist again.

If she fought him, he would only tighten his grip, so she tried to remain calm, even though her heart was beating right out of her chest and her breathing had become choppy and shallow.

Why did he have this effect on her? He shouldn't.

"Stella."

And why the fuck did her name on his lips and the way he was holding her make her lose her breath? "Let me go."

It was impossible to hide her reaction to him. Which put her at a disadvantage.

Even so, she would not give in.

If she did, everything around her would collapse. Again.

She would lose control of her life. Lose control of what was hers.

She'd lose everything.

She did not need a man like Trip in her life.

She didn't need a fucking man at all.

And the fucking balls on him...

She lifted her chin and met his eyes directly. "Let. Me. Go."

"What were you dreamin' about, Stella?"

She jerked her arm, but he held tight.

"Same thing I've been dreamin' about every night?" His anger had softened a bit, but it was still there, barely simmering beneath the surface.

"Depends. Are you dreaming about when you pushed an eleven-year-old girl so hard she cracked her head open on a concrete block wall? Is that what you're dreaming?"

The fingers on the back of her neck tightened and the ones around her wrist twitched.

"Let me go, Trip."

"I was fuckin' fifteen, Stella."

"And that makes it okay?"

"No, it doesn't make it fuckin' okay. But what fifteen-year-old kid wants a little girl chasin' him around tryin' to kiss him and demandin' he marry her?"

None. She knew that now and she knew that later once she was old enough to know better.

"Try kissin' me now. Bet you won't get that same response."

What? "You know what? It would be the same result. It'd be like slamming my head against a fucking concrete wall. Back then I thought you were the greatest, now I see you as you really are."

"And how's that?"

She could see it in his face. Him putting up a wall, becoming guarded. And a muscle in his tight jaw jumped.

"Someone with nothing and nobody. Someone scrambling to make something out of nothing because you don't have shit to show for the last thirty-five years."

As she tried pulling away from him again, he spun them

until her ass was against the back counter and his hips had her pinned.

His brown eyes glittered fiercely. "Sounds fuckin' familiar, Stella. What do you have to show for your thirty-one years on this goddamn Earth? This run-down goddamn bar that was handed to you? A mountain of debt? What? What do you have to show? No man. No kids. No fuckin' nothin'. So, before you start throwin' stones, you better move outta your own goddamn glass house."

She sucked in a sharp breath. "Fuck you, Trip."

The motherfucker smiled.

And that didn't cool down her anger at all. "You just walk in here out of fucking nowhere, and then think you're going to be some fucking hero and help the damsel in distress? For what? What the hell do you expect to get out of this?"

"Told you what."

What she didn't want to give him. "A portion of the bar."

"Half of the bar."

Half... Suddenly, she couldn't breathe. "And I'll say it again... Fuck. You. Trip."

"Give me half and you'll have more fuckin' money in your pocket than you do now."

"Right."

"Swear it. You'll have free or cheap labor—"

"Prospects—"

"Money to invest in fixin' up this shithole—"

"I don't want to turn this into a fucking biker bar, Trip."

"It doesn't have to be a fuckin' biker bar, Stella! Fuck! You're so goddamn stubborn."

She wasn't the only one. "Because you want me to give up half of everything that belongs to me. Just like that, you walk in twenty fucking years later and you want half." Like she was in the middle of a bad divorce.

"Let me help you."

Fuck that. "No."

Trip closed his eyes and his nostrils flared. His fingers had flexed on her wrists, which were pinned between their bodies.

She shoved at him, but he didn't budge. "Back off."

His eyes opened and their gazes locked. "If I back up, you're gonna knee me in the nuts."

"And you'd deserve it because I still owe you one."

He dropped his head until his mouth was just above hers.

Like at the barn. Like in her dream.

Though, with two different results.

His warm breath beat rapidly against her lips. His jaw was working and his eyes so intense, they seared her. "If you fuckin' think I hurt you on purpose, you'd be fuckin' wrong."

She blinked back the sting in her eyes.

She had already cried enough tears to last a lifetime. She wasn't going to cry over this man, or any other man, ever again.

She stared at his parted lips as he challenged her, "Try to kiss me again, Stella. You know you wanna."

No. No. No. Don't fall down that fucking rabbit hole.

"I don't want anything to do with you."

His eyelids got heavy and those lips of his, the ones she couldn't pull her gaze from, curled at the corners.

He knew she was lying.

Because even though she would be leaping into that bottomless pit, she wanted nothing more than to feel those lips on hers. What the little girl inside her wanted back then and was denied. What the woman who she was today dreamed about after the other day in the barn.

That little girl had thought the sun rose and set in that boy.

Now she was too jaded to think that.

She'd been dead inside for over a year. When she wasn't angry or sad, she was numb.

But sex with Trip might make her feel alive once more.

Might.

And that right there was too much of a risk. Because with sex, there were always complications.

She worried Trip would think he owned her afterward. Women were no more than property to bikers. She'd seen it. Even with her mother. With the rest of the original ol' ladies, too.

And he might use that as a way to get his hands on her bar.

Her bar.

No longer Pete's.

Not the club's.

Not Trip's.

This was her fucking bar, and no one was taking it from her. No one was ever taking away what was hers again.

And one night with Trip wasn't worth the risk of losing it. No matter how alive it would make her feel. No matter how much it would remind her that the world hadn't stopped that day. At least for everyone else.

Even so, she was the captain of her own destiny now and if she went down with the ship... Then so be it.

"Fuck you," she forced out.

"Yeah, you wanna do that, too."

"You are so fucking full of yourself."

"Yeah."

Yeah. The arrogant asshole didn't even bother to deny it. "Let me get your change so you can get the fuck out of my bar."

"Keep the fuckin' change. You need it more than me."

That blade sliced deep. "I don't need your fucking charity."

He shook his head, regret in his eyes and his tone. "We all used to be family once."

Stella's blood ran cold. "Family doesn't hurt family." But she knew that was a complete lie. The pain family could inflict was always the worst and sometimes the deepest.

"You need to fuckin' let that go."

"Which part? Where you hurt me? What your father did? What Razor did? What happened to Ox and all the rest of our so-called *family*?"

"I'm only responsible for the first one. The rest I had nothin' to do with, Stella. You fuckin' know that. I'm done apologizin' for what I did. You can't forgive me, then..." He shrugged. "Then fuck you, don't forgive me. Don't give a shit, let that eat at you just like the rest of the past. Me? I'm movin' forward, makin' amends, makin' somethin' outta my life. You wanna sit alone in this dingy fuckin' bar feelin' sorry for yourself? Do it while listenin' to a few Joan Jett songs, then get the fuck over it and move the fuck on. Now, I'm done askin' and I'm just takin'."

What the fuck did *that* mean?

He let her wrist go, but still kept his hand firmly around the back of her neck and her pinned to the counter with his body as he reached into his cut and pulled out a worn, folded piece of lined notebook paper. He shoved it against her chest and her fingers automatically grabbed at it, but he didn't let go. He held onto it as he kept talking.

"The Fury is mine. That means half of this bar is mine. If you don't believe me, that's the agreement Pete signed with Buck thirty years ago. The club financed the whole fuckin' bar, Stella. The whole goddamn thing. The agreement was Pete and the club split the profits fifty-fifty. And for the last twenty fuckin' years, Pete kept all of the fuckin' profits. You don't want me collectin' that debt, Stella. Swear to fuck, you don't. So the best thing for you to do is to put my fuckin' name on the deed next to yours and... let... me... fuckin'... help... you."

The last was said only inches away from her face, which she was sure was as white as a ghost, since all the blood had drained from it.

She wondered if what Trip said was true, whether the paper in his hand was legally-binding. She was afraid to look at it. Afraid to think about what all he just said meant.

She knew the club helped Pete buy the bar, she had no idea that they had paid for the whole thing.

Fuck. If it wasn't for Trip coming back to Manning Grove and opening those wounds, no one would've known. If it wasn't for him, she wouldn't be in this situation right now, losing the one thing she had left.

The *only* thing she had left.

Without the bar she had absolutely *nothing*.

No home. No job. No future.

She dropped her head and tried to breathe. Tried to still her spinning thoughts.

This was all his fault for coming back.

This was all Trip's fault for digging up the past.

Her father never told her.

No one ever told her.

Christ, the rug was just pulled out from beneath her again. Her future unsure, questionable.

She couldn't start over again. She couldn't.

She would be forced to give him half the bar. Forced to deal with him on a regular basis.

She tried to swallow the sob that rushed up from her chest. She couldn't contain her sign of weakness, so she turned it into a scream instead as she slammed both hands into his chest. "Bastard!"

He grunted at the force of her hit but didn't move back. Instead, he pinned her tighter against the counter.

"You fucking bastard! You knew this all along, didn't you?"

"No—"

"You knew this and were playing me!"

"No, Stella—"

"You did. This was just a game to you. A power play."

"No, just wanted—"

"*You* wanted," she hissed. "*You*. Fuck Stella, right?"

"Stella."

"You know what I want?" Before he could answer, she slammed him in the chest again with both palms, causing another loud grunt. "I want you out of my fucking bar. I want you out of my life." She was now screaming in his face.

She couldn't stop. She couldn't. Her fear, her rage, her frustration was bubbling up and over. Leaking. Escaping. Like the steam from a pressure cooker. She couldn't contain it because if she did, she'd explode.

Her heart was beating so hard, so fast, she swore she was going to have a heart attack.

A heart that had been irrevocably broken, then withered and died.

"Not leavin' the bar."

She couldn't take any more loss because she had nothing left to lose.

Nothing.

Trip just claimed the last thing she was clinging to.

"Then I will. I'll get my shit and get out. You can have it." *But you can't have me.*

"Stella..."

"Get out of my way." As she went to slam him again, to break free from him, from the chains he was trying to bind her in, he grabbed her wrists in a grip so tight she winced.

He got up into her face and growled, "Learned the hard

way twenty fuckin' years ago not to put my hands on a female, but you're fuckin' pushin' my patience, woman."

"Good. Because I have zero fucks left to give. I'm fresh out."

"You better dig deep and find some, woman, because I need you to run this fuckin' bar and help me make it a success. The club needs the money and so do you."

"Once again, Trip... *You* need. My life does not revolve around your needs."

"No, it revolves around yours. And you're too fuckin' stubborn to see it."

"Let me go so I can go pack up my shit."

"You're not goin' anywhere."

She knew one way to get him to free her. And he was too close to knee him in the nuts.

She relaxed every muscle in her body, raised her face to his, and whispered her challenge. "Who's going to stop me? You?"

Anger quickly disappeared from his eyes and heat took its place. His look was wary but interested. And she immediately felt his body change. One particular part was starting to press hard against her belly.

"Yeah," he murmured. "Me."

She ran her tongue over her bottom lip then tucked that lip between her teeth. His eyes followed every one of those movements.

Typical fucking male. Dangle a bit of sex in front of him and he was putty in her hands. Thinking with his dick and not his brain.

"You can let me go and the bar could be all yours and the club's."

"Don't wanna let you go, Stella. Want you to stay."

She wanted to demand why. She would hand the bar over to him free and clear. "You don't need me."

"The fuck I don't."

His words were soft but sharply edged at the same time. She ignored some of the implications behind them.

He would never own her. She was not property. She wouldn't be used or passed around.

She had grown up watching women be forced to do things they didn't want to do.

She would never be that woman.

Never.

Chapter Six

He wasn't sure what Stella was trying to pull. One minute she was hard and resistant, the next soft and compliant.

Sort of.

He wasn't falling for that bullshit.

He hadn't wanted to use the agreement against her, but she'd forced his hand. He would've preferred she'd let him help her by her own choice.

But fuck no.

If he had any fucking sense in his head, he'd let her do what she threatened. Pack up her shit and leave. He could turn this bar around without her by using the MC to run it. It could be profitable for both the bar and the club.

He couldn't imagine she'd just walk away.

But, worse, he couldn't let her.

Did he want her? Fuck yes.

Did she want him?

Both in the barn and even now, he saw the pulse pounding along the delicate line of her throat. It wasn't from fear.

Fuck no.

He was stirring something deep down inside her, the same as she was doing to him.

He came back to Manning Grove to get his life in order, to rebuild the club. He did not come back to find a woman. He didn't need that complication, he had too much work to do.

But Stella wasn't just any woman. She knew the ins and outs of an MC. She came from Fury blood.

She also had a passion and determination he admired. She was like a pit bull hanging on to the throat of this bar, until she had nothing left. She would starve to death before letting go.

He knew this not only because of what Dutch had told him—the man could flap his gums—but by what he saw in her.

Her grit.

It was the same as his.

She was the kind of woman who could stand by his side and help him rebuild. A woman who would not need constant reassurances, would not want to play relationship head games or keep him on a leash.

He would not take this bar from her. Which meant she'd have to stay.

But she needed to see the only way out of the hole she had fallen into was to take his offered hand. Because anyone else would come in, take the bar, and kick her ass out the door.

And then she'd truly have nothing.

Instead, he wanted to give her something.

However, he needed something from her in return.

The first and most important thing so he could do that, would be for her to stop fighting him.

With the look she was now giving him and the way her body had gone soft against his, anybody not thinking clearly would think she was being compliant. Accepting. Resigned.

But Trip knew it was a trap.

Even so... Did he want her? Fuck yes.

Did he want to get his nuts knocked into next Tuesday? Fuck no.

She was cunning. But then, so was he. So, he recognized her tactic.

However, he did not appreciate it. Not at fucking all.

But two could play that goddamn game.

"Then go." He released her and twisted his hips away to make sure his sac wasn't in her strike zone. "Get your shit and get the fuck outta here. But let me say this. You walk away, don't fuckin' come back. You walk away, you give it all up. Gave you a chance to make somethin' from nothin' and you just fuckin' shit on it." He jerked his chin toward the rear exit of Crazy Pete's. "So fuckin' go." He added fuel to the fire. "Had a year to get this place turned around, you failed. I'll do it in a couple of months without you bein' in the way."

As he turned to walk away, to completely dismiss her, he heard her sharp intake of breath.

He braced.

The rush of booted feet, the howl of frustration, then the impact of her against his back. Fists pounded him, more of an annoyance than anything. But it wasn't until she yanked his leather skull cap off his head and grabbed a fistful of his hair, just about ripping it out of his scalp, that he decided it was time to end this shit.

Time for him to get things straight with her.

Time to lay out the rules.

Because she was not leaving that bar, or even town, if he had anything to say about it.

He spun on his heel and brought a fist up to break her grip on his hair. And when he did, he clamped his hands on her wrists, trying to control her flailing arms. Her face was nothing but a twisted mask of pain, frustration and exhaustion.

He recognized it because he'd been there. He'd been in her shoes.

Somehow he needed to convince her that he wasn't the bad guy. He wasn't out to hurt her. Or take what little she was clinging to.

When her boot made contact with his shin, making him suck in a breath and then release it in a loud, "Fuck!" he... was... done.

Completely fucking done.

He jerked her around and shoved her against the back counter, bending her over, pinning her hands under her chest and holding her down. With one hand he grabbed a handful of her hair and used it to yank her head up. He dropped his next to hers. "You fuckin' done?"

Her answer was her spitting at him. With his hand to the back of her head, he forced her right cheek against the counter, holding her still. "You ain't fuckin' done. Tell me when you're done."

"I'm not letting you take what's mine, Trip. So, fuck you."

"We're back to that again? We already established whose fuckin' bar it is. So, you can fight me all you like. I can do this all fuckin' night, Stella. And I know you won't last all night because I can see how fuckin' exhausted you are. Can see the shadows under your eyes and the desperation in them, too."

"Fuck... you," she hissed between gritted teeth.

He put his mouth against her ear, whispering, "I'd be happy to give you what you want, Stella. Just add a few words to that demand."

"Fuck... you."

"Still missin' those words," he growled, then sank his teeth into the top curve of her left ear. He tongued the small hoops that pierced the upper curve of cartilage. "You wanted a kiss all those years ago, I can give you so much more than that. Just say the words."

"You'll just take what you want." Her words barely discernible between her panting. "Just like the bar."

She was stoking his flames by poking at the embers, trying to create an out of control bonfire within him.

But prison had taught him a lot of things.

One being how to control his temper. The reason he'd ended up in a concrete box in the first place. The reason he'd ended up in the hole time after time until he learned that hard lesson.

"Fuck that. Not endin' up back in the joint, just so you can get me outta your hair. Not gonna work. Pussy ain't worth prison. No matter how tight, sweet or wet it is."

Her jaw was clenched but her words came out more breathless than pissed. "You think I want you, but you're wrong."

No, he wasn't wrong. Another lesson learned the hard way. How to read people. It kept his throat from being sliced and his asshole from being stretched.

"No? How hard are your nipples right now, Stella? How wet's that pussy? How much do you want me to rip down your jeans and fuck you hard just like this? From behind." By tilting his hips, he showed her just how hard he was for her. How much he wanted her.

But he wouldn't take her. Not like that.

A whimper then a shuddered breath escaped her lips and her eyes squeezed shut.

"You don't want this?"

She spoke no answer but her heavy breathing gave her away. And that wasn't the only thing. Her ass began to rock against his hard dick.

"Tell me you don't want this. You tell me and I'll fuckin'

stop, let you go and you can get your shit and get the fuck out."

She growled and ground against him even harder.

Yeah, right. She didn't want him to let her go. But she needed to be a pain in his fucking ass right to the very end. Because she was too stubborn to admit she was wrong. She was too stubborn to admit outright what she wanted.

She liked to fight, to give as good as she got. To make things more difficult than they had to be. She'd never be sweet and pliable. Everything would always be trying with her.

Every-*fucking*-thing.

But she had no idea how he fucking ate that shit up. That her being defiant made him even hungrier.

He lived for challenges. That was how he'd survived in the Marines and also in prison.

He fought hard for what he had, everything he wanted.

And he'd fight hard for her.

If she didn't want to admit out loud she wanted him, then fuck her. She didn't need to. Her movements and the noises she made gave her away.

"Want that dick, Stella?"

Again, no answer.

"Gotta tell me you want it, or you ain't gettin' it. Need to hear it loud and fuckin' clear. Won't give up my freedom for a quick fuck."

"I can't... can't give it. You need... to take it."

All the air rushed from his lungs. Was that consent? There was no fucking way he was fucking her without her consent. No fucking way.

"Just take it!" she screamed.

Goddamn.

Did that mean she wanted him to give it to her hard and rough?

This better not be a damn trap. "Stella..."

"Stop being a pussy and just fucking take it!"

Fuck.

His brain might still be unsure, but his cock wasn't. His dick was an enthusiastic *all-systems-a-go*.

If he had a lick of fucking sense, he should just walk away from her. He wanted her but he wasn't sure it was worth the risk.

"Goddamn you, Trip, just fuck me!"

For fuck's sake, that was pretty fucking clear.

She began to squirm. He thought she was trying to get free and was about to let her go, when she managed to shove her jeans and panties down to mid-thigh, exposing...

Fuck.

The roots of the tree tattooed onto her back became visible along the top curves of her ass and those roots spread all the way from one hip to the other... But it was that ass...

His balls tightened uncomfortably as he released her and stepped back. He gave her plenty of time and freedom to change her mind as he purposely took his time to pull out his wallet, snag a wrap and tuck it between his teeth. The jangle of his belt buckle as he unfastened it made her body jerk against the counter, but she didn't straighten, she didn't bolt. She didn't make a move to escape. In fact, she widened her stance as far as her dropped jeans would allow, then she settled in. Waiting.

His heart beat furiously as he dropped his own jeans to his knees, rolled the wrap down his throbbing cock, and shuffled forward again.

Sliding a finger down her tempting crease, he ignored the tightening of her anus as he slid over it until he found her slick heat. Just like he thought.

Her breathing was loud, ragged and quick. His was the same. But he held it as he slipped the head of his cock between her lips until he found his target.

The spot that would change everything.

Fuck. He should walk away from this. Sex between them would create problems. More than they had already. It could take the mess they were dealing with and turn it into a full-blown disaster.

But if that happened, he would deal with it. Like everything else.

Because Stella might be a pain in his ass, but she was going to be his pain in the ass.

"What the fuck are you waiting for?"

Damn. If she wanted to be like that...

He seated the tip where it needed to be, dug his fingers into her hips and slammed it home. He actually had to pause, take a breath, gather his scattered brain cells. Because, *fuck*, it had been a few months. In fact, the last pussy he had was when he was down in Shadow Valley.

But this wasn't a sweet butt. This wasn't just any pussy.

This was Stella.

She was soaking wet and the inside of her hot, slick pussy rippled around his dick, massaging it. Squeezing it to the point where if she kept that up, he'd fucking blow his load way before he was ready to.

But she wasn't going to get that satisfaction. Fuck no.

"You're gonna make me work for this. So, it better be worth my fuckin' while."

"Shut up and do it."

He gritted his teeth and almost pulled out. That would show her.

But then that would fuck him, too. And not in a good way.

Since after this, there was no way he was letting her go anywhere, they had plenty of time to get shit straight between them. But now was not it.

Instead, he gave her what she wanted. What he had fantasized about since the first time he walked back into

Crazy Pete's and saw her. Even before he realized who she was.

With each pounding thrust, their skin slapped together, her ass rippled, and air rushed from her parted lips. Her fingers now free from being trapped beneath her were digging into the counter. Her cheek was still pressed to the countertop, her eyes closed, her back arched, as she gave him full access to her ass.

"Harder."

That single word was enough to cause a build up of pressure within him. He was riding the edge already, so he couldn't give it to her much harder than he had been. If he did, he would shatter in seconds. He was struggling to keep his shit together. But he also wasn't slowing down. He wasn't making it sweet.

He was giving it to her how he wanted to, how she wanted it. Because her growl of defiance was long gone. Every deep plunge caused a whimper she tried to muffle. A cry she tried to hide.

Why the fuck she'd want to do that, he had no fucking clue.

But he wasn't holding back. With each slam of his hips, she milked his dick, pulling a low groan from him. In a desperate attempt to make it last, he'd pull out, pause, before powering forward once again with a grunt.

He wanted to see her face, see her tits, take her mouth. But that wasn't going to happen. Not tonight. No, because this was a fucking power play between them. A way to break the tension. To claim what would be his.

Fuck that. What *was* his.

She could fight him on that. But she would lose.

"That pussy's mine. Claimin' it right now. That ass and mouth will be mine, too."

Her next "fuck you" came out on a ragged breath, the exclamation point a gasp.

"Yeah, I'm fuckin' you and you can't get enough of it, can you? You like my dick in your cunt. You want more."

"Can't give me more, can you? Not without breaking."

Jesus fuck. "Think you're goddamn tough. Won't ever be tougher than me."

"That's where you're wrong, Trip. I've got nothing left to lose."

His pace stuttered and almost came to a halt.

He knew what that was like, too, having nothing left to lose. It could make someone dangerous from their desperation, their will to survive.

"Told you. You can't give me what I want," she taunted him.

"Bullshit." He took a handful of her long black hair with those goddamn blue highlights and gripped it tight. He yanked her head up, forcing a gasp from her and her eyes to open. "Want it hard? Want it fast? Want it until it hurts? You fuckin' got it."

"Shut up and do it," she hissed.

Even getting fucked, she still hung onto the anger. Still provoked him. She wanted him to hurt her.

Why? Why the fuck did she want that?

Why would anybody prefer the pain over pleasure?

She reached back and grabbed his forearms, digging her black-painted nails into his flesh, ripping his skin.

He grabbed her hands, torquing them up behind her back until he knew it had to hurt. His arms had been held like that one too many times, right before the cold metal cuffs took his freedom.

He couldn't give her the bite of handcuffs, but he could make her hurt in other ways. If that's what she wanted...

He took both her wrists in one hand, holding them mid-back, ripped her hair to the side and bit the back of her neck hard.

She cried out but didn't tell him to stop as he drove his dick into her even harder.

It was raw. It was brutal and this wasn't what he had wanted.

But it was her words now driving him on. Encouraging him to continue on one breath, while cursing him with the next.

He wanted to bring her to orgasm, but she was fucking with his head. Her teeth were bared when she sneered, "You can't make me come."

He'd had enough. "Fuck you," he growled. He released her wrists, jammed his hand between her and the counter, found her swollen, slick clit and pinched it so hard, she bucked against him.

He ripped her head back again by her hair and sank his teeth into the side of her neck almost hard enough to draw blood.

She exploded around him, cursing him, the intensity of her orgasm pushing him to his own.

He drove deep one more time, grunted against her skin, around the hold his teeth had, as his balls emptied. Never in his life had he had such an intense release, his dick pulsing like it had its own heart as he filled the wrap.

After a few moments, he released both his hold on her neck and her hair and tried to catch his breath. His heart was pounding so hard, his thoughts in such a tailspin, he couldn't move.

Not yet.

His whole being had splintered and he was having a hard time gathering the pieces.

What the fuck had happened? What the fuck did this all mean?

"Get the fuck off me."

Nothing, apparently. "Gimme a sec."

She began to scream, "Get off me! Get off me! Get off me!" causing him to wince.

What the fuck was wrong with her?

He straightened and stared down at her as he secured the wrap at the base with his fingers and carefully pulled out, hoping it didn't spill inside her because it was that full.

Before he could pull it off and get rid of it, she spun around and shoved him hard, making him stumble back.

"I hate you!"

Tears were streaming down her face faster than she could wipe them away. She gave up and jerked up her jeans, securing them, her face pale, her eyes holding a whole mix of things Trip couldn't even begin to decipher.

"Stella..." He slipped the condom off, knotted it and tossed it into a garbage pail tucked under the bar nearby.

"Get out of my bar. Get out of my life." No anger drove those words. Instead it was desolation. Loss. Giving up.

"Stella—"

She pointed toward the door, the tears coming unchecked now. "Get the fuck out."

He yanked up his jeans. "I'm not fuckin' leavin' you like this."

"I don't need you."

The deep-seated disgust and pain in those words twisted in his chest. Were they for him? Or herself?

And then it hit him...

It wasn't him she'd wanted, him she'd needed.

It was punishment. She had needed the harsh punishment for some reason.

Jesus fuck.

She had used him.

Used him to get whatever she needed.

She sucked in a deep but shaky breath, then screamed, "GET OUT!"

Before he could catch her, she collapsed to the floor.

"Stella!"

He dropped to his knees next to her, sweeping her long hair out of her face. She was conscious but her eyes were empty, even though she was still sobbing hard enough that each one wracked her body.

"Jesus fuck, woman," he murmured, scared she had some sort of mental break.

Had he drove her to it? Was this his fault? Had he pushed her too hard?

It was never his intent to hurt her.

For fuck's sake, if he caused this...

"I can't do it anymore," she cried. "I can't."

"Hey—"

"I can't take anymore. I can't."

"Stella—"

She wasn't hearing him.

"I can't. I have nothing left."

She wasn't seeing him.

"I'm empty. I'm empty. I have nothing left."

She rolled to her side in the narrow space between the front and back bar. Pulling her knees into her chest, she pressed her face to them and wrapped her arms around her head.

"I have... nothing left," came on a broken sob and it fucking pierced his heart.

He scooped her curled up body into his arms, her fingers automatically burrowing into his shirt under his cut.

"Nothing," she repeated, her voice thin as she clung to him.

He strode to the door leading to the storage area behind the bar and kicked it open. Without missing a stride, he carried her through the dark but clearly empty area which should be full. With boxes of liquor. Empty kegs. Cases of beer. Cases of snack foods. The things needed to run a successful bar. There was none of it.

He'd deal with that problem later.

But now he was dealing with the woman in his arms.

Right now she was his priority.

He carried her up the back steps to the apartment above the bar. He didn't want to kick the door in and break the lock, so he hoped it was unsecured.

It was.

By shifting her in his arms, he managed to both hang onto her and open the door, using his boot to slam it shut behind him.

A light over the stove was the only light in the dark apartment until he spotted a switch by the door. He flipped it and muttered, "Jesus fuck," under his breath.

The apartment was a complete shithole.

The furniture, the décor, the wallpaper and carpet from the early '80s, if that.

The place was like an efficiency. There was no separate bedroom. Everything was in one open space and not a big one at that.

A bed was in one corner, in another an outdated galley kitchen with the old almond-colored appliances, and next to that was what looked like a door to a bathroom, which hung crookedly on its hinges.

That was it.

It was neat and orderly, but everything was old, worn and outdated.

He moved to the bed, wondering how old the mattress and box spring were, but the only other choice was to put her on the old plaid couch, and he figured her sheets were cleaner than that.

He gently placed her on the bed and she once again curled up into a ball, no longer sobbing, but trying to hide her quiet crying.

With a little wrangling, he got her knee-high leather boots unzipped and one at a time, he tugged them off, tossing them to the floor. Then he shrugged out of his cut, placing it on a rickety wooden chair next to the bed. He was too scared to sit in it to remove his own boots, so he sat on the edge of the bed and unlaced them, tugging them off. The whole time his eyes stayed glued on her.

He couldn't see her face because it was tucked in her arms, but it sounded as if her crying stopped, though her breathing was still unsteady and her body curled tight.

He didn't bother to pull back what looked like a hand-quilted bedspread, probably one from the local Amish and also the nicest thing in the apartment. The rest of it could be burned without a great loss.

He spooned her, his chest to her back, and snaked an arm around her waist, pulling her tightly against him. He nuzzled his nose into her hair and breathed deeply.

He didn't know what had happened and wasn't going to ask. He figured most of it was from her bone-deep exhaustion and being overwhelmed by a failing business.

He promised her silently that would change.

She had hit bottom, so there was no place left to go but up.

She didn't want his help, but at this point, he wouldn't give her the choice not to accept it. Otherwise, she was right. She'd have nothing left.

Right now, she still owned half a bar and she had him.

And with him came the club.

Eventually, her tense body relaxed into his, but he didn't loosen his hold. Even when he suspected she'd fallen asleep.

He remained there, holding tight, wanting to protect her, even though that might be the last thing she wanted.

When they were kids, the club was supposed to be family. It ended up being anything but.

Brothers became enemies. Kids became strangers.

He had witnessed the tight-knit family that the Dirty Angels were and he wanted that. Craved that. He needed that sense of family, of belonging, of having loyal brothers at his back.

But he also needed a strong woman at his side, something each and every one of those Angels had.

They were not treated as lessors, but almost as equals. They held more power in their hands than anyone would admit to out loud.

But it was there. Unmistakable.

What was shown to the world and what happened behind closed doors were two different things. But they were all better and stronger for it.

And that was what he wanted.

He watched how women were treated by the Originals. How they were used and abused. One could argue that those women chose that life. That they knew the way. What was to be expected.

It still didn't make it right.

And it helped erode what should've been a strong club, a power to be reckoned with. It wasn't the only reason, but Trip was pretty sure it was part of it.

It was one thing to have sweet butts, women who want to be used for whatever reason, it was another to disrespect an ol' lady. Trip determined right there and then not to have any of that shit poisoning his club.

The woman in his arms, though...

This woman was going to be his ol' lady, his goddamn queen. She was going to stand next to him while he rebuilt what the past destroyed.

She just didn't know it yet.

He waited long enough to make sure sleep had pulled her deep. That she wouldn't be restless.

And once he was assured of that, he decided to give her space.

It wasn't a good idea for him to stay, as much as he

wanted to. It was better he be gone when she woke up. Give her time to digest everything that went down.

The bar.

The sex.

Her meltdown.

Which seemed to be a long time coming and badly needed.

You could only be a fortress for so long, eventually those walls were going to crack from the constant battles. And once they did, when there was a lull in the war, you stepped back, evaluated the damage and then worked on getting those cracks repaired before the next onslaught.

He hoped when morning came and she faced a new day, she'd see things more clearly.

That she was no longer alone in that fight.

She'd have help repairing those cracks and rebuilding her father's bar.

No, not Pete's bar, her bar.

He shook his head.

Their bar.

He was now determined more than ever to turn it around. To make it work, to make it successful once again. Like Buck and Pete had wanted.

She might not like it, but in the end, she'd see it was for the best.

Hopefully, he could convince Sig of the same. His brother might not like what Trip was doing, but in the end, maybe he'd see Trip was doing his best to help him out.

He only fucking hoped Sig would accept that olive branch. If not, at least he'd given it a shot.

Trip slipped carefully from the old, lumpy mattress, tugged on his boots and his cut and locked her apartment door behind him as he left.

He made a mental note that her locks were a joke and

needed to be upgraded if she was going to remain living there.

He half-jogged down the steps and back out into the bar area. Heading immediately toward the front door, he secured it for the night, then went behind the bar. He found where she'd tucked the bulging checkbook binder and grabbed it, shaking his head with how many bills she was behind on.

It wasn't one month's worth or even two. It was many. He didn't bother to look at the balance of her checking account, because he knew it wasn't enough.

Tucking it under his arm, he turned out all the lights except for the ones lighting up the back bar and then slipped out of the rear emergency exit.

Tomorrow was a new day.

And he had a lot of fucking work to do.

Chapter Seven

He was running on gas fumes since he couldn't sleep after leaving Stella last night. When he finally gave up trying, he headed back downstairs to the kitchen and sat at the farmhouse table his grandfather had built with his own hands, sorting through all the invoices and bills for Crazy Pete's.

If he couldn't sleep before, the grand total of what was owed, the amount in which both Stella and the bar were behind, might keep him up for a week straight. He had a hard time wrapping his tired brain around it. And now he understood one reason for Stella's meltdown, but he was pretty fucking sure that wasn't the only reason.

He also found the property tax bill tucked into the back of the checkbook. Hiding it wasn't going to make it go away, but at least it wasn't due for a couple of months yet. Plus, he could pay it late without too much of a penalty, if needed.

No matter what, it would get paid, because he was not letting the tax collector put that property up for a sheriff's sale. Thank fuck the club had paid cash for the building back in the day, so there was no threat of foreclosure. He couldn't find any mortgage payments due in those torn-open pile of envelopes which would indicate she or Pete financed the property to pull out some cash.

While normally it might have been smart to do—to pull out some equity and invest it back into the bar—the way the finances were currently sitting, it might have been the last nail in the bar-sized coffin.

His stomach had been tied in knots as he tried to pay some of the bills with what he had left in his own accounts. The one he opened for the club, the business accounts he opened for both the motel and the repo business, and even his own personal account.

A mountain still remained.

Sometime in the early morning hours, he'd switched from beer to coffee. And as he drank what was probably his fifth cup, his cell phone had rung, causing a whole new knot in his gut.

He wasn't sure how this afternoon would go. He'd figured it was best to think the worst and if it ended up being better than that, then great. If it ended up being a complete shit show, then...

Yeah, it would be a complete fucking shit show.

He currently straddled his sled, the engine's vibrations soothing his nerves because if he didn't admit he was anxious as all fuck, then he was stupid, too.

His asshole was slightly puckered but less than the day he walked into SCI Camp Hill, where he was housed for a couple of months before being transferred to a unit at the prison in Huntingdon.

Now he was free. And planned to keep it that way.

Now Sig was free. Trip wanted to keep it that way, too.

What Sig wanted was a whole other story and Trip had no fucking clue what it was.

It only took Deacon a little over a week to locate his brother. But as soon as he got the call earlier this morning and heard the address, Trip knew he couldn't put off this reunion, since his brother could hit the road and disappear again at any time.

Trip didn't think a shittier motel existed than The Grove Inn, but he was clearly wrong. The one before him looked like it should be condemned. In fact, a couple of the rooms had plywood instead of windows.

How Deacon found Sig here, Trip didn't ask. But he was definitely impressed with the man's skill and it cemented the fact the new Fury member would be an asset for both the MC and his repo business.

It also impressed Trip that Deacon had convinced Judge to wear a Fury cut and sit at the table in his father's old spot. So that right there got him Trip's utmost respect.

Unfortunately, Judge still had a burr up his ass, but hopefully the big man would pull it out sometime soon.

Trip eyed the rusty, beat-up Ford truck, the one parked directly in front of room number twelve. In the bed of that truck sat a Harley that was definitely in worse shape than the pickup.

He and Sig were three years apart and had grown up as best friends, not having any clue they were brothers until...

Until... Sig found out the hard way they were.

They both did.

Nothing in life had been easy for either of them, but Trip was determined to change that, too.

So here he was, hoping he could convince Sig to join him on that ride.

Trip just hoped to fuck he didn't get plugged in the chest with a .45 while he tried to do so.

He'd been sitting in the parking lot for over fifteen minutes, kind of hoping Sig would walk out and Trip could call him over. But the curtains remained closed, the motel quiet and he couldn't sit there forever.

He kept going over in his head what he needed to say and how quickly he needed to say it before Sig slammed the door in his face. Not before plugging Trip in the chest with that .45.

Yeah, Trip wasn't sure knocking on the door of a room in a sketchy motel was a smart idea. But he didn't have Sig's number, if the man even had a fucking phone.

From what Deacon said, Sig had been sprung from a prison in upstate New York not even a week ago. Trip imagined his brother was getting some sleep in which he could finally close both eyes safely.

Trip had slept with one eye open himself during his six years of confinement.

While he only had one long unplanned vacation without a view, from what he'd heard and what Deacon confirmed, Sig had taken multiple. Too many to count on both hands and at too many windowless concrete and razor-wired resorts to list.

Trip didn't care. He wanted to move forward and put the past behind them.

Though, everyone he'd come across so far had made that impossible.

He was sure this afternoon would go no differently.

Even so, he needed to get this over with, so he untucked his nuts, shut off the sled, and dismounted. After a second of indecision, he pulled off his leather skull cap, hanging it over the bike's throttle, and shook out his hair, hoping Sig would recognize him.

As he strode across the lot, he tucked his keys in his front pocket and straightened his cut. Stopping in front of the door, he hesitated long enough to take a long, deep breath, then he raised his fist and pounded on the door with the heel of his hand.

He knew Sig was inside because the door was thin and, as he had approached, he could hear two voices. Not just a man's but a woman's, too.

So, sleep wasn't probably the only thing Sig was catching up on.

The sounds from inside continued without interruption, so he pounded again and heard a "fuck" barked out followed by a grumble.

Then a bunch of chatter.

"This better be fuckin' good," came clearly through the door as Trip heard the slide of the chain lock and the click of the cheap deadbolt being twisted before the door swung open wide.

The room was dark behind Sig, leaving Trip at a disadvantage. But his brother, the one he hadn't seen in almost twenty years, undoubtedly stood in front of him, squinting because of the afternoon sun behind Trip.

That meant Sig might be too blinded by the light to recognize Trip off the bat.

And though he hadn't seen Sig in two decades, he never saw him like he was right at that moment. Totally fucking naked with a hard-on.

Living in prison and even during his time in the Marines, privacy was at a premium—Trip saw more cock, balls and assholes than he ever wanted to see—so it was no big thing. Only Sig wasn't in prison anymore and Trip didn't want to see his brother's fucking dick, which was pointed directly at him like a compass pointing west.

"Got a pair of fuckin' jeans?"

"Got some goddamn balls knockin' on my door and disturbin' us after I told the fuckin' office we weren't to be bothered."

"Who is it, Siggy?" came a female voice behind him.

Siggy? Trip couldn't see much since his brother's body blocked most of the open doorway. But if the woman was as naked as Sig, which was Trip's educated guess, maybe it was better he couldn't see into the room.

"Is it food? I'm fucking starving!"

Trip's eyebrows raised as that female voice was not the same as the first one. He grinned. "Is there a third?"

"Not sure who the fuck you are, but since you ain't carryin' any bags of food, I got a feelin' you're lost." As Sig went to close the door, Trip slid his boot into the jam to prevent that.

"You know who I am," Trip said.

"Can't say I do," Sig answered, lifting his gaze from Trip's offending boot and squinting up at him. Those narrowed eyes landed and stuck on Trip's chest. "Why you wearin' that cut?"

Sig's gaze rose over Trip's shoulder and Trip knew exactly what he was looking at.

"That fuckin' sled kinda looks familiar."

"It should."

Sig's eyes slid back to him and Trip stood his ground as the man studied Trip's face. Trip did the same since he really didn't want to keep looking at Sig's now sinking battleship.

Trip gave him a quick once over, stopping above the waist. His hair, the same color as both his and their father's was shorter than Trip's. Surprisingly a lot shorter, like the sides had been shaved and were just beginning to grow out. The top was longer but still not long at all. A beard, also shorter than Trip's, covered his face. He had a large tattoo along the right side of his neck, starting at his hairline and making its way down his body to consist of a full sleeve on his right arm, one part of it a large phoenix which covered his right shoulder and pec.

How fucking fucked was that? Trip considered the resurrection of the Fury similar to a phoenix rising from the ashes.

And his fucking half-brother bore that very tattoo.

Other smaller tattoos, like sayings, decorated his torso

and left arm but Trip wasn't going to take the time to read and decipher them all.

The man had no beer gut like their father had sported, either. It seemed as though Sig had worked on his body in prison just like Trip. Sig wasn't quite as built, but he was close.

What caught his attention next was the ink over Sig's heart. Two angel wings with a name in between them, but before he could ask the meaning of that, Sig growled, "Yeah, got some goddamn huge balls showin' the fuck up here. Huntin' me the fuck down. Either that or you're fuckin' stupid. And I don't remember you bein' fuckin' stupid, Trip, but a lot could change in twenty fuckin' years. Maybe someone cracked your head against a concrete wall, and you lost some of your fuckin' sense. That what happened?"

Trip schooled his face so he wouldn't cringe at the reminder of what he'd done to Stella when they were kids. "No."

"Then you better have a good goddamn reason for you to be not only standin' here but interruptin' me gettin' fuckin' laid."

"Got a good reason," Trip muttered.

"Then let's hear it."

"Wanna put some clothes on or at least move from the doorway?"

"Why? Shouldn't take long."

"Not really in the mood to be talkin' into your mini microphone."

Sig tilted his head and grabbed his junk, shaking it. "Was always bigger than yours."

"Siggy, who is it?" came one of the female voices again.

Sig stepped back, jerked his head in an unspoken invitation and Trip wondered if it was smart to go inside. But he did and then he questioned that choice again when Sig hit the lights.

Yeah, there were only two and they were both totally fucking naked and neither one of them cared that he'd entered the room.

In fact, they didn't care that they were touching each other in front of a stranger, either.

They weren't bad looking girls, but they were young. A mirror smeared with coke residue sat on one of the particle board nightstands. A few crushed beer cans and a few that still appeared full littered the room. All the bed coverings were in a pile on the floor so both women were laying together on just the fitted sheet which had some spots on it. Trip wasn't too keen on discovering what those spots were.

He had a good guess.

Both girls' pussies were shaved bare and one was playing with the other.

"Some hot shit right there, right?"

"Yeah, if you like teens." And wanted to end back behind bars.

"They're legal."

"You sure?"

"You girls legal?" Sig asked them.

"Yeah," they both answered in unison as they kissed each other.

"See?" Sig asked, moving toward the bed and sitting on the edge. With his knees spread Trip got an eyeful.

"Got somethin' you can put on?"

"Why, big brother? A little nakedness bother you?" He twisted his head to the girls behind him. "Toss me my smokes."

One of them got up onto her hands and knees and moved toward the far nightstand. As she did so, Trip swore he could see right through her gaping pussy to her throat.

He decided it was best to keep his eyes on Sig, neck up.

"Want some of that? Don't mind sharin' since we're blood and all that."

"I'm good."

Sig held out the pack of Marlboros the girl had handed him. "Smoke?"

Trip shook his head. "Got my own."

Sig plugged a cigarette between his lips, lit it with a pack of matches from the motel and then studied him as he inhaled the smoke deep into his lungs and held it there.

As he talked the smoke rolled out of his mouth. "Why you here?"

"Was hopin' to reconnect."

Sig leaned a forearm on his bare thigh and studied the lit end of his cigarette for a long moment. "Right," he murmured. He lifted his brown eyes to Trip. "Why now?"

"Had a room at Huntingdon for the last six years, that kinda restricted my travel and ability to socialize."

"Yeah?"

Had Sig not known? "Granddaddy didn't tell you?"

"Didn't talk to him. Wasn't my granddaddy, was yours."

"He was yours, too, Sig."

"Let's just say, after everything went down and the truth came out, *Granddaddy* didn't put me on his Christmas card list." Sig took a long drag of his cigarette, his eyes narrowing on Trip. "Also didn't put me in that will." He emptied the smoke from his lungs and one of the girls pasted herself to him, grinding her tits against his back and stroking Sig's chest. "You here to make it right and give me my half?"

"Here to make you an offer."

Sig snorted and shook his head. "If it ain't half, ain't much of an offer." He lifted the hand not holding his cigarette and snapped his fingers over his shoulder. "Pam," he called out.

"Paula," the one not hanging all over Sig corrected.

"Whatever," he grumbled. "Your sister's gettin' me hard

pushin' those little titties of hers on me, get down on the floor and suck my dick while I'm talkin'."

Trip went solid, waiting for the girl to tell him to go to hell, but he was wrong. So goddamn wrong. She eagerly scrambled off the bed, fell to her knees between his legs and began to Hoover him like his dick was as dirty as the fucking carpet she was kneeling on.

Damn. Seeing Sig's dick was bad enough, seeing him getting head by some chick who may not even be eighteen yet...

Time for him to split.

He dug into his wallet and pulled one of the cards he had made up for the repo business and tossed it onto the mattress. "Gonna leave my number. You let me know when you got time to talk. See you're too busy for business right now."

As he spun on his boot heel, Sig stopped him. "See you stole good ol' Dad's cut."

Trip remained facing the door when he answered, "Didn't steal it. Found it."

"Why the fuck would you wanna wear that?"

Trip dropped his head and stared as his boots as he heard slurping sounds behind him. He wanted to have this conversation with Sig, but not like this.

He figured Sig was doing it on purpose, just to be an asshole. Trying to push Trip. He tightened his jaw. "Lemme know when she's done."

"If you were in the joint that long, sure you watched a lot of tongue and mouth action. Probably got some done to you and gave some yourself."

"Wasn't my thing."

"No? Long bids tend to make it one's thing."

"It woulda taken a lot longer bid than six years."

"Six years is a long fuckin' time unless you kept catchin' charges inside."

Trip lifted his head, trying to ignore Sig's groan of, "Fuck yeah, that's it." He stared at the door, which was just a couple feet away.

He needed to go. He did not need to get caught in a motel room with underage girls, if that's what they were, and drugs.

Six years had been six years too many.

"You on parole?" Trip tossed over his shoulder.

Trip didn't get an answer, so he had to assume he was on the tail end of that head job.

Jesus fuck.

They were close when they were young and had done some stupid shit, but this took the fucking cake.

A few seconds later, Sig's voice, sounding a little too satisfied, filled the room. "Forget that I watched that sweet butt suck you off in a corner of the warehouse one night when you were fourteen. Also forget that same fuckin' sweet butt popped your fuckin' cherry at one of the roasts in front of everyone not six months later. Every fuckin' one at that party egged her on. And then when she was done with you, she ate your load right out of her own cunt."

Jesus.

Fuckin'.

Shit.

He had tried to forget that night. Though, a first time like that was hard to forget.

His own father had encouraged that sweet butt to do it.

Her name might have been Shelly. He didn't know and, at the time, he didn't care.

"Tried to get her to do me. She ruffled my hair and said I was too fuckin' young. Always missin' out."

"You were eleven at the time."

"Yeah? And I could get hard. So, what does it matter?"

Trip needed to go. He needed to go. Why the fuck was he still standing there?

Ice slid through his veins as those memories surged through him. "Was Stella at that roast?"

"Stella, that little pain in the ass bitch who wouldn't leave us alone? Don't fuckin' know and, anyway, why does it matter?"

"It doesn't," Trip lied under his breath.

Trip heard a rustling behind him. "All right, big brother, got some jeans on and you got a few before I'm ready to fuck Patty and Pam."

"I'm Paula and she's Penny," one of the females corrected him.

Sig kept talking. "If you don't wanna watch then I suggest you say what you came here to say."

Trip took a peek over his shoulder. Sig wasn't lying. He had pulled on some jeans, though they weren't fastened. The two girls now had the mirror on the bed between them, using a credit card to scrape some coke into several lines.

Trip had to close his eyes from those neat white rows. He hadn't done that shit in years and he wasn't about to start again.

A little weed was one thing. A few shots of whiskey and a six-pack was another. But he was not touching that shit again. He had better things to spend his money on besides throwing it down an endless pit, when one line, three lines, five lines weren't enough.

Trip jerked his chin toward the females who were now taking turns snorting the lines with a rolled up twenty. "You do that shit?"

"Not much anymore. My dick breaks when I do. I'd rather lose myself in sweet hot pussy than be all coked out."

Good. Because he was not having that shit at the barn or even on the farm. He was not going back to prison because of someone else's bad habit.

"So... Tick. Tock. Talk."

Trip sighed. "Resurrecting the club."

"Kinda figured that when you walked in here wearin' that bullshit. Especially since it's your name above that president's patch and not Buck's."

"Got a spot for you." Trip lifted his palm to stop Sig before he flat-out turned him down. "Got an apartment for you. A job. A family. Or," he shrugged and looked around the messy room, "if you prefer fleabag motels, got one of those, too."

Sig snorted. "What family?"

"Need me to answer that?"

Sig shook his head. "Then you're givin' me my half."

"Not givin' you half. Gotta earn it."

Sig snorted again. "Like you did." He followed up that insult by spitting a hocker onto the dirty motel room carpet.

"Bustin' my ass to get shit rollin', Sig. If you think I'm just bein' handed everything, you'd be fuckin' wrong. Got a place for you. At the table as VP. At the barn. Place to start fresh. Also, need help runnin' one of my businesses."

"Your businesses," Sig echoed.

"The repo business."

"Well, damn. Good ol' Dad's business. So again, half mine."

"Sure, if you got half the money for the fuckin' license, the bond, the repairs for the wrecker. Plus, half the money so I can buy a rollback, too. Got that money to spare?"

Sig's nostrils flared and his mouth got tight as he looked away. "Everything I got's in that pickup truck out there."

"Right. So, *my* business. Got a motel and half a bar, too."

Sig's bloodshot brown eyes slid back to him. "Half a bar?"

"Crazy Pete's."

His brother chewed on that for a few seconds before asking, "How's Pete?"

"Dead."

"Fuck," Sig muttered, raking fingers through the longer hair on top of his head. "Never forget the day he and Buck kicked your fuckin' ass. Thought you were dead for a while there. Mighta shed a tear for you, too, if I remember correctly. All because of that pain in the ass Stella—"

"Yeah," Trip cut him off. "Didn't die. Here I am. Own half of Pete's bar."

"The club owned half."

Trip nodded. "I'm claimin' that half."

Sig cocked a brow. "Who's claiming the other half since Pete's dead?"

"Stella."

"Fuck. She back?"

"She's back." *Damn*, he needed a cigarette. Or something stronger. "Claimin' her, too."

Sig's eyes met his and he didn't bother to hide the surprise in them. "How long have you been tappin' that?"

Trip ignored that question. "So, you in?"

"Got pussy and booze?"

"Not yet. But workin' on it."

Sig lifted his hand and lifted a finger. "No pussy." He lifted a second one. "No booze." Then a third. "Gotta work to get what's mine. Not likin' the sound of all that. And anyway, why the fuck would I wanna live in that fuckin' backward-assed town? Couldn't get outta there fast enough."

"Roof over your head."

"Got one of those."

"No rent. No roaches. No bed bugs."

"Yeah. That could be a plus," he said, scratching at his beard.

"Tellin' you now, though. No hard shit. No jailbait. Nothing that's gonna get our asses thrown back in the pen."

"Not sure I'm likin' the sound of that, either."

"What part? The part where your ass remains free?"

"When there's rules, you ain't free."

"When you're free, there's always fuckin' rules to remain that way," he reminded his brother, who should know that only so well. "Can you leave New York?"

The motel room they were standing in was just over the border of Pennsylvania into New York. He might not be able to leave the state depending on the condition of his parole.

"Didn't say I was takin' you up on your offer."

"Didn't say you weren't, either."

"Not sure why you feel the need to make that offer."

"You're blood," Trip answered.

"So? If you think blood was important back then, then you weren't payin' the fuck attention."

"Was important, just ignored." Trip wasn't sure how true that was, since blood wasn't always family and family wasn't always blood. A solid MC was family. The BFMC Originals should have been family. Turned out they weren't. Once again, he was using what he witnessed with the Dirty Angels MC as his goal. They were all tight. They were all family. They would die for each other, not plug a hole into each other's backs.

"Dutch in?"

Sig's question pulled him out of his thoughts. "Yeah."

"You talk to Rook?"

"Not yet. Dutch said he's in Lycoming County."

"You gonna talk to him?"

That was at the top of his mile-long to-do list. Along with trying to find a way to make some quick scratch to fill not only the club's coffers but his own. "That's my plan. Dutch said he gets out soon."

"Judge?"

"Judge is in."

"Yeah?"

"Yeah."

"Who else?"

"Judge's cousin, Deacon. A couple prospects. Cage."

"Cage?"

"Dutch's youngest boy. Remember him?"

"That kid was a pain in the ass, too. Just like that gash you're now bangin'."

Trip's blood began to simmer. "Seems he still is. And Stella ain't gash. Fuckin' call her that again, we're gonna have a problem."

"Whatever you say, big brother." Sig pulled a joint out of the pack of Marlboros and lit it. He offered it to Trip.

Trip stared at it for a second, tempted, then shook his head. He needed to get back. If he got stoned, he'd have no motivation to do shit later. And he had a hell of a lot of work to do.

With Sig or without him.

Sig took another hit, jerked his head at one of the girls and she crawled over to him and pressed her lips to his. Sig shotgunned the smoke into her mouth.

Paula, Pam or whatever the sister's name was—if they were sisters—came over and pinned her naked self to his other side and Sig repeated the gesture.

Sig held the joint out and one of the girls took a hit and shotgunned the other one, then added a whole bunch of tongue to it.

Fuck. Trip hoped they weren't really sisters.

Sig put his arm around both of them and pulled them into his lap. "Times up, big brother. You stayin' and watchin'?"

"You got my card. Think about it, Sig." With that, Trip turned around and got the fuck out of there before he changed his mind about offering Sig a place to land.

Chapter Eight

IT HAD BEEN three days since her meltdown, and though she hadn't wanted to see Trip, she was surprised he hadn't stopped in at the bar.

In one way she was relieved, in another, not so much.

But now she needed answers and to set some rules.

She also needed to collect what he took so she could take care of business.

During those three days, as she cleaned glasses, the bar top, straightened chairs, wiped down tables and took inventory, she had gone back and forth about staying and trying to make a go of the bar with Trip's—or the club's—help or simply writing the whole thing off, handing it over and trying to find somewhere else to once again plant some roots.

Because right now, without those roots, she felt about to topple.

Like the other night.

When she fell to the floor, everything inside her had shattered like a glass hitting concrete. And it took her over a day to sweep up those pieces and try to glue herself back together.

What happened between her and Trip...

She wished it hadn't and she hoped he'd let it go. She doubted he would, but she could still hope.

Even so, here she was, standing on his porch in front of that beautiful rustic door of his farmhouse.

The property was quiet; no construction could be heard. Most likely because it was Sunday and that was the Amish's day of worship. To them, it was a day dedicated to rest and God.

For Stella, it was one day she gave herself off since the bar was closed. One day she tried to get more than four hours of sleep.

The only problem with having the bar closed was her hands became idle and her mind began to wander, and memories she worked so hard to keep at bay tended to swallow her whole.

So, in the end, every Sunday, instead of relaxing and recharging, she found something to do with the bar. Especially since something always needed to be done.

To the far left, through the antique etched glass panels on the door, she caught some movement inside. She lifted her hand to knock and hoped he was alone, and she wasn't interrupting anything.

Before she could put her fist to the panel to announce her arrival, she heard, "Door's open," loud and clear.

Door's open.

Did he know it was her standing out there?

"Stella, door's open."

Yep, he knew it was her. How? She had no idea.

She opened the door and stood there, unsure whether going inside was a good idea. But she had come out to the farm for a reason and she needed to show strength instead of the weakness she showed the other night.

She refused to be the wounded doe and let Trip, who

she considered the predator, take her down. She would fight to the very end.

Or, at least, that's what she told herself. In reality, she was afraid she was too tired to fight anymore.

"Lettin' the skeeters in, Stel."

Stel. He'd never called her that before.

She took a deep inhale and stepped over the threshold, closing the door behind her.

He had to have every damn window in the house open, which let the spring breeze sweep through. That was probably why he knew she was there. There was nothing quiet about her Jeep coming up his rutted dirt and stone driveway.

Like typical old farmhouses, the main entrance to the house was the back door, the one she had entered through and also faced the barn. It had taken her directly into a country kitchen.

The large, rustic room needed some fresh paint, but that was all it needed. Other than that, it was gorgeous. Just like the man standing in bare feet and only wearing jeans at the old six-burner white porcelain gas stove that had to be from the fifties. The only new appliance seemed to be the fridge, but it was in a fifties style. It blended in perfectly with the cabinets, the handmade farm table and the more than century old wide-planked knotty wood floors.

Stella would kill for a kitchen like this.

And a family to sit around that table, while she stood where Trip did, making them pancakes.

Trip wasn't making pancakes, but she could smell bacon and heard what might be eggs sizzling in a cast iron skillet.

Without turning around, he asked, "Hungry?"

She considered him, his bare back and the Blood Fury colors taking up that whole, muscular landscape. He'd had the colors permanently inked into his skin even before he knew whether the club would rise again.

He was that fucking confident.

Or maybe just that cocky.

Either way, the man knew what he wanted and went after it with everything he had.

"Don't got a cat," he muttered, forking the bacon from a cast iron grill that covered two of the burners onto some stacked paper towels to drain.

Her gaze circled the floor, wondering what cat he was talking about.

"Don't got a cat," he repeated again. He twisted his head to glance at her over his bare, broad shoulder. The one Stella wanted to sink her teeth into as she was clawing his back.

A flash of him fucking her in the bar while bent over the counter swept through her and her knees almost buckled.

That night she had wanted him to hurt her, to make her feel something. He didn't, but he did cause damage she was afraid she wouldn't recover from.

Her wanting him.

Just like she had when they were kids.

While it had been obsessive back then, now it was more out of curiosity. If the sex was that good when it shouldn't have been, she wondered how good it would be when she was in a different mindset. When they both were.

Note to self: none of that was the reason she was there.

Was it?

Could she have had him just drop off the bills and her checkbook or had one of the guys come pick it up? Just like she could've had Dutch deliver Pete's cut to him over a week ago?

Or was she just looking for an excuse to see him? Be around him?

That thought bothered her.

He was everything she was not looking for in a man. If she was even looking, which she wasn't.

He turned around and curled his fingers around his hips, shooting her a look of concern. "Want me to kill that cat?"

She shook herself mentally. "What cat are you talking about?"

"The one that's got your fuckin' tongue. Never known you to be so fuckin' quiet." He walked over to the large table and jerked out a wood chair. "Take a load off. Gonna get you food so you don't pass out."

Surprised, she put the back of her hand to her forehead. "Do I look pale?"

"No, your face is red, and your nipples are hard, makin' me wonder what the fuck you were thinkin' about when you were so quiet."

"Just how good that bacon smells," she lied.

One side of his mouth lifted into a half-grin and the corners of his dark brown eyes wrinkled. "Yeah, that might be it." He tapped the chair and she approached. As she settled into it, he got close to her ear and murmured, "But I doubt it."

Her breath caught and he moved away.

"Coffee?"

She scooted the chair back. "I can get it."

"Sit. Takin' care of you this mornin'."

"I don't need taken care of," she reminded him.

"Will be plenty of mornin's where you'll be takin' care of me. And I'm not just talkin' 'bout breakfast."

Uh... what? "I'm sorry?"

He went over to what looked like a new coffeemaker in one corner of the black marbled soapstone counter. "Nothin' to be sorry 'bout."

"No, I meant... I think I misheard what you said."

He returned with a steaming large mug in his hand. He put it in front of her and asked, "You take shit in your coffee?"

"Not shit, but cream and stevia."

"Stevia? What the fuck's that?"

"Sugar will be fine."

He dug around in the fridge and brought out a small carton of whole milk, put it on the table as he passed, then a few seconds later, dropped a spoon and a small generic bag of white sugar off as he headed back to the stove.

"Trip," Stella murmured as she added a heaping spoonful of sugar and poured the few drops of milk that remained in the bottom of the container. She shook her head. Just like a man to put the milk container back in the fridge empty.

"Stella..."

She lifted her gaze from her mug as he put a plate in front of her. "Hmm?"

"Said my name, then stopped."

Stella stared at the plate in front of her. Hash browns heavily decorated with ketchup, two fried eggs, also covered in ketchup, and three slices of bacon, thankfully not covered in ketchup.

Her husband had used Tabasco on his eggs, not ketchup. Stella preferred just a little salt and pepper. She never understood the whole condiments on an egg thing.

Trip straddled the chair across from her, then lowered his own plate—a mountain of hash browns, three fried eggs, six slices of bacon and she swore a half bottle's worth of ketchup—in front of himself, along with a full mug of black coffee.

He forked a good portion of perfectly crispy shredded potatoes into his mouth, some ketchup catching at the corner of his lip.

She swallowed hard as his tongue slid out and swept it away.

She dropped her gaze back to her plate, picked up a slice of crispy bacon and bit into it. Her eyes closed. She hadn't had good bacon in a long time. She couldn't afford it. Most mornings she made oatmeal. By buying it in bulk, it was cheap and filling. Occasionally she had toast. But bacon? Too much of a splurge.

And she had missed it.

Without opening her eyes, she shoved the other half of the strip into her mouth and took her time chewing it, savoring the smoky but sweet taste. Maple. That's what the sweetness was.

"If only a woman's face would look like that while suckin' my dick."

Stella's eyes popped open and met Trip's. "Is that a joke?"

"If you saw your face while you ate that fuckin' bacon, then you'd know it wasn't."

She busied herself with chasing the bacon down with a mouthful of coffee. That was good, too. Trip hadn't used a generic bag of coffee to make that pot.

"Coffee must be good, too."

"It's okay."

Trip grinned around a mouthful of eggs. "Eggs are from the Amish. They've been bringin' me a dozen or two every week when they come out to work. Gonna get a regular supply of 'em from them, along with some of their meats and dairy. Possibly even some veggies and fruit they grow. Keep the kitchen in the barn stocked with shit so the guys don't only have a diet of whiskey, beer, pussy and pot."

She choked on the bite of egg she was chewing. She helped it down with another gulp of coffee.

"Speakin' of pussy..."

He surged from his chair, came around the table, and before she could react, he drove his fingers into the hair by her ears, fisted them and pulled her head back, dropping his.

Her objection of what he was about to do became muffled when his lips crushed hers. He tasted like a delicious mix of coffee, bacon and sweetness as their tongues touched. When he pushed forward, she pushed back.

She shouldn't be enjoying the kiss, but it was rough and thorough, just how she liked them. But the problem wasn't the kiss. It was with who was kissing her.

When he was done, he pulled away just slightly, letting her catch her breath, but left his fingers tangled tightly in her hair, enough to feel that delicious pull. Enough to not only make her scalp tingle but everything else, too.

His gaze locked with hers as his low voice sent heat spiraling into her belly. "You never got that kiss twenty years ago. I never got it the other night. Now that we got that outta the way, I can concentrate on breakfast."

He released her and her eyes followed him as he went back to his seat and sat down, then shoved another forkful of eggs into his mouth.

The mouth that had made her nipples pebble and her pussy clench hard.

That mouth.

The mouth that had bitten her the other night and left bruises in its path. Reminders that what they had done had been a mistake.

"It was a mistake."

He finished chewing, lifted his mug to his lips and took a long sip. When he was done, he said, "Yeah, you're right. It was." He put the mug down next to his plate and sat back in his chair, tilting his head as he studied her across the table. "Our fathers—both yours and mine—taught me to never put my hands on a woman in anger. And that was my fuckin' mistake."

"It wasn't just the—"

"Both times I've done it, it's been with you."

His expression turned troubled. Was it guilt?

"Why is that, Trip?"

He shoved his last piece of bacon into his mouth and said nothing.

She pushed her chair back and rose, grabbing her plate. She scraped what she didn't eat—couldn't, after that kiss—into the trash and went to the sink. She needed some space between them when they discussed what she came to talk about. "We need to talk about the other night."

"Probably shouldn't."

His chair scraped back, but she remained facing the sink, bracing herself.

Damn it, he was going to close that space she created. She needed to talk fast. "I just want to make it clear." She turned and saw him on the move, heading toward her, carrying his now empty plate. "What we did meant nothing. I need to remind you that you don't own me. I'm not property. I'm not an ol' lady. I'm not a sweet butt, patch whore or a piece. Not even a backpack."

His face remained neutral as he brushed against her, putting his plate in the sink. "Got it."

Her blood began to hum with how close he was. Since he still faced the sink, his right hip was pinned to her left. "It was just a slip-up. I was tired, frustrated and stressed. And then you showed up and..."

"'Kay."

She expected him to move away, but he remained, the heat from his bare torso searing her side through her well-worn, but treasured, Nirvana tank top. She should move away but she couldn't. It was like he was a magnet and she was metal.

She fought that strong pull and forced herself to continue. "But that's all it was. A mistake." More of a reminder to herself than one to him.

"All right."

He was being suspiciously agreeable. "Now we got that

straight, we can move on. Figure out what happens to the bar from here."

"Agreed."

"Good. I don't want to fight about this."

"No fight."

"Good," she repeated on a relieved breath. She went to step away and his hand became a blur as he snagged her wrist.

He spun around and yanked her to face him. "You done?"

"What?" Being this close she had to look up to read his face. To see if he was angry or annoyed.

"You done with the shit you came to say?"

"Yes. But that's not the only reason why I'm here."

A grin slowly crossed his face. "Figured that."

She didn't like that grin; she knew what it meant. "Guess you ignored everything I said about that night being a mistake."

"Pretty much."

Too fucking arrogant. "Just so you know, I meant it."

"Guess you ignored it when I said you'll be takin' care of me most mornings."

"I did ignore that, yes."

"Well, don't."

"I didn't come here for that; I came for my checkbook and bills."

"Took 'em."

"No shit, but I need to pay them, Trip. If I don't, I'll lose the bar."

"*We'll* lose the bar. I paid the worst ones." He released her wrist to scrape a hand through his hair. The lines around his eyes crinkling but not from a grin this time. "I couldn't pay 'em all."

Since she was now free from his grip, she took a step

back, trying to create the space she so desperately needed. "I'll pay you back."

"Yeah, you will."

"I just don't know how soon—"

He kept talking over her. "But not in cash."

She lifted her chin and pulled her shoulders back. "I'm not a patch whore, Trip. Never will be. If that's what you want, then fuck you."

His jaw worked. "Said nothin' about you bein' a patch whore. Do I want you in my bed? Fuck yes. Do I want you ridin' a bunch of dick like a sweet butt? Fuck no."

"But you want me to pay off my debt to you by sleeping with you."

"Has nothin' to do with sleepin', but no, didn't say that, either."

She threw her hands up and then dropped them, slapping her palms against her outer thighs in frustration. "Then what the fuck do you want from me?"

"What else you got?"

Once again, he was being a dick since he already knew the answer to that.

Nothing, she had nothing. And now only half a bar. Officially, his name might not be on the deed yet, but he had a paper stating the club owned half. Stella couldn't afford to fight that if he decided to take it to court. Even if she won, she'd end up losing. Having to hire an attorney would just put her in the hole even more.

"Nothing. You want the bar, take the fucking bar." Her fingers curled so hard into the sides of her thighs, her nails dug into her skin even through her jeans. "I don't have the strength to fight anymore."

She hated to admit that, but it needed to be said. He needed to get where she was coming from.

He pursed his lips and dragged a hand down his

bearded jaw. "An eleven-year-old Stella was a determined fuckin' bitch. Where'd she go?"

"Life happened, Trip." It had kicked her in the gut so hard she couldn't breathe. It got so bad, at one point she hadn't even wanted it to continue.

Her tenacity barely remained strong enough to keep her sucking in one breath at a time. And that was what she'd done. Took one breath, then another, each measured until she got through that day. Slowly she got through one day, one week, one month until she could tolerate the pain.

"Yeah, life happened. And when someone kicks you in the nuts, you hold on to 'em 'til you can breathe again, then you stand the fuck up and kick that motherfucker's ass. That's what the fuck I'm doin' here with all this, with the farm, the club, the motel, and now the bar. Don't need to do it by yourself, Stel. You don't. I got your back."

"Why? Just because you want to pilfer the profits for the club's coffers?"

"Not pilferin' when I own half."

"You know what I mean."

"I'll give you the checkbook back, but not the bills. Gonna pay them all off as soon as I can."

"And again, how am I going to pay you back? Even if you own half, I owe you half of those bills."

"You owe more than that, Stella. Like I said the other night, for twenty years Pete put all the profits into his own pocket. You're lucky I'm only takin' half."

Right. She was *lucky*.

She was lucky this man was walking in and taking over like he alone owned not only the bar, but also her.

He was sadly mistaken.

She closed her eyes and inhaled deeply through her nose, held it, then let it go, hoping it would relieve some of her tension. It didn't. She rubbed at the invisible band that squeezed her chest. Her gut churned as she forced herself to say, "I'll just walk away. It's for the best. Like you had said, I had a year to turn the bar around and I failed."

"Not lettin' you walk away."

Again, he spoke like he owned her, like she was club property. She had witnessed that mentality firsthand as a child growing up a part of the Fury. "It's not up to you, Trip."

This time when he closed the gap between them, he didn't grab her wrist, instead his face was soft—which was even harder to deal with than when he was angry—and he tucked his thumb under her chin, raising her face to his.

"You're not goin' anywhere. Need you to stay and manage the bar, Stella. Need your help. I got too many irons in the fire already and not enough hands. Will help you get it turned around, but you'll be runnin' it."

"With some strong *suggestions* from you, right?"

"When they're needed. Thinkin' if you got cash flowin' in to fix shit up and a bit of help so it's not all on your shoulders, then you'll do all right without me steppin' in too often."

"Too often," she repeated under her breath.

"Thing is, once I find you some prospects, you won't be closin' the bar every night. In fact, you won't be closin' it at all. You'll be managin' it, not doin' the heavy liftin'. Want you in my bed every night at a decent hour."

Whoa. What kind of drugs was he doing? "Trip, I'm not going to be in your bed. I'm not paying back the debt that way."

"Got nothin' to do with the debt, baby. Nothin' at all."

Baby. She shook her head like she was stuck in some twilight zone. "You're not getting what I'm putting down, Trip."

His fingers tightened on her chin. "No, baby, *you're* not gettin' what I'm puttin' down."

The intensity in his eyes, the growl in his voice made her

lose her breath. The meaning behind his words closed her throat. "You..." She tried to swallow past the constriction. "You..." *Jesus Christ.* "You can't just claim me. I'm not a part of the club."

"Were born into it. You're still a part of the club."

"My mother freed us when we left twenty years ago. I don't want anything to do with it."

"Too fuckin' bad."

He must be living in some sort of fantasy world. Panic began to set in, her heart thumping furiously in her chest. "No, that's not how real life works, Trip."

"In my world, it does."

"Not in mine."

"Yours is the same as mine."

He was definitely deluded. "No."

"Yes, Stella."

"You're fucking crazy."

A slow smile crossed his face. "Maybe so."

"That's nothing to be proud of, Trip."

"Got a plan, Stella, and you're a part of that plan."

"Since when?"

"Since the moment I walked into Crazy Pete's and found you instead of Pete."

She stared at him for a long moment. He didn't look crazy, but he was fucking bat-shit crazy.

She needed to get the hell out of there.

Once again, she'd made a mistake coming out to the farm to talk to him. Not only did Trip need his head examined, so did she.

Because the life she had escaped all those years ago was suddenly beginning to control her all over again.

And she refused to let that happen. Even if he promised things would be different.

Because he hadn't.

She jerked her chin from his grasp. "Give me my stuff and I'll get out of here."

"Will give you the checkbook but not the bills."

"I don't want to owe you more than I already do."

"Baby, that's one thing you're not gettin'. You don't owe me fuckin' shit. Just need your help makin' the bar a success. It'll benefit both of us, as well as the club."

And that would be fine if he didn't want anything else. But he did. He outright stated it more than once. "I'll make you a deal."

"Not in a position to deal, Stella."

The fuck she wasn't. "I'll stay and manage the bar, consider your suggestions, accept the help of whoever you can find—as long as they're more help than a hindrance—but that's all you're getting from me. Nothing else."

He sucked at his teeth and scrubbed at his beard.

"Nothing else, Trip," she repeated more firmly.

"Know that's not what you really want," he finally said.

"What you want and what I want are two different things."

"Doubt that."

When he took a step closer, she took a step back.

"Gonna prove you wrong."

The large kitchen suddenly felt way too small. Even with the windows open, the oxygen in the house seemed to be gone. Her surroundings became a vacuum which held her fast. Her heart squeezed as he took another step, closing the gap between them. She scrambled backward and her ass hit the kitchen table, stopping her escape.

"Lookin' for a strong woman to stand by my side, baby, and that's you."

"No." She wasn't strong, not anymore. Her strength had been sucked from her, leaving her an empty shell. "I'm not her."

"Yeah, Stella, that's you."

"You think I'm strong but I'm not." She wasn't who he thought. She needed him to see that. To look elsewhere. She could not be who he wanted.

"Bullshit."

"Every fucking day's a struggle, Trip."

"And you keep wakin' up. That right there takes strength."

Holy shit. He needed to remain a complete asshole and not say stuff like that. Otherwise, he'd easily chip away at the armor she wore to keep him at bay.

But him paying the outstanding bills, telling her he'd have her back, reminding her how strong she used to be...

Giving her the hope she could be that strong again.

Like he was doing with the club, she needed to rise up and grab life by the balls.

"Whatever the fuck it was that drove you to crumble the other night didn't crush you. Don't know what the fuck it is or was, but know it wasn't just the bar. Got your fuckin' back, Stella, to fight whatever haunts you."

No. She couldn't rely on someone else to do it for her.

She needed to do it herself.

She needed to dig deep and pull herself out of the depths of despair. To find the sun behind those dark clouds.

And if the pressure of making the bar successful wasn't weighing so heavily on her, if she had help with relieving some of that weight, maybe she could do just that. Fill that hollowness inside her with something other than sorrow and regret.

The only solution that was realistic was letting Trip help her and to stop fighting it.

But it scared her. The knowledge he wanted so much more than to just help her.

He wanted all of her. And she wasn't sure if she could ever give him that.

She was born into a club where the females were put into boxes.

Ol' ladies, where they became a member's main bitch. She couldn't even say the brothers' one and only, because she'd seen with her own eyes that wasn't true. Faithfulness was lacking.

Sweet butts, the so-called patch whores, who did whatever wherever with whomever. If one of the brothers wanted head, she dropped to her knees and gave him head. If they wanted to gang bang her, she spread her legs and let them take their turns. Otherwise, if she didn't do what one of the patched members asked, she was either banned from the club or worse.

The house mouse, usually a female underage or barely of legal age, used to take care of a member's domestic needs in every way but sexual. But Stella wondered now how many of the teenagers and young women she remembered had been getting used in more ways than was expected.

The backpacks. Usually the occasional hang-arounds. A female hoping to get her claws into one of the patched bikers. Or a female allowed to come along for one of the club runs but she didn't belong to one biker. She was only a toy for the day.

She was thankful her mother had taken her away not long after Trip cracked her head open. Because if she had stayed...

She might have ended up in one of those boxes.

Now Trip wanted to put her in one. He never said the words ol' lady and if he wanted her to stand by his side, she had no idea to what extent. An ol' lady usually had no power within an MC. No females did. Worse, they usually stood behind their man, not next to him.

Women in an MC were nothing but property. And the men did with them what they wanted.

Why women volunteered for that shit, accepted it willingly, she'd never know. Why her mother did? The answer, when she had asked, was her mother loved her father. And she said Pete treated her well. But that didn't add up since her mother grabbed Stella and escaped Manning Grove during all the turmoil. If her mother loved her father, why would she just leave?

She never got that answer no matter how many times she'd asked it. And Stella's only guess was to save herself and her daughter from the violence that was sweeping through the club.

Why her father and mother didn't reconnect later when the dust had settled...

Again, another question that had gone unanswered. And would forever be a mystery.

"Stella." Trip's deep voice saying her name brought her back to his kitchen.

And her current situation.

Which was Trip's long fingers curled around the side of her neck, his thumb pressing under her jaw as he searched her face. She wondered what she'd revealed while she was lost in thought.

Whatever it was had etched concern on his face.

In one way, he could make her life so much easier.

In another, he could make it so much harder.

To get the first, she knew she wouldn't be able to avoid the second.

Especially when he dropped his head and once again took her mouth in a crushing kiss.

Chapter Nine

He wanted to throw her over the table, pound her from behind like he did at the bar the other night. But then, he also wanted to throw her over his shoulder, carry her upstairs and eat her pussy out until she came all over his face.

He wanted to take her rough and relentlessly but also wanted to be gentle and take his time, discovering and appreciating every inch of her.

He decided he'd do both.

And if he got his way, he'd be able to do either one on a regular basis.

The thought of only fucking sweet butts didn't do it for him. When he was fifteen—hell, even younger—they got him hard and he wanted every single one of them. With how they dressed and how they acted, what teenaged boy with raging hormones didn't?

Now that he was thirty-five, he couldn't swallow the idea of fucking any of them.

Not that the club had any right now anyway.

But they'd show up. They always did. They'd do whatever was demanded of them, no matter how perverse, in hopes of being allowed to hang around the club or becoming an ol' lady. In hopes of securing a coveted spot on the back of a brother's sled.

It was one thing to bust a nut in a sweet butt, it was another to make her your permanent piece. Nobody wanted to go home to a woman who'd fucked, sucked, and more, all your brothers. No brother wanted a woman like that being the mother of his kids.

Why they thought they'd had a shot? Trip never knew as he watched sweet butt after sweet butt getting bent over and accepting the load from a line of brothers, waiting to give it to her.

He'd watched that and much worse.

At the time, he wasn't a patched brother, still too young to even prospect, so he couldn't participate.

Besides that sweet butt being told by the president, his own father, to pop his cherry, Trip wasn't allowed to touch any of them.

Stella would never be one of those. But she *would* be his.

And his alone.

He deepened the kiss when she didn't try to pull away, didn't make a sound except for a low groan he captured in his mouth. In fact, it was her tongue that invaded his mouth and found his first. Touching, tasting, not tentative at all.

She wasn't holding back which proved she wanted him, too.

Only he didn't want this to turn into what happened the other night, where she goaded him into being rough.

There was nothing wrong with rough if that's what she wanted, it just had to be for the right reasons.

Being punished for something that happened in her past —whatever it was— wasn't one of them. One of her hands curled around his waist, the other slid up his chest, skimming over one of his nipples before pausing on his throat, then a second later moving up along his jaw, and into his hair. She took a handful and he waited for the sharp pain of her ripping on it to free herself.

But it never happened. Instead, she tugged him forward, bringing him closer until his dick, now hard and throbbing in his jeans pressed into her belly.

She was not soft because she was too thin. She probably couldn't afford to eat like she should.

He would remedy that, too.

He loved the softness of a woman's belly, the wide curve of a hip, the heaviness of a breast, the roundness of her ass. Flesh he could grab and hold onto, squeeze and bite.

The ecstasy on Stella's face when she ate that slice of bacon...

He wanted to see that every morning. He never wanted her to worry about where her next meal was coming from. Never wanted her to have to choose a booze invoice over a grocery bill again.

That shit was going to end immediately.

Without breaking the kiss, he tugged her tank up her belly, shoving her bra up and over her tits until they were free of the restraint. He swore the tips of her nipples were as hard as his dick as he thumbed one and then the other.

The urge to taste them, suck them, bite them became so overwhelming he broke his mouth free and slid his nose down her jaw, her throat and with one hand holding the cotton of both her tank and bra out of the way, he cupped one, pinched the nipple between his finger and then sucked it deep into his mouth.

His teeth scraped the tip as he squeezed her tit hard, her back arching and her breath rushing from her on a cry.

Taking small bites, he worked his way to the other one, sinking his teeth gently into the soft swell first and then sucking the nipple hard.

The fingers from both of her hands were now threaded

into his hair, her nails digging into his scalp, not to discourage him, but to encourage him to continue.

He pulled his mouth away just enough to growl, "Shirt off," before going back to taking one puckered nipple into his mouth then the other.

Her shirt and bra were ripped over her head, leaving his hand free to slide along the waist of her jeans.

He hadn't seen her completely naked the other night, he only got to see her ass and the back of her thighs. This morning he wanted to see all of her. Every fucking inch.

But before he could thumb the button of her jeans free from its hole, a pounding on the door made him freeze. Stella stiffened, too.

He was going to kill whoever the fuck it was.

He needed to remember that this property would be no longer his own and people would be in and out on a regular basis as well as living on site. Having sex in the kitchen in view of the door probably wasn't a good idea unless he wanted a possible audience.

He did not.

And he was pretty sure Stella didn't, either.

He straightened as she held her discarded tank and bra in front of her tits.

With a flushed face, she focused on the door behind him.

He closed his eyes, reined in his fury at being interrupted and turned, but tossed over his shoulder, "Put on the tank, leave off the bra. We're not done."

He gave her a few seconds to do just that as he also stared at the large figure on the other side of the door. He was pretty sure his body was blocking the man's view of Stella until she got herself covered.

Then he strode to the door and yanked it open, ready to rip someone a new asshole.

He rethought that really quick-like when he saw who it was.

He'd been in plenty of fights, and he'd kicked a lot of asses, but he knew his limits.

The club's new enforcer was one of them.

Plus, it wouldn't be smart causing bad blood from the get-go when things were just starting to come together.

So, to cool his boiling blood, he sucked a deep breath in through his nose, counted to five and released it. A habit he'd gotten into when trying to control his temper, so his six years inside didn't turn into life without fucking parole.

"Brother," he greeted, glad his voice didn't shake with his dissipating anger.

Judge jerked his chin up in response. "Deacon's here with his shit." His green eyes slid past Trip to where Stella was and stuck there. One brow lifted slowly as he looked at Trip for a second before his gaze returned to a quiet Stella. "Hey, Stella."

"Hey, Judge." She sounded a bit breathy, which made him bristle, but when she cleared her throat and asked, "Where are the babies?" it was back to normal.

Judge's expression didn't change much but enough so Trip knew the man hadn't missed the change in her voice, either. "In the truck."

"Give them a scratch for me."

"Will let 'em out when we get down to the barn if you wanna give 'em one yourself. Just stopped in on the way to give Trip a head's up we're here."

Trip was pretty fucking certain that Stella wasn't going to head down to the barn to give the fucking dogs a scratch.

The only scratches she was going to dole out would be on his back. And he needed Judge to get lost for that to happen. "He can have whatever room he wants."

"Thinkin' he wants one of the apartments."

"Thought you wanted one of 'em."

"Yeah, but he wants the other one before it's claimed."

"Savin' the one for—"

"Sig," Judge finished for him.

"Sig?" he heard behind him.

Judge's eyes again landed on Stella behind him. "Had the same reaction." They came back to Trip. "Savin' an apartment for someone who might not even fuckin' show up."

"He'll show."

"Got a lot of fuckin' confidence, brother."

"He'll show," Trip repeated, hoping he was right.

"If he don't land behind bars again. He's like a fuckin' boomerang when it comes to prison."

"That's a good reason for him to come home."

Judge shook his head. "You didn't see his sheet."

"You did?"

"Yeah. Was only one piece of the puzzle Deke used to find him." Judge leaned in closer and lowered his normally booming voice. "Your agg assault with a deadly weapon's child's play for him."

Fuck. Trip needed to tell Stella about the charge he caught and why he did time, but he wanted to be the one to tell her. Not Judge.

"Want a copy of it along with Rook's."

Judge nodded. "When you goin' to see 'im?"

"When I get a chance but before he gets sprung, in case he thinks about not comin' straight home."

"Yeah, smart. He's another one who gets pinched just by crossin' the fuckin' street." Judge wasn't joking.

"If I know their weaknesses, we might be able to keep them out."

"What about your own?"

He locked gazes with Judge. "Got it under control."

"Yeah, you opened that door ready to tear me a new asshole. Just a warnin', I already like the one I have, so I'll do what I gotta do to make sure that doesn't happen."

"This club needs to be solid, Judge. Fighting amongst

ourselves will burn it to the ground again. Not gonna let that happen."

"Then you'll keep your shit together."

Trip gave him a single nod. "No other choice."

Judge gave him a single nod back. "Yeah. I hear you."

"You never landed anywhere, at least."

The monster of a man simply tilted his head and grumbled, "Just never got caught."

"Guess that's the key."

"That's the fuckin' key."

"Speaking of keys. For now, the barn and bunkhouse won't be locked. But there's individual locks on all the rooms. The key to your apartment's up there on the counter. The keys to the rooms downstairs are in each individual room. Like I said, he can pick whichever room he wants since he's the first one movin' in."

"Apartment ready?"

"Just needs another coat of paint. Doin' that this week."

"Good fuckin' deal. Tellin' the landlord I'm out at the end of the month. As soon as the paint's dry I'm movin' in. It'll save me a shitload of scratch. And the dogs will love it out here."

"TV and internet are scheduled for next week, too."

Judge grinned. "Sounds like a fuckin' palace."

"If a little cable and Wi-Fi's gonna make it a palace, then you're gonna feel like a fuckin' king."

They clasped hands and bumped shoulders.

"Glad your ass is on board."

"Don't make me regret it," Judge threw over his shoulder as he jogged down the porch steps and cut across the grass to a waiting pickup truck with some furniture and a big screen TV in the back.

Seeing the new cut on Judge's back gave Trip a sense of satisfaction and also one of coming home.

The Originals might have made a fucked-up family, but

it was a family even so. Trip wanted to not only build on that but make it better.

He saw the mistakes made. They just needed to avoid those same mistakes. Though, that might be easier said than done.

Deacon flicked a cigarette out the truck's window and shot him a two-finger flick in greeting. Trip returned it and shut the door, making sure to lock it, just in case.

When he turned, he realized why Judge hadn't said anything to Stella as he left.

She was gone.

The loud rattle of her Jeep as it made its way down his long lane came through the open windows. He rushed to the front door—the door he never used—and saw it was unlocked.

She had snuck out the front.

Son of a bitch.

He opened it just in time to see the Cherokee turn right onto the paved road. He slammed the door and locked it, a weight pressing heavily on his chest.

He turned slowly, his eyes immediately landing on his grandfather's roll-top desk.

Just what he expected. The checkbook binder and the pile of bills were gone.

"For fuck's sake," he growled, pressing the heel of his palm to his forehead, which was suddenly pounding.

His temperature was spiking, and he needed to cool off. He needed to get it under control before it swallowed him whole.

Because once it did that, there was no telling what he'd do.

HER CHIN RESTED in her palm as she frowned at the peanut butter and jelly sandwich sitting on the chipped plate in front of her. Two bites were missing from one corner, but that was it.

She couldn't stomach eating anymore. It churned with what happened earlier. With the knowledge if she hadn't escaped when she had, she would have let Trip do whatever he wanted to her.

And she would have welcomed it then. But regretted it later.

She had no choice when it came to Trip and the club being involved in the bar. That choice had been taken from her.

However, she did have a choice about landing in his bed. Or his kitchen table.

Or the bar's back counter.

She had been grateful Judge had showed up when he did. It gave her a chance to escape undetected, though the club's new Sergeant at Arms saw what she was doing and didn't tip off Trip.

Thank fuck.

She owed Judge a beer or two on the house.

He probably wouldn't accept it because, when he came in, he always over tipped her, knowing she desperately needed the money.

Like she was nothing but a fucking charity case.

She had come back to Manning Grove in an effort to get her life in order. To start fresh. But all it did was bog her down more. It took the monkey on her back and turned it into King Kong. The weight becoming unbearable.

Trip had asked her what happened to the eleven-year old determined bitch.

She still existed. Stella just needed to drag her back out and dust her off.

A loud pounding at the rear door downstairs not only

jerked her out of her thoughts but made her jump. It sounded like the police were using a battering ram.

With her heart racing, she slipped off the stool at the counter and made her way to the window to glance down at the parking spots behind the bar.

There was room for four vehicles, hers and three employees, if she had them, which she didn't. But even if she did, on a Sunday night only her Jeep would fill one spot since the bar was closed.

Something that, if she got help, she might be able to change.

Next to her vehicle, a very old wrecker took up two of those spots.

She couldn't see the rear door to see who was pounding on it unless she stuck her head out of the window.

But she knew.

She remembered that tow truck since Buck had run a repo business when he was still alive. And she also recognized the painted but faded name on the side: Buck You Recovery.

A teenage Trip had always vowed when he turned eighteen, he would wear a prospect cut for the MC and help his pop with the repo business.

He thought that was his future.

Instead, his father ended up shot in the back, Trip got dragged to Wisconsin and then he joined the Marines at eighteen. At least that was what Pete had told her on one of their rare father-daughter conversations and she was curious enough to ask.

Judge's father, Ox, also helped Buck with the "recovery" business, by doing "collections," just not of the legal type. The club offered so-called "protection" to the town's business owners for a monthly fee. It wasn't optional, even though there was nothing to protect them from. It wasn't like the townsfolk were getting shaken down by the mafia or gangs running the streets wreaking havoc. The only shake-downs and havoc created were from the BFMC itself, arguably a gang in its own rite.

She heard more pounding and "Stella" being yelled just like in *A Streetcar Named Desire*. Her mother's favorite movie.

"Fuck," she muttered under her breath as Trip stepped back far enough to where she could see him. He jabbed a finger toward the door, not looking any kind of pleased.

Well, she wasn't happy about this interruption, either.

She winced when the window sash complained loudly as she struggled to lift it. It got stuck open halfway, but it was enough for her to yell down, "Go away, Trip."

He plugged his hands on his hips under his cut and tilted his head, his hair not restrained by any kind of hat or skull cap since he hadn't ridden his bike.

The fact that he looked hot as fuck annoyed her even more.

"Not goin' anywhere. Save some time for both of us and open the fuckin' door."

"That's not smart."

"As part owner of this fuckin' place, I demand access."

I demand access.

Stella rolled her eyes. Well, that just made her want to run right down and let him in. "I'll get you a key made next week."

"Want a key today. Come down and open the fuckin' door. Can't afford to replace it if I kick it the fuck in."

"You won't."

"Try me."

"Goddamn it," she whispered as she jimmied the window sash free enough to close it.

She slipped on her flip flops since there was no way she was heading into the bar barefooted. She hurried down the steps, through the storage room and toward the rear of the bar where Trip was waiting. Most likely impatiently.

With her hand on the door's panic bar, she paused, dropped her head and sucked in a breath. Then as she pushed the bar, she lifted her chin to show a confidence she did not feel, unlatching the door.

Her mouth dropped open and she fell back as he barreled past her, practically shoving her out of the way with what looked like a half dozen plastic grocery bags draped over each arm.

He didn't slow his roll and kept heading down the short hallway.

She quickly secured the door and followed, the slap of her flip flops on her feet the only sound as he disappeared into the storage room.

"Hey!" she yelled as she scrambled to catch up and barely saw him disappear up the steps. "Hey!"

Holy fuck, this man was trying her patience.

She ripped off her flip flops and ran up the steps, shoved open the door to her apartment and then whipped her shoes at him as he stood with his back to her at the tiny counter of her galley kitchen.

Her cheap foam flip flops fell to the floor two feet from him in an unsatisfying flutter.

He finished sliding the bags off his arm and onto the counter. Twelve bags of groceries barely fit in her limited space, so he had to pile some on top of others.

"What the fuck, Trip!" she yelled at him as she stomped over to where he was pulling things out of the bags. "What the fuck are you doing?"

"Told you we weren't done. You left knowin' that." With that he continued to pull out items, shoving them into her chest, where she automatically grabbed them.

"Again, Trip. You don't own me. I'm not your property."

"Right."

No, no, no. Not "right." Wrong.

She stared at what he'd handed her so far. Two packs of

maple-flavored bacon, what looked and felt like two butcher-wrapped steaks and a bag of expensive coffee.

What the fuck?

"Put that shit away, then help with the rest."

"I don't need your help." Talking to him was like talking to a brick wall. It was not only frustrating, it was pointless.

The man did not fucking listen.

Trip's hand stilled deep inside one of the bags and he lifted his dark brown eyes to hers. "Say that again?" He slipped his hand out, empty this time, and raised it, palm out. He jerked his chin toward her barely eaten PB and J. "Two bites of that fuckin' sandwich."

"You interrupted my dinner."

"A PB and J doesn't count as fuckin' dinner, Stella. Saw your ribs showin' earlier when I was suckin' your tits. Too fuckin' skinny." He snagged the two packages of bacon from her arms and went over to the fridge.

Damn it.

He flung open the door and jerked both hands up and out in an exasperated move before tossing the bacon onto one of the shelves and turning to face her. "It's fuckin' empty."

Stella let her gaze slide over the mountain of bags as she told her next lie. "I haven't had a chance to go shopping."

"Goddamn it, woman, don't fuckin' lie to me. *Ever.*" The last was said with extreme annoyance. "Don't like fuckin' liars."

She stood there in stunned silence, unsure what to do or say. Because whatever she did or said would go ignored.

He went back to the bags and yanked out a waxed paper bag which filled that tiny corner of the apartment with a smell so damn delicious, her stomach growled. She slapped a hand to it to quiet it.

It pretty much gave her the finger just like Trip.

He unrolled the top of the bag, glanced inside, sniffed

and smiled. "Now that's what you need." He picked the PB and J off the plate and chucked it into the trash can sitting at the end of the short counter. He dug out two large, still steaming pieces of fried chicken and dropped them on her plate. "Sit the fuck down and eat those."

"Thought you wanted me to help you."

"Eat first."

"You'll be finished before I'm done eating."

"Think I'm capable of puttin' away some fuckin' groceries. Just like I was when I went to fuckin' Walmart to get 'em for you."

She bet that was a sight. Him pushing a grocery cart wearing that fucking cut.

She closed her eyes.

She was being an ungrateful bitch.

But she didn't like what he had done without asking. Being pushy. Forcing her to accept his help without her agreeing to it.

If she accepted any help from him, she would be beholden to him.

She didn't want to owe him anything.

She didn't want to owe anyone anything, not just Trip.

Even so, plenty of other people in this town knew she was struggling and not one of them had brought her groceries. Not one.

She opened her eyes again as the plastic bags rustled. He was digging more stuff out and stacking some of the non-perishable items in one corner. Crackers, cookies, soups and more. She didn't have a lot of storage; the kitchen was so small that there was barely any space available to keep canned or dry goods here. But there was plenty of space down in the storage room, if she needed it.

Since moving in, she hadn't needed it. Plus, she was worried about mice.

"Eat the damn chicken, Stella, before I feed it to you."

"I'm fine."

He went solid, his back still to her. Then he spun on his heels and took the two large steps separating them and yanked the top of her tank down enough to show her collarbones. He ran a finger over one of them. "This is not fine." He jerked the hem of her tank top up and spanned one side of her rib cage with his fingers. "This is not fuckin' fine."

She slapped his hands away. When she escaped his house, she hadn't taken the time to put her bra back on and since she was the thinnest she'd ever been, since before...

Well, before...

She really could get away without wearing one since her breasts had shrunk a bit.

She knew she was too thin not only because of seeing it in the mirror, but because her clothes were hanging off her and even sometimes had to use a belt to keep jeans up.

She used to love to eat and cook. She even used to love to bake. Especially birthday cakes for...

She hadn't died that day but everything inside her had.

Too many times she wondered if she even had the strength to go on. But somehow, she had enough to take that next breath, to wake up that next morning, no matter how hard it was.

Things were slightly better now than right after the day her world went dark.

But it had been a long time since she'd felt joy.

And eating was just something she now had to force herself to do. Life had lost its flavor and now remained tasteless.

She'd hoped that having the bar to concentrate on, put all her energy into, would have helped.

It didn't. It was almost as depressing as everything she'd escaped.

But would never forget. That she couldn't do.

She pulled away from him and slid onto the stool,

staring at the chicken long enough that her mouth began to water. The smell filled her nostrils as she lifted one of the thighs up and took a big bite.

Just like the bacon this morning, this had to be the best tasting fried chicken she ever had.

She knew that wasn't true. But maybe her taste buds were finally reawakening.

Trip watched her take a few bites of the chicken, then with a nod he went back to putting the groceries away, partially filling her fridge and freezer with enough food for the week and then some, if she was careful.

When he was done, he snagged her cell phone off the counter, which had been next to her plate, and held it up to her face to unlock it by using the facial recognition feature before she could block him.

"Trip!" She was removing that method to unlock her cell as soon as she could.

Once again, he ignored her, did something on her phone and a few seconds later a phone rang in his pocket. He put hers back where he found it, and dug out his own, fiddling with it.

The man was cunning, that was for sure. Now he had her phone number, which she'd had no plans to give to him.

When he was done, he slipped the phone back into the inside pocket of his cut, leaned back against the counter and crossed his arms over his chest, making the muscles in his arms bulge.

She took a bite of the chicken before she took a bite of him. He might be a bossy asshole, but he sure was a tempting one. Those muscles, that scruff on his face, that hair. All the shit that attracted her should be negated by the cut on his back and his attitude.

Not to mention, all the crap that went along with being a woman in the MC life.

She was lucky she escaped at a young enough age, but

then she turned around and ended up married to a bad boy anyway, just not of the biker variety.

She knew better than to get involved with another one.

The first one almost killed her without trying.

"Once I get you help, bar's gonna be open on Sundays. Gettin' large screen TVs and the NFL ticket. NHL. All the fucking sports that cause people to drink. Startin' now, you're doin' daily drink specials and Happy Hour. Also, gonna start a dart league. A pool league. Anything to encourage people to come back. The bar's a dump. So, we're redoin' it. New pool tables and all the shit that goes along with that. New tables, new chairs. Refinish the bar top, replace those old, torn stools. New lighting so it doesn't look like a fuckin' cave. New paint. New flooring."

"I don't have that money, Trip," she said around another bite of chicken.

"Gonna have it."

Sure. And pigs were going to sprout wings and fly, too. "All that work will take time."

"Gonna get the Amish who did the barn and bunkhouse to come out and do the work. They like to start early, so that'll work out. Get 'em in, and then you open a bit later every day 'til it's all done."

"Still need to pay them."

"Yeah."

"Yeah? How am I going to do that?"

"*We*, Stella."

"And the answer to that is?"

"Gonna hold off workin' on the motel 'til the bar's self-sufficient. Then I'll worry 'bout it. But not 'til then. Once you're moved out, gonna also fix up this apartment and get one or more of the prospects to move in, or even a member. Someone to not only help at the bar but keep an eye on it."

Hold up. "Once I've moved out?"

Again, he ignored her.

He tilted his head in thought. "Maybe a member, then he can keep the prospects in line. Make sure they ain't fuckin' up."

"Umm. I live here, Trip. This is my home."

"It's a dump."

"But it's my dump."

"And half of it will still be your dump, but it's not where you're gonna sleep."

Stella dropped the half-eaten chicken thigh onto the plate, picked up the plate, slipped off the stool and took it to the sink. She slowly and carefully washed her hands, using that time to try to loosen the tightness that pulled at her chest.

He was suddenly next to her, in her space, holding the dish towel. She stared at it for a second, then lifted her gaze to him before taking it and drying off her hands.

"That sink in yet?" he asked.

"Trip, you need to stop. I don't understand why you're doing this. The bar I do, but me?" She shook her head. "There's no reason for it. We made a mistake, it's now over and let's move on."

He dropped his head until his breath was beating off her lips, but he didn't kiss her. No. He let that warm breath sweep along her jaw and up her cheek as he slid his nose along hers. "You were born club property," he said softly but firmly into her ear. "I'm reclaiming what belongs to the club. That means you belong to me."

That means you belong to me.

Was it wrong that heat rushed through her and everything clenched tight? Her nipples, her pussy, everything except her lips which parted, and a ragged breath escaped.

Yes, it was wrong. So, so wrong. "Sounds like slavery to me."

"Then you weren't listenin'."

"I heard you, Trip, loud and clear. As much as you want

to think you can 'claim' someone, you can't own a person. Not without their consent. Hell, maybe not even with their consent."

"Then tell me no, baby. Tell me that's not what you want. Tell me you didn't feel what I did in my kitchen this mornin'. And don't lie."

"Having sex with someone is not even remotely similar to having someone claim them."

"Isn't it?"

"Maybe if you're into some kinky shit."

"Maybe I'm into some kinky shit."

Stella pulled her head back so she could look at his face. Her hand which she had pressed against his chest to give them as much space as possible, curled into his T-shirt, gripping it hard. "Are you?"

"No, but if you are, I'm willin' to try whatever the fuck you're into."

Holy shit, this man! He was fucking crazy!

She pressed her lips tightly together and pushed at him. He didn't budge. Of course not.

"I can tell you what I'm not into... You being a bossy motherfucker and trying to control my life. You're not asking, you're telling. That's bossy. And I don't like it."

"Don't you?"

She sucked in her stomach as his callused fingertips traced the waistband of the leggings she had put on earlier. They slid lower until he cupped her mound. She was afraid he'd discover just how damp the crotch of the stretchy cotton was.

Because even though she didn't want to be claimed as some biker's woman or ol' lady, she definitely wanted to have sex with Trip again.

As crazy as that was.

Her brain reminded her it was a mistake and would make things even messier, but her body disagreed. Besides the other night downstairs in the bar and again this morning in his kitchen, her blood hadn't pumped like that in a long time.

Also during that time, her black and white world had taken on a little color. Just like when the top of the morning sun hit the horizon. Creating enough light to start chasing away the darkness.

He dropped his head until his mouth lightly touched hers and he gripped her mound tighter. "Want my mouth on you there. Want you moanin' my name as I eat you 'til you come. Want you beggin' me to give you my dick. Want you drippin' wet as you claw my back and bite me hard enough to leave a mark because you're losin' your fuckin' mind as I fuck you."

His tongue slid quickly along her bottom lip, then was gone. Simply a taste before he devoured her.

"But when I do all that, when I take you like that, wanna know it's all mine and only mine. I don't fuckin' share, baby. Want *my* name on your lips as you come and no other man's."

"We hardly know each other, Trip. We're different people than we were twenty years ago."

"Know what I see and know what I want. Also know what I'm feelin'." His middle finger slipped deeper between her thighs tracing the damp line of cotton. "And what I'm feelin' doesn't lie."

"Can you give me space to breathe, to think?"

"Nothin' to think about."

"There's so much to think about, Trip."

So much happened in the last two decades. He was no longer a fifteen-year-old boy and she certainly wasn't an eleven-year-old girl. He hadn't even wanted—or, *hell*, liked—her back then. He and Sig and most of the other boys considered her and the other girls pests.

So, what changed?

It certainly wasn't her sparkling personality.

And he said she was too skinny. Plus, she was so broke, her meals basically consisted of oatmeal or peanut butter and jelly sandwiches.

What did he see in her that made him want to claim her?

She just couldn't wrap her head around it.

She needed to switch gears and help him understand exactly what he said. How he said it. See how wrong it was.

Because while she wanted to have sex with him, she did not want to sell her soul to the devil. "Your father took what he wanted, whenever he wanted. As did a lot of who you call the Originals. But that was his downfall. Do you want to end up just like him?"

Trip tipped his head back and stared at the ceiling. A long moment later he dropped it and pulled away, giving them at least a few inches of space. But he was still too close. "You're right. Goin' about this the wrong way."

"You shouldn't be going about this at all. I've got nothing to give you, Trip. Nothing. You're trying to claim someone who won't make you stronger, but who might pull you down."

"Bullshit."

"Trip," she whispered as she closed her eyes. "Listen..." She had to make him understand without revealing what needed to remain buried.

Her eyes flicked open as his fingers grabbed her chin and he yanked her face up. "No, you fuckin' listen. Know what I fuckin' see in you, Stella. I see it clearly. Maybe you don't. Not sure what fucked up your head, but I still see who you are deep inside. That stubbornness, that determination. That's who I need at my side. A woman like that. Someone fuckin' loyal. Someone who's got my back. Someone who's got a spine of fuckin' steel and balls to match. That's you."

"No."

"Yeah, baby, it's you."

"It used to be. Not anymore."

"Think we had a conversation about when life kicks you in the nuts. The pain has passed, Stella, now you gotta rise up and fight back."

"You don't even know..."

"Right. I don't know. I wanna know and you're gonna tell me." He lifted a hand to cut off her protest. "When you're ready."

What, he wasn't going to demand she spill her guts?

"We're stronger together, Stella," he said softly.

"How do you know that?"

"I just do."

"That's not even a good answer."

"But it's an answer."

"Holy shit," she muttered under her breath. She shook her head, trying to shake the craziness out of it. Was this really happening? "We only had sex once, Trip, and now your hinting at me moving in with you."

"Not hinting. And we're gonna change that other fact, too."

"We are?"

"Yeah, baby, we are. You fuckin' snuck off before I could finish what I started."

"That was the point, Trip."

His eyelids got heavy and he gave her a slow grin. "Didn't like what I was doin'?" She opened her mouth and he pressed his finger to her lips. "Told you I don't like liars."

She decided not to lie. "It was the first time in a long time that I've felt alive."

"You're definitely alive, baby, and I'll prove it to you."

He took her mouth, burying his fingers into her hair, arching her neck back as he increased the pressure of his lips. The hand over her leggings at her pussy squeezed so hard it made her gasp, but it also made her throb.

And want so much more.

Their tongues tangled and their breathing caught when he removed his hand to only slide it between the fabric and her skin. She wore no panties, nothing stopped him from reaching his destination.

His middle finger pressed on her clit, then circled it a couple of times before continuing lower, separating her folds which were getting slicker by the second.

Cupping her, he slid that long finger of his into her. She couldn't hide her body's reaction to him and his Neanderthal-like mentality.

Claim.

Eat.

Fuck.

He just needed to grunt, club her over the head and toss her over his shoulder, and evolution had gone backward millions of years.

If this was anybody else but Trip, she wouldn't be tolerating it. But with him? For some reason, she was.

At eleven she had foolishly pursued a boy who wanted nothing to do with her.

Now, the tables have turned.

Chapter Ten

HAD THE TABLES TURNED? While, yes, Trip's relentless pursuit of her was unexpected, was it all one-sided? Had the last twenty years purged him from her system?

Her body was saying otherwise as he continued to make her breathless with not only his kiss but with what he was doing with his fingers.

And what he was doing was about to make her come.

Unlike the time in the bar, no anger or frustration was behind it for either one of them. No need for anything but the pleasure he was bringing.

She missed being touched like this, letting everything go except for what was currently happening.

Losing herself in Trip instead of her memories.

She hadn't been this wet in forever. Not since her relationship with her husband had been new and exciting.

Before things began to change.

Trip pulled away just enough to end the kiss. "You were with me. Now you're not."

She realized his hand had stilled, though two of his fingers remained inside her and his thumb on her clit. He began to move them again and she sucked in a sharp breath.

"You with me?"

"Yes," she breathed, closing her eyes and dropping her head back far enough it pressed against one of the kitchen cabinets. "Yes," she repeated as he began to plunge his fingers in and out of her wetness faster.

"Gimme your mouth," he demanded.

She lifted her head and opened her eyes to see him focused on her lips. "Kiss me."

His nostrils flared and a little growl escaped him as he captured her lips again. Their tongues clashed and her fingers gripped his face, encouraging him to kiss her harder, deeper. Somehow swallow her whole.

She needed to lose herself within him. Even if for a short while.

She shouldn't want this.

She shouldn't want this.

She shouldn't want this.

But she did.

And she wasn't going to tell him to stop. It wasn't going to end with their kiss. It wasn't going to end with him making her come with his hand.

A few seconds later, heat exploded from her center, radiating to every outer edge of her body, pulling not only a groan from her but one from him as she convulsed around his fingers.

Their breathing was ragged but he didn't let her mouth go, even when he pulled his hand free from her leggings and hooked her around the back of her thighs, lifting her up.

She held on by wrapping her legs and arms around him and he moved to her bed. When his legs hit the mattress, he let them both topple. Her mouth only became free for a second, enough for her to gasp at the impact of his heavy body landing on hers. He took it again, his fingers digging into her hair, his lips moving, his tongue exploring, like he owned her mouth.

And at that moment, he did.

Where he learned to kiss like that, she had no idea, but it was driving her wild enough that she wouldn't be surprised if she came again. Or maybe it was the thought that his hard cock—which was pressed into her thigh—would soon be inside her.

Either way, she was holding onto the edge by her fingernails. Fingernails she wanted to dig into his back when they both came.

That wouldn't happen until he was undressed. He had way too many clothes on.

She twisted her head to break free. She was practically panting when she demanded, "Fuck me."

That got him moving. He surged up, stripping himself of his cut and tossing it onto a nearby chair. Next, he pulled his T-shirt over his head and threw that onto the floor. His hands dropped to his belt and she followed their every movement as he unfastened it, popped open the button and unzipped his jeans.

He scrambled off the bed to his feet, his eyes not leaving hers. "Get naked."

She wanted to watch him get undressed first.

He bent over, unlaced his boots and toed them both off, yanked off his socks and then shucked his jeans, leaving them right where they landed with a loud jangle from his belt buckle and chain wallet as they hit the floor.

She didn't get to see him like this the other night. She had been facing away from him and he'd only dropped his jeans enough to fuck her.

Now she saw everything.

And he was fucking breathtaking.

His thick cock, which pointed right at her, in a nest of trimmed dark hair, and his even thicker thighs. He circled the root of his cock with his hand and began to stroke it, his dark gaze catching hers.

"You're not naked," he growled.

She wasn't sure if she could do that, get naked while he watched. He had said she was too skinny, plus she wanted to put off that other conversation as long as possible. If it was up to her, she'd never have it. But she had a feeling it wouldn't be up to her.

So, to avoid him from seeing her all at once from a distance, she said, "I want you to do it." She'd prefer if it was dark when he did it, but the April early evening sun was still high in the sky and the curtains were so thin, they didn't even darken the studio apartment when closed.

He climbed back onto the bed and walked up her body using his hands and knees, his erection swinging heavily as he did so.

She didn't know where she wanted to look more. His cock, which had a thick string of precum hanging from the tip, making her want to lick it off, or his face. The intensity of his dark eyes and the predatory expression he wore...

It made heat swirl in her belly as well as goosebumps explode over her skin.

He looked as if he was hungry and she was his next meal.

"Wanna taste that wet pussy but it's not gonna happen this time, baby. Next time, though. Promise. Will make you come a couple times with my mouth. Is that good?"

Was which part good? The next time part? Or the part where she'll have at least two orgasms by him eating her out?

She guessed the first one was needed for the second one. And the first one was the problem. By having sex with him, she was dropping her guard enough to let him in, and she was afraid that would be all he needed to take over.

Like he was doing with the bar.

He ripped her tank top over her head but as he tucked

his thumbs into the waistband of her leggings, she twisted until she was lying flat on her belly.

He hesitated.

And she knew why.

He was looking at the tattoo that took up even more landscape on her back than the BFMC colors did on his.

He was no longer in a rush to remove her leggings. Instead he remained silent and his finger traced down her spine. She knew he was reading the word "perseverance" that was written down the center of the trunk of the large Tree of Life tattoo.

She held her breath when his fingers hesitated on the fallen leaf at the base of the tree.

Please don't ask. Not yet.

Not yet.

She released the air she was holding deep within her lungs when he moved on, catching the waistband and rolling her leggings down her thighs, working them over her knees, calves and then her feet.

His broad, warm hands slid up her bare skin from her ankles to the top of her thighs, where he gripped her hips, and pressed his mouth to the very top of her crease, where one of the tree roots ended.

"That's a lot of ink," he murmured against her skin.

"Yeah," she murmured back.

"Took a lot of time."

"Yeah."

"Your full sleeve alone... Know how long it takes. The time and money invested."

"Yeah." She could afford it then. She couldn't afford it now.

Most of it had been done years ago, starting when she was eighteen, one small piece after the other, until the sleeve on her left arm was done in full color, unlike his sleeve of black and gray.

The tree was also in color, but done in watercolor, so it was a softer look for the green leaves and the brown trunk. PERSEVERANCE was in solid black. The only part in grayscale was the fallen leaf with Kade's name in it.

She had that done, along with the lettering, a lot later...

After.

He ran his tongue up her spine and when he was finished, he said, "The word's a good reminder, unless you don't heed it, Stel."

She had gotten it to keep herself breathing when she wanted to do nothing but stop. To remind herself that one day it would get better, she just needed to get herself to that day.

She almost didn't... until she persevered.

He straddled her hips, swept her hair from her neck and replaced it with his face. His mouth moved along her neck and around the curve of her ear. "Need to grab a wrap and for you to turn over, baby. Not doin' it from behind today. Wanna see your face, want to feel your nails, your mouth. Yeah?"

"Yeah," she breathed.

She shouldn't want that, too, but she did.

She wouldn't fight him this time. Not like the other night.

Her crappy bed shook violently as he moved off her to grab his jeans and wallet. A few seconds later he was back. She heard the tear of the condom wrapper and the bed moved again as he rolled it on. She squeezed her thighs together in anticipation. The slipperiness between them confirmed she was soaked.

Why did she want him? Why? She didn't need more complications in her life. She certainly didn't need them in a man like him.

She had vowed she was done with men like Trip.

And here she was, about to roll over and let him into her life.

"Baby, turn over." He rose enough to give her the room to do so.

And because he was straddling that area, she hoped he wouldn't see what she wanted to hide.

The reminder of what she'd lost.

As soon as she rolled over, she curled up and grabbed his face with both hands, falling back to the mattress and pulling him with her.

She took his mouth, while her fingers gripped the wiry hairs of his beard. She swallowed his groan, spread her legs and bent her knees.

He tried to break away, but she held him there. His next groan turned into a growl as he reached between them, lined up his cock and pressed the crown just barely between her folds.

Pushing her hips up, she tried to force him deeper, but he held back, not letting her impale herself.

And that's what she needed, him to fill her up, to take her completely.

He jerked his beard free of her fingers, which had to hurt. Just as she suspected, he was not going to let her take control. She doubted Trip would ever allow that. And if he did, it would be on his terms, not hers.

With both of his palms planted in the mattress right above her shoulders, he stared down at her, his brown eyes dark.

She waited for him to say something, but he didn't. He just continued to stare at her, as if almost being able to see her soul.

Which scared her. Her eyes slid to the side to avoid his. "Trip," she whispered.

"Baby, look at me."

You're everything I don't want, what I don't need whispered through her head.

"Look at me." The words were still said softly but much more demanding.

"I can't," she breathed.

"You want me?" he asked.

She should say no, but she couldn't. She closed her eyes. "Yes."

"Then look at me."

She gave herself a second to breathe before opening her eyes and meeting his. And the moment she did, he slid all the way inside her until he was completely buried.

He remained deep. His chest pumping but his hips still.

"What are you doing?"

"Takin' a moment to appreciate you, baby. Don't look away... Eyes on me. Look, I like it rough, too, but now's not the time for that. If you're expectin' me to just pound it out to get it over with, give you what you want and then get out? Ain't gonna happen. Not today. Wanna take my time, show you—"

"Stop."

His head lifted, his nostrils flared, and his lips flattened as he began to withdraw from her.

Her hands gripped his ass, stopping him. "No, not that. What you're saying. Please, let's just fuck. That's it. Nothing more."

"With me, you get more."

She swallowed back a scream of *I don't want more!* "We'll talk after."

"After, you'll want me gone."

He was right. Afterward she'd want him gone. She'd want her space. "I can't be who you want me to be."

"Bullshit." He thrust inside her again. "Fuck first, talk later."

"Thank you." He seemed annoyed that she thanked

him, so she left one hand gripping his ass and curled the other around the back of his head and pulled him down. "Kiss me again. You're good at it."

His smile was smothered by their kiss.

She moaned as he began to move. This wasn't a pounding like the other night. This was way more than that. She swore the flex of his hips took her to heights she never went before.

She dug her heels into the back of his thighs, matching his movements. Her fingers slid from the back of his head down his spine, her nails scraping along his heated skin as he powered deep.

Kissing wasn't the only thing he was good at.

Damn.

It wasn't long before their kissing was interrupted by her throwing her head back and crying out his name as she came. But as soon as the orgasm faded away, he captured her mouth and began all over again. Thrusting deep, but steady, stealing her breath with his kiss.

This wasn't just fucking, it was more.

She could not fall for him. If she did, she might end up back where she was, on a path to the darkness. Unexpected and devastating.

And she swore she'd never take that path again.

SHE WAS hot and wet and... *Fuck*, her orgasm had been intense. So much so, that he had to fight not to come when she did.

But he wanted to hold off. Make it last as long as he could. He needed to show her he didn't just want sex from her, and she shouldn't just want sex from him.

They could be a powerful team.

He wanted to be there to help her through whatever was

bogging her down and she could do the same for him when he needed it.

Because there was no fucking doubt he would need it. Resurrecting the Fury along with everything else was starting to wear on him. The pressure was beginning to overwhelm him. Not only because of that endless to-do list but because of all the financial shit.

He had never been good with money, but now he was forced to be. If he had known the bar was such a shit show before he bought the motel, he wouldn't have bought it. He would've dumped the money he got from selling the warehouse right into Crazy Pete's.

So now he was wrestling with getting the wrecker rolling for the repo business so he could start bringing in some cash there, taking that cash and reinvesting it into not only the bar but also the motel.

Plus, trying to finish getting the barn and bunkhouse not only set up but filled with bodies. Bodies who could also bring in scratch. Bodies who could take some of the brunt of the heavy lifting.

He'd been trying to do too much by himself.

And though, it was coming together, it was a slow go.

But at the end of the night when he was fucking exhausted, he wanted to fall into bed with Stella.

When his temper was at his breaking point, he needed to sink into her wet heat.

When he was wondering how the fuck he would get out of bed the next morning, he wanted to turn his head and see her sleeping next to him.

Safe and secure.

Not hungry, not wanting for anything.

He'd fallen fast for his ex-wife, which had been his biggest mistake, besides him doing something stupid to land in prison.

Because of that, he knew better to fall fast for Stella. But, *fuck him*, if he wasn't doing just that.

At the time, he'd gotten married young, but he wasn't so young anymore. He hoped now that he'd lived a life full of experience, between the Marines and prison, he'd become a much better judge of character. That he could see through someone faster now than he could at eighteen, twenty or even twenty-five.

He only hoped he was right. Because he was not dealing with the shit he was forced to with his ex-wife again.

Never fucking again.

And this was why he was determined to claim Stella. To make sure she was his. Because like he told her, the fuck if he was going to share his woman. And he would not land behind bars again for one, either.

But, *fuck him*, he was building a new life, a better one, and he wanted someone besides his club brothers to share that with.

And for some reason, the minute he saw Stella, the very second he realized who she was, he knew it was her.

Maybe stupid, but definitely fucking true.

He could be making another big fucking mistake, but it didn't feel like that in his gut.

But for now, he needed to get out of his head, concentrate on the woman beneath him and prove to them both that this was right.

Her nails were digging into his back as she clung tightly to him, her mouth near his ear, panting, moaning, whimpering as he drove into her over and over. That sound was better than any song that had hit number one on the charts.

Hearing his name on her lips as her hips rose to meet his, cemented everything he thought.

He dropped his head and sucked one of her nipples into his mouth, flicking the tip with his tongue. Then he did the same with the other.

With his wandering thoughts now collected, he realized she needed to come again soon, or she wouldn't get that chance until next time.

Next time.

And the next.

And the next.

He had come home to Manning Grove, but he had found home inside of her.

He had felt driven to come back to a place with bad memories. And maybe it was to right all the wrongs.

Including the one with her.

Chapter Eleven

TRIP STARED at the brown water stain above him. That stain meant there was a current leak in the roof, or one in the past that had been fixed. He hoped it was the latter. He really didn't want to add a new fucking roof, or even a roof repair, to his already long list.

His chest tightened with the thought of one more thing he might have to come up with money for.

He wanted to keep Stella from drowning, but he might have to do some serious treading water himself to keep from all of it dragging him down, too.

In the end, whatever it was would get done. As soon as he could swing it.

Even though their skin was covered in a sheen of sweat and their breathing a bit ragged from the last orgasm he pulled from her, as well as his own, he was pissed at himself for not tucking a second wrap in his wallet. Because the fuck if he wasn't staying the night this time.

He'd prefer they head back to the farm and sleep in his awesome bed, unlike her lumpy piece of shit, but he doubted Stella would go. Or she might agree to it and, once he was out of her apartment, slam the door behind him. He was not risking that. Not tonight.

But he also wanted to fuck her again. Maybe even twice more, but that wasn't going to happen without a wrap.

He wanted to ask her if she had any, but he wasn't sure how he'd react to the answer if she said yes. If she had some that could mean she had fucked someone since she came back to town, was fucking someone, or planned to fuck someone. Someone who was not him.

And that thought made his blood begin to rush again, almost as much as when he was fucking her. He knew his limits when it came to his temper and one hard limit was his woman fucking someone else. Or her even thinking about it.

So, until he convinced her to move in with him, he needed to tuck more than one wrap in his wallet or even his cut.

She rolled up and out of bed. Keeping her back to him, she snagged his T-shirt from the floor and tugged it over her head as she headed to the door near the kitchen, which he assumed was the bathroom. She disappeared inside and shut the door.

He scrambled to the edge of the bed and jerked her nightstand drawer open, quickly searching it for wraps. None. Not even one.

In one way he was relieved, in the other, he wasn't happy they wouldn't get a chance to fuck again. But his fingers did find something deep in the back of the drawer. He pulled it out and held it up.

A bright pink vibrator. It wasn't the typical vibrator he'd seen; this one had a slight curve and three buttons. He smiled. While he might not be able to fuck her, there were other options for later.

He tucked it back in the drawer and slammed it shut as he heard the bathroom door opening. He jackknifed from the bed and headed in that direction on his way to break the seal.

"Shirt off when you get back in bed," he said in passing.

He figured her non-response was a silent "fuck you" to his demand.

After doing his thing in the bathroom, he opened the door and was surprised to find she had shucked his shirt, placing it neatly over the chair where his cut was. Problem was, she had climbed back into bed and pulled a sheet over her, covering herself anyway.

In truth, he thought she'd get dressed and when he came out, she'd be pointing toward the door and ordering him to get the fuck out.

While the sheet wasn't ideal, it was better than her kicking him out.

Not that he would've left. Because they still had shit to talk about before he ate her pussy.

She watched him approach the bed, her expression turning suspicious due to his grin he didn't bother to hide. He felt her light blue eyes on him as he pulled the handmade quilt off, so it wouldn't get ruined later, and lifted the sheet, sliding in. Once he was under it, he rolled into her side and slowly began to tug the sheet down. "If I wanted you covered up, woulda been fine with you wearin' my shirt."

Her fingers wouldn't release it, causing them to play tug of war. "I can't sleep without a sheet."

"We're not sleepin' anytime soon. It's early, plenty of time before we need to catch some ZZZ's."

"We?"

"Pretty sure that's what I said."

"You're planning on taking a nap here?"

"Stayin' the night. Plan on makin' you breakfast in the mornin' to make sure you eat."

Her lips thinned. "I don't need you to fatten me up like a lamb going to slaughter."

"Yeah, baby, you do. The fatten part, not the slaughter. Though, I did kill it when I fucked you."

"Damn. Ego much?"

"I didn't kill it? Did I suck?"

She sighed and rolled her eyes. "I didn't say that."

He tugged on the sheet again and she gripped it tighter. "We were just fuckin' naked a few minutes ago. What are you hidin'?"

"Nothing."

"Told you I don't like liars."

Her white knuckled fingers twitched but she still didn't let go. He flopped onto his back, tucking one bent arm behind his head, and sighed. "Fine. Takin' a nap, then we're goin' at it again."

"Do you have another condom?"

"Nope."

"Then we won't be going at it again."

"Plenty of other things we can do without me gettin' you knocked up."

He twisted his head to stare at her when the bed shook, and she went as stiff as a board next to him. The color in her face from their recent activity had disappeared and her eyes were squeezed shut.

He studied the long black hair with the blue stripes in it, which spilled over her pillow, the nose ring, the full sleeve of tattoos. Things she had changed about herself since he last saw her when they were kids.

He wondered what other changes had happened to make her want to hide herself and cause that kind of reaction to what he said.

He rolled onto his side again and propped his head in his hand, facing her. "Baby, said we'd talk after. There's shit

I need to tell you and I'm sure there's shit you need to tell me."

Her eyes opened but she didn't look at him, she focused on the ceiling instead. Avoiding him. Avoiding whatever it was.

"Why?"

"'Cause I want everything out in the fuckin' open, that's why. Gonna be partners, gonna need to trust each other."

"Partners in the bar."

He blew out a frustrated breath. "Yeah. In the bar, Stel." *For fuck's sake.* Not just in the goddamn bar...

"What do you need to tell me?"

"Are you interested, or you askin' just to get it over with?"

"Does it matter? I'm sure I'm going to hear it no matter what."

"Whatever, Stella." He flopped to his back again, scraping a hand through his hair. "Jesus fuck."

He was surprised when she rolled into him this time. Her breasts pressed into his ribs and she planted her hand on his chest. "All the original members of the Fury kept their shit close to the vest. Why do you feel the need to tell me... whatever it is you're going to tell me?"

"'Cause I need you to understand where I'm comin' from."

"You mean why you're pursuing me so hard even though I'm not interested?"

He lifted his head. She wasn't interested. That's what she just said. "Wet spot on the bed says otherwise."

When she flipped onto her back, he followed, taking the opportunity to tear the sheet off her before she could stop him. "Ready to make another one?"

"Trip!"

He ignored her "outrage" and sucked a nipple none-too-gently into his mouth. He twisted the other one with his fingers, causing her back to arch.

"Think that's a yes," he murmured against the curve of her tit before sinking his teeth in gently and then licking where he bit her.

He let his fingers slide down her smooth skin to her belly ring. He followed his fingers with his mouth, tonguing the piercing when he got there.

He let his hand go on ahead without him, finding the small dark patch of hair at the top of her pussy and he brushed his palm over it.

"Trip," she said in a half warning, half moan when his fingers teased her, and he settled his weight between her legs. As he lowered his head to taste her, her fingers grabbed his hair and tugged. "Kiss me."

He raised his eyes to her and grinned. "Gonna. Down here." He lost his grin as he saw the worry in her eyes. No, it wasn't worry. It was panic and she had her bottom lip crushed between her teeth.

What the fuck?

He dropped his gaze and saw what she'd been trying to hide. And she'd been damn good about doing that until now. How he'd missed it...

His fingertip followed the slight curve of the scar, then moved to travel along her stretch marks. Not fresh. Old. Pale. Like the scar.

For as thin as she was it didn't make sense to him why she'd have stretch marks. All radiating from some loose skin on her lower belly. He pursed his lips and studied the scar again.

And then he went cold.

This was why she wanted to kiss him when they fucked. It kept him occupied so he wouldn't explore her elsewhere.

So she could avoid the questions.

Because he certainly fucking had them.

And if she thought she'd get away without answering them, she was dead fucking wrong.

"Where is he?"

Not once had she mentioned a baby or a child. And she certainly wasn't hiding one in this studio apartment.

Did she lose custody of her child, or even children?

The possibility of her already being a mother never even crossed his mind.

"Where is he?" He pressed his hand to her lower belly. "Or she?"

His questions, those unavoidable questions, made ice slither through her veins and her heart seize. Against her will, he was taking her back to a place and time she didn't want to go.

She knew the conversation would need to be had, especially since they'd had sex and she was sure Trip planned on them having more.

Or, actually, Trip planned on them doing much more than having sex. But right now, she was only on board with the sex part. And even that was questionable.

The rest...?

She had not only returned to Manning Grove but had avoided dating and anything that would cause questions or looks. Or even whispers. Because right after it happened, she swore everyone was staring at her, pointing and whispering. Either with an accusatory look or one of sympathy.

She hadn't welcomed either.

In one month, she had lost too much. But that saying, "when one door closes, another one opens," was true... in a way. Though, she hadn't been expecting that first door to slam shut, catching her fingers in the jamb and causing excruciating pain. The cause of the other door opening wasn't a happy occasion, either. But it *was* a door she escaped through. To a place she could lick her wounds and hope to recover. Eventually.

But coming back to Manning Grove and taking over her late father's bar gave her something to concentrate on, instead of sitting in a room with the lights off and the curtains closed, wondering if she could continue.

While she was lost in thought, Trip had moved back to her side, pulling the sheet up over them, and remained surprisingly quiet.

If she was going to be partners with him in business, he needed to know why some days for her might be worse than others. Why some days she might be barely functioning. Those had been occurring less with time, but there was no guarantee they would completely go away.

She needed to forget the bad and remember the good, the only problem was the bad memories kept slamming her in the chest like a sledgehammer.

He also needed to understand why she wasn't looking for a man, and even if she was, why it wouldn't be someone like him.

She closed her stinging eyes and took a moment to gather her thoughts, swallowing around the tightness in her throat. Somehow, she got the words out. Words she hadn't said out loud in over a year. "I had a son."

She wished those four words were enough to satisfy him, but she knew better. It wouldn't be enough to satisfy his curiosity. It wouldn't be enough for him to understand.

His hand was still pressed to her lower belly, even though the sheet now covered them both. But that was the only place he touched her. "Had."

That single word held so much. Sadness. Confusion. Even a touch of anger. Like he was waiting to hear the rest before he decided how he should feel about what she revealed.

"He died." By saying it, she couldn't ignore the truth.

"Stella," he whispered, the tone of his voice changing to tortured. Like what she said actually hurt him.

He'd never feel the pain more than she did. Not even a fraction of it.

She covered her eyes with her hand, fighting back the tears that threatened. And she let the dark emptiness engulf her as she just let the words roll from her. "You carry your child inside you. Shelter him for nine months. And when he's born, even though it's painful and unpleasant, all that disappears the second you hear him cry and announce loudly he's ready to meet the world. You created that little person. It's the best day of your life. Nothing can ever beat it. Nothing. You brought a piece of yourself into your own world, as well as others. And then you protect him as he learns to roll over, to crawl, to walk. And then..."

The fingers along her lower belly twitched. "And then?"

Her chest felt like it was caving in, crushing her. "It's gone in a flash. In less time it took for him to come into the world, he's taken from you. Gone. That light that shone so brightly the first time I held him was gone. Extinguished. Darkened. I'd never hold him, kiss him, hear him say "Mommy" again. Just... *gone.* Nothing left to hold onto but memories. A hole in your heart so big it seems impossible to fill, so you don't even try. You try to go on. One day. The next. Then the next. You exist. Nothing else. You even wonder if you want to continue. I brought a piece of me into the world and he was stolen from me. Never to be returned."

Something tore deep inside of her as she relived that day and that phone call all over again. The call that caused her to throw her phone, to smash it against the wall. She wanted to believe if she wasn't holding it, if she couldn't hear it, it didn't happen. And if she couldn't hear the voice on the other end, they couldn't give her the details.

She had collapsed to the floor and curled up in a ball,

covering her ears with her hands, not wanting to hear anything.

Because they had to be wrong. It had to be a mistake.

He'd walk in the door at any moment, yelling about how he was hungry and asking if he could have a snack.

But it wasn't him that walked in, it was her mother, who sat on the floor with her, telling her to breathe. Confirming her nightmare was real.

The person on the other end of the phone hadn't been lying. It wasn't a bad prank.

It was true.

It was true and there was nothing she could do to bring him back.

Not one fucking thing.

"Jesus Christ, baby," Trip murmured against the side of her head, where he had his nose buried. "Can't even fuckin' imagine."

She waited for him to ask how it happened. But he didn't, he only held her tight. But she needed to finish because eventually he'd want to know, and she never wanted to talk about it again.

If he wanted to hear about Kade's first eight years of life, if he wanted to see photos, his drawings, his handmade cards, and the rest of the things she had saved, that was one thing. But she never wanted to talk about that last day ever again.

That meant it was now or never.

"My son was the best thing that came from my marriage. We got married young. I had just turned twenty. Some say that you end up with men like your father. Well, that was my first mistake."

While he wasn't a member of an MC, he had a similar attitude. She and some of her girlfriends used fake ID's to get into a bar. It was something they did all the time, but one night they got into a bar for free using their ID's and flashing their tits to the bouncer.

They laughed about it and had a blast since men were buying them drinks plus the rock band on stage was awesome.

They spent the night dancing and having a great time, and when the band ended its last set, the drummer squeezed between her and her best friend, offering to buy them a drink. But it was only Stella he had eyes for.

And those eyes. They were what drew her. A richer blue than hers, a gorgeous contrast to his dark hair that was so long it skimmed his shoulders. But it was the way he smiled at her that had sucked her in.

It was genuine.

That night they hooked up. And then every other night for weeks when he wasn't out of town for gigs.

Eventually, he begged her to join him when his band traveled. At twenty, sex and love seemed more important than a steady job. So, she agreed and gave up her job, moved into his apartment with him and whenever he was on the road, she went along.

Everything was fun until reality began to set in. She ignored his excessive drinking and drug use since she figured that was normal for guys who played rock and roll. While she drank and smoked, plus partook in a little pot herself, as the months went along, he began to do it more excessively. Even after voicing her concerns, he blew her off by saying he was fine and had everything under control.

Then at twenty-one, she found out she was pregnant. She stopped smoking and drinking and begged Kellan to stop, too.

He promised he would. And he did for a while, then he'd fall into old habits when he'd go back on the road, leaving her and Kade at home.

When it got bad, she'd threaten to leave, and he'd clean up his act once again.

For a while.

It never stuck.

Eventually, she changed the locks and filed for divorce, not wanting Kade to be raised around a bad influence. She didn't want her son believing that being falling down drunk and so stoned you barely functioned was normal.

When he was served with divorce papers, he swore he'd clean up his act and go to rehab. He wanted back in the house and in his family's life. She told him she was not accepting him back until he was clean and sober for at least six months.

Even so, he somehow convinced the judge to allow him unsupervised visits while they were separated. Probably showed him his chip for being thirty days sober. The same one he showed her when he promised he was sober and on the path to coming back home.

But he lied.

He. Fucking. Lied.

Like so many addicts do.

He lied to get what he wanted. Which was time with his son.

Kade loved his father, loved spending time with him. But it still worried her every time she had no choice but to let him go. She knew Kellan loved their son and would never purposely hurt him. She had to hang on to that fact when Kellan would pick him up for the two days a week he had fought for.

But she worried. And her gut instinct was right.

Kade had texted her pictures of him and his father in a jon boat on the Susquehanna River, one he'd borrowed from another band member. Her son had the biggest smile on his face when she received the picture of him holding his "monster" catch of a tiny catfish. The first fish he ever caught besides a sunfish.

It turned out to be his last.

What wasn't caught in any of those pictures was the twelve pack Kellan had taken along.

What wasn't caught in those pictures was the fact that Kellan had no experience in taking a boat out on his own, a fact he forgot to mention and was important since the Susquehanna River was so dangerous.

What wasn't caught in those pictures was the fact that the river was very high and rushing more than normal. Or how close they were to the Dock Street Dam near Harrisburg. Or that even though Kellan had thrown the anchor, he hadn't realized the boat was drifting down river.

Until it was too late.

That dam had claimed too many lives.

Including her son's.

And his father's.

She didn't need the toxicology report to know why.

No, she knew. Even though she was told there were several circumstances for the accident besides him being drunk.

But she didn't care about the rest of the reasons.

It didn't matter.

All she knew was, she never should have let Kade go.

In the end, it was her fault for allowing it.

Even her mother agreed.

"I never should have let him go. Never. It's just as much my fault. I should've known he'd been lying to me. Lying to everyone. That he hadn't stopped drinking. He only learned to hide it better."

"This won't begin to cover it, but gotta say it. First, your mother can fuck off. None of us are perfect, especially her, because I remember her. Even so, we all fuck up, Stella. Do shit we regret. Shit we wish we could take back or have a chance to do all over again. However, you can't blame yourself for what happened."

He could say it but that didn't make it true.

"Didn't the fucker have a vest on your kid?"

She closed her eyes and those photos she'd been texted flashed through her mind once again. How happy he was.

"He was wearing one in the pictures. The investigator said it might have been too loose and the strong churn of the water at the dam... ripped it off him, trapping him under water. It wasn't until the next day they recovered him down river." She swallowed hard to stop the bile from coming back up. "I had to identify his body, as well as Kellan's." She hadn't been able to stop the bile from rising that day, either.

His death was devastating enough, but identifying her own son was even worse.

She had collapsed that day, too, and even though she hadn't eaten a thing, her body tried to expel what didn't exist.

She ended up in bed, barely existing on only air and tears for a week.

She ignored the knocks on the door and the phone calls.

She'd even missed the call from Max Bryson, the Chief of Police for Manning Grove, regretfully informing her that Pete had finally succumbed to his cancer.

Which was why her father had been buried without her. Which was why he'd been buried without his cut.

He also died without knowing his grandson would be waiting for him on the other side.

"Jesus fuck," Trip muttered as she trailed off.

She hadn't even been aware she was speaking her thoughts out loud.

He pulled her against him so tightly she had no choice but to burrow into him. She didn't fight it, she welcomed his heat which engulfed her, the circle of his arms and the weight of his heavy thigh over hers. It all created a comfort she hadn't felt in a long time.

That dark hole she'd stared into over the last year, suddenly didn't feel so bottomless and insurmountable.

She hadn't talked about this with anyone since leaving the Harrisburg area. She'd kept it buried deep inside.

But now she had lifted the lid and released it.

While not quite a relief, it was something.

And like Trip said, something was better than nothing.

Maybe he was fucking right.

Chapter Twelve

HE SLID a small mountain of scrambled eggs onto the plate next to the toasted buttered bagel and crispy bacon he placed there moments before.

She sat on the stool at the tiny counter, staring at it all. "I can't eat all that. I'm fine with coffee."

Trip finished scraping the remainder of the eggs from the pan onto his own plate. "Bullshit. You need to eat."

"I'll eat later."

He dumped the pan into the sink with a clatter and came around the counter to take the other stool. "It's non-negotiable."

She put her mug of coffee down with a clunk. "You can't force me to eat, Trip."

He cocked one brow at her before shoving a forkful of eggs into his mouth. "The fuck I can't."

She fingered the fork which laid next to her full plate, avoiding his gaze.

"Need you to keep your strength up. Got a lot of work to do to turn the bar around."

"Money is required to turn it around, Trip. In case

you've forgotten, I don't have it. I have a feeling you don't have it, either."

He didn't fucking forget. He bit off a piece of sesame seed bagel and chewed it. "Got my first repo job today. That'll start bringin' in some scratch."

"Rob Peter to pay Paul," she muttered as she picked up her fork and stabbed at the eggs but didn't put any in her mouth. "How'd you get the license since you did time?"

That reminded him that he never got to tell her what he wanted to tell her. Another time. Soon, though.

"Eat a bite and I'll tell you."

She shot him a look but lifted her fork to her mouth.

He waited until she swallowed the bite of eggs, then answered, "Deacon."

Her brows raised. "You put the business license in Deacon's name?"

"No choice. Coulda put it in yours if you hadn't been fightin'."

"Fighting what?"

"What's inevitable."

She put her fork down.

Fuck.

She ran the pad of her index finger along the rim of her coffee mug but said nothing. Which disturbed him more than if she argued.

"Time doesn't heal all wounds, Trip," she whispered, lifting the mug to her lips. When she was done taking a couple sips, she put it down and placed a hand to her lower belly which was once again covered in leggings.

Leggings which he did not approve of since he preferred her in just his T-shirt. However, he had to wear his shirt since as soon as they were done with breakfast and he made sure she ate something, he needed to jet.

Not that he wanted to, he just needed to get his ass in

gear to make sure the bar's debt didn't swallow him whole, too.

"Wanna explain that?" he said around a whole piece of bacon he'd accordioned into his mouth.

He stopped chewing when she said, "That's not the only scar I have."

He jerked when she unexpectedly grabbed his hand. It took everything he had not to yank it free when she raised it to the back of her head. Singling out his index finger, she ran it along a ridge hidden in her hair.

Jesus fuck.

"I was a stupid fuckin' kid, Stella." Was he never going to live that shit down?

"I know you didn't mean to split my head open, Trip. But you did because you lost your temper. Makes me wonder about that temper. And if it was the reason you ended up in prison."

Again, a reminder they needed to have that discussion.

When she released his finger, he kept his hand there, cupping the back of her head, and turning her to face him. "Promise you. I'll never fuckin' hurt you like that again."

"You sure? There are more ways to hurt someone than just physically."

"How 'bout I tell Judge he can kick my fuckin' ass if I ever hurt you again. All you gotta do is let him know I caused you pain in one way or another and I won't fight that fuckin' beat down."

Her eyes got big for a second, then they narrowed on him. "Judge could kill you. Especially if you didn't fight back."

"No fuckin' shit."

"That's crazy."

"Just don't go runnin' to him because you got bent that I left the toilet seat up or some stupid shit like that."

Was that a grin?

Yeah, it was, and she covered it by taking another bite of eggs. *Thank fuck.*

He combed his fingers through her long black silky hair that fell loose around her shoulders. She'd had dark hair when she was a kid, but it wasn't black like it was now. Which meant the color was as fake as the blue stripes.

He didn't hate it, so if she loved it, then he could live with it.

He burrowed his hand under the fall of her hair and curled his fingers around her neck, tugging her closer. "Gimme that mouth."

She rolled her eyes at his demand but didn't fight him when he leaned in and brushed his lips over hers. When he pulled away, he mumbled, "Eat," and went back to his own breakfast.

As he ate, he watched her out of the corner of his eye to make sure she did the same until at least half the food on her plate was gone.

Half was better than nothing.

Tonight he'd bring her a good dinner, even though she would be working the bar. Unfortunately, the bar might be so quiet they probably wouldn't get interrupted while they ate, anyway.

Afterward he'd stick around long enough to help her close the bar and make sure she ended up in his bed at the farm tonight. Then he'd work on getting her to land in his bed every night.

Also tonight, after they ate, might be a good time to bring up the reason he'd landed in prison. His worry was the reason he went to prison was too much like what started the avalanche that took down the Fury.

His other worry was it had all been due to his temper, which was her concern. He'd admit it because he wasn't going to lie to her, but just needed to convince her that he had that shit under control.

She had his promise he wouldn't hurt her.

He'd do his fucking best to keep that promise.

She just needed to give him that chance.

TRIP SCRUBBED the towel over his wet hair, then paused. He tipped his head to the side and listened more carefully.

Pounding.

On the back door.

Whenever the club could afford it, he was having cameras installed everywhere. The lane, the house, the barn, the outbuildings. Even in some areas of the bunkhouse. This way he and Judge, and whoever else, could pull up those cameras on their phones whenever they needed to.

The Fury might not have any enemies at the moment, but that could change at any time. Especially if the local pigs got a skewer up their ass about something.

In the past, the Fury and the 5-0 had a bad relationship since the members were shaking down the local business owners. At the time, the Originals outnumbered the cops. Now, things were switched, and they outnumbered the Fury. Whether that would change, Trip hoped so, but he still wanted to keep the peace with them, if possible. Especially since he had to deal with them for his repo business to keep it legit.

He hoped to fuck all the cops who dealt with Buck, Ox and the rest of them had retired or kicked the bucket. If not, Trip was going to have to make nice and do some major ass kissing.

And he did not like the taste of a pig's ass.

He'd find out soon enough since he was headed to their pig pen shortly. But not before he found out who was still pounding on his back door and bellowing, "Yo."

He snagged his discarded jeans off the floor and tugged

them on as he moved out of his bedroom, down the hall and by the time he hit the kitchen downstairs they were fastened.

He twisted the deadbolt and yanked open the door, ready to ream out whoever was being a dick.

He swallowed his words and frowned at the man who stood grinning at him, wearing a fucking Fury cut.

Trip's gaze dropped to the name patch.

Ozzy.

His eyes slid to the right to read the patches which said, "Manning Grove" and "Original."

What the fuck?

Who the fuck was this guy?

"Got a lot of fuckin' nerve to wear a cut that don't belong to you," Trip growled.

The man jerked his chin toward something behind Trip in the kitchen. "You mean like you?"

Trip ground his molars. His cut was hanging over the back of one of the chairs at the kitchen table. "That belongs to me."

"Bet it was Buck's, though. Am I right?" When Trip didn't answer, the guy continued. "Back then, it was always 'finders' keepers.' Pussy, booze, scratch, drugs, whatever. Didn't apply to our sleds or our cuts, though. Those were sacred."

"It was handed down."

The man, who planted his hands on his hips, dropped his head, shook it and snorted. "Right." He lifted it again and met Trip's gaze. "A cut's supposed to be buried with a brother."

"Should be. Not always possible," Trip muttered. "Who are you and what the fuck you doin' here?"

"Guess you don't remember me."

Trip let his gaze slide over the man's face. He had to be in his late thirties, maybe even early forties, which meant he was young when the Fury imploded. But Trip couldn't say he remembered the man. He was wearing a black leather skull cap, so Trip couldn't tell what color his hair was, but from where Trip stood, his eyes appeared some sort of gray.

That didn't shake any memory loose. Nor did the name Ozzy.

"Dutch put the word out. Said the Blood Fury's gonna rise from the bloody wreckage. Or maybe he said from the ashes. Like one of those fuckin' birds."

Trip had no clue who this motherfucker was and hesitated to say shit about the club. "Yeah."

"Want in."

He wanted in. Just like that.

"Gimme a sec." Trip pulled out the cell phone he'd tucked into his back pocket on the way out of his room. He held it up and snapped a photo of the man, who grumbled a curse as he did so. He sent the photo to both Judge and Dutch at the same time. *Know this MFer?*

A few seconds later Dutch texted him back with a laughing emoji and the words: *Yeah. A fuckn asshole. But 1 thats doable w/ a lil lube.*

Judge's answering text quickly followed: *No fuckn clue.*

Before Trip was done reading Judge's text another one came in from Dutch. *Need a sec, there U fuckn go.* Followed by a thumb's up emoji.

Where the fuck the old man learned emojis and text speak... Trip shook his head. But what did he mean by "need a sec?"

Need a sec for what?

Then it hit Trip.

"Satisfied?" Ozzy—if that was his name—asked with a crooked grin.

"Nope."

"Was a member when you were a fuckin' snot-nosed kid."

Trip sucked at his teeth. "Don't look old enough to call me a snot-nosed kid."

"Right. Lied about my age. Became prospect at seventeen, patched at eighteen. Think you were about fourteen at the time. A pain in the ass, though. Cocky little shit."

Trip set his jaw. "And you think you're gonna walk the fuck right back in where you left off? Why shouldn't you prospect now?"

He'd already told Dutch that former members and blood of former members wouldn't need to prospect. But since he was prez, he could be a "cocky little shit."

Ozzy shrugged out of his cut, and, with one hand, ripped his shirt over his head. He turned to show Trip his bare back. "Just got my rockers when shit went down. Ink was still fresh on my skin."

Those colors were no longer fresh. But that cut, those colors... Trip's gaze landed on the super sweet Harley parked next to his.

Like Dutch said, with a little lube, any asshole might do. He'd rather have a club full of assholes than one of pussies.

Trip's gaze slid back to Ozzy when the man turned back around to face him, pulling his shirt back over his head and sliding on his cut.

"Guess you planned on walkin' the fuck back in," Trip said.

"I can roll if you wanna be a dick. Got better things to do than work my fuckin' ass off for nothin'."

"Won't be for nothin'."

"Yeah, tell that to my eighteen-year-old self. Spent a year lickin' boots and takin' it up the ass. When I finally got my rockers, got fucked again but without a tube of lube in sight. My ass and my attitude got a bit raw from that fuckin'."

Trip pursed his lips and agreed that had to have sucked. Spend a year being a prospect, being shit all over, treated like a slave, lower than dog shit, and then when you finally made it, all your suffering meant nothing.

"I hear ya."

"Do you, though?"

"Yeah, I do. Shit's gonna be different this time."

"Dutch mentioned your pie in the sky fuckin' thinkin'. Willin' to stick around to see if you're right."

"I'm always right."

Ozzy grinned. "Like I said, cocky little shit. See things didn't fuckin' change."

"One thing did."

"What's that."

"No longer little."

Ozzy pulled his shoulders back and looked down his nose at him. "Right. Me, neither."

Trip ignored the unspoken challenge. "Where'd you land?"

"Ran free for a while. Eventually hooked up with a club out west."

"Why aren't you stickin' there?"

"Was a support club to the Fifty Calibers. Fucked up and got caught runnin' guns. While doin' time, my girl found other dicks to spin on. Got out, found her strung out and my so-called brothers were passin' her around like a fuck toy. Her choice to keep the high. Not my choice in a steady piece. Went nomad again. Now, here I am, lookin' to settle since my ass is gettin' too old for that lone wolf shit."

While he didn't look too broken up about losing his girl, Trip understood what kind of betrayal it was for your woman to be sucking and fucking dick other than your own.

"Got a place to crash?"

"Nope."

"A job?"

"Nope. Just got back to town."

"Got any construction experience?"

"Loads." Ozzy lifted his hands, which were rough. "These hands ain't Ivory soft for a reason. Done it all. You name it, I've fuckin' done it."

"Know how to run a crew?"

"For construction? Yeah."

"For a motel."

"Like housekeepers and shit? Sounds like cake."

"Construction, too. Bought The Grove Inn. It's a steaming pile of shit. Need to polish that shit to a diamond. Put scratch in the club coffers, put scratch in your pocket."

Ozzy's brows rose. "Used to fuck all the time in that motel. They rented by the hour."

"Yeah, that ain't happenin' now. Once it's fixed up, want to attract renters who've got money. The better the rooms are, the more we can charge."

"Hear you on that. It got a manager's apartment?"

"Yeah, but it's a total shit show. That'll need redone, too. Got a cheap room for you in the bunkhouse. Food, booze—"

Ozzy's eyes lit up. "Pussy?"

"Not yet."

"What club don't have pussy?"

"One that's just gettin' reestablished."

Ozzy nodded. "Okay, place to stay, manage the motel, fix it up. Who's the construction crew?"

"Hopin' prospects once we get 'em. 'Til then, there's some local Amish workin' for me. Redid the barn, built the bunkhouse, gonna be workin' on Crazy Pete's bar."

"Crazy Pete," Ozzy murmured. "That ol' fucker still around?"

Trip shook his head. "Cancer got 'im."

Ozzy dragged a hand down his face. "Fuck."

"Yeah. A little over a year ago."

"Club took over the bar?"

Trip stared at him for a moment, not sure if he should

mention Stella. "Yeah. It's the club's. That needs turned around, too, like the motel."

"Who's managin' that?"

"Got that covered for now."

"Yeah?"

"Yeah," Trip said with finality.

"That it?"

"Nope," Trip answered. "Need someone to sit at the table as Secretary."

Ozzy got quiet for a long moment.

That couldn't be the breaking point for the guy. Trip just dumped a whole shitload of responsibility on someone he didn't know. Being the club secretary wasn't much more.

Finally, the man smiled and said, "No you don't."

Trip smiled and offered his hand. They clasped palms and bumped shoulders. "Welcome, brother."

"Fuck, that sounds good. Missed the brotherhood. Will be good to have others at my back."

"If all goes well, you'll have a bunch of 'em. Loyalty's priority. Buildin' a solid family here, not a cluster-fuck."

"A cluster. Like the old days."

"Right."

Ozzy glanced over his shoulder at the barn. "Where am I layin' my head? Been ridin' the past twenty-four hours straight. About to drop."

Trip jerked his chin toward the barn. "Take your sled 'round back. Lemme pull on a shirt and some boots and I'll meet you there, get you settled. Will introduce you to Deacon, our Treasurer, if he's there. Got a couple prospects, two of Dutch's mechanics, livin' in the bunkhouse, too. They should be at work, though."

"Great. Will get a little shut-eye and then head out to the motel to check out what needs done."

Didn't sound like the man was lazy if he was willing to

go the same day he rode into town. Trip liked that. Gave him some hope.

"Got a repo job I need to do after gettin' you settled. But should be done before you wake up and we can head over there together later."

"Cool, brother. See you in a bit," Ozzy said as he turned on his boot heel and jogged down the couple steps from the porch, heading over to his sled.

Trip crossed his arms and smiled as the deep rumble of his new Secretary's sled settled in his bones.

Shit was finally coming together.

Now, he just needed Stella on board.

Chapter Thirteen

TRIP DIDN'T WASTE time hauling his ass out of the police station and back to his wrecker. He hated the fact he needed to report each repo job he was doing. But he also didn't want to get his repo license revoked for not following the law when he just got the fucking thing.

All because of Deacon. *Thank fuck.*

Even so, he got the fucking willies just standing in the PD's lobby and talking to the lady at the front desk.

Last time he was in a pig pen, he'd been wearing a pair of metal bracelets that clashed with his outfit.

He also had a busted lip and some broken ribs from when the pigs had kicked the shit out of him. But then, he hadn't gone willingly. He realized later he was lucky they only tased his ass instead of shooting him.

When he got to the tow truck, he yanked open the door, grabbed his cut and slid it on. He'd flip it inside out once he climbed back in, but for now, he needed a fucking smoke. And fuck the pigs if they didn't like him representing in their parking lot. They were going to have to get used to seeing those colors around town since the club was growing.

He dug out the tin from the inner pocket, pulled out a hand-rolled and used his H-D Zippo to light it.

After taking a long hit, he leaned against the fender and let the pure tobacco, free of any extra bullshit, fill his lungs, immediately settling his nerves.

Closing his eyes, he let the smoke roll out of his open mouth. The Amish grew some A-plus shit. Now if they only grew some quality bud, he'd be set.

His chuckle was interrupted by a loud, "*Ooo. Ooo. Hellooooo* there, handsome!"

What the fuck?

His eyes popped open and he saw a man flouncing toward him.

Flouncing.

How the fuck did he even know that word? He shouldn't, but it defined how the man moved, who was heading in his direction at a fast clip. The man's narrow hips swung with flair and confidence. He looked to be in his late thirties, wore a huge smile on his face and a predatory look in his eyes.

As he stopped in front of Trip, he raked his gaze up and down Trip's body and purred, "Fresh meat."

Trip frowned. That frown deepened when he, whoever the fuck he was, ripped Trip's baseball cap off his head and ran his fingers through Trip's hair.

"Yo!" Trip yelled, jerking his head away and snatching his hat back, but before he could tug it back on his head, the man announced, "Hats cause bald spots. They don't let the scalp breathe. And you going bald would be a sin. You've got a great head of hair even though you need a trim. Just the ends. It just so happens I know the perfect fella to do it."

I bet.

The guy pressed a hand to his own chest and curtsied. "I'm Teddy. I am the proprietor of and *extreeeemely* gifted hairdresser at Manes on Main." He did a snipping motion with two fingers, then pointed in Trip's direction. "And *youuuuu* are my newest client." He clapped his hands together and bounced on his toes with way too much excitement.

"I am?"

"Of course," he read Trip's name patch, "*Trip*. Interesting name. Nobody better than me to keep those pretty locks of yours at their best."

"I do it myself," Trip informed him, earning him a loud gasp.

Teddy slapped a hand over his mouth and his eyes went wide. "Oh no. Unacceptable."

Trip tugged his hat back on his head and when he took another deep drag of his cigarette, Teddy leaned even closer, inhaled loudly, then sighed. "Can I bum a hit, handsome?"

For as cheap as he got his hand-rolleds from the Amish, he didn't mind giving the man a whole one. He dug into his tin, handed one over and lit the cigarette for him. Teddy wrapped his hand around Trip's as he did so, and the man's fingers slid over his seductively when Teddy finally released him.

"I'm straight," Trip felt the sudden need to announce.

"I'm not," Teddy answered with a wink and a smile. As he took his first long drag, he glanced around the parking lot like he was afraid of being caught. "Don't tell anyone. I quit. My S.O. doesn't like me smoking."

Trip lifted an eyebrow. "S.O.?"

Teddy flapped a hand around in the air. "Significant other, silly. Though, if he finds out, he may give me a good spanking." He grinned and leaned into Trip again. "He's really good at that." Then the man eyeballed Trip again. "You probably are, too." He sighed. "But, alas, I'm taken."

On his second slower drag, his eyes rolled back and so did his head. He slowly and sensually let the smoke escape from between his lips. "Holy shit," Teddy breathed like he just had the best orgasm of his life. "That's the best thing I've had in my mouth in a long time." After a moment, he lifted his head and curved his hand around the side of his mouth, saying in a loud whisper, "Just don't tell Adam." Then he added an exaggerated wink.

Since Trip didn't know who Adam was, there was no risk of that.

"*Anywhooo*. Like I said, I own Manes on Main. Remember that." Teddy poked Trip's chest with a pointed finger. "*Ooo*. You've got some hard muscles there. Anyway, you look smart enough to figure out where my salon is located. You need to let me trim you up. First one's on the house since you're new in town." He brushed a knuckle down Trip's bearded jaw. "And I can clean this up, too. Way too handsome to let yourself look like an unkempt gorilla."

Trip's lips twitched but he fought to keep a straight face as he blew out another stream of smoke. "Gorilla's shave?"

"My type does. I do love me a jealous gorilla." He sucked in a breath to continue but got distracted. "*Ohhhh*, shit. Speaking of... Here comes mine." He pasted on a huge smile.

Trip turned his head to see a cop taking long, quick and very determined strides in their direction. And not looking any kind of pleased with Trip talking to Teddy.

"Act natural. Like you don't want to kiss me or anything." Teddy quickly pinched the lit end of the hand-rolled and handed it back to him, trying to hide that action from the cop with his body. "Wait! I need a mint." He slapped the pockets of his skinny jeans. "Damn. You got a mint in that filthy vest? Or gum? Anythin— *Heeeey*, baby," he purred and went up on his toes to plant a kiss on the cop's cheek, who wore a look of suspicion. "Was I supposed to meet you here for our lunch date or was it the diner? Did I screw that up?" He once again curved his hand around the side of his mouth and stage whispered, "Or was it supposed to be for a bit of afternoon delight?"

Good thing Teddy was asking the cop that question and not Trip. He didn't feel like getting in a knock-down fight with a jealous man in uniform over another man.

That was not on the day's agenda.

Teddy plucked playfully at the pig's uniform shirt which had a tag stating his last name was Bryson. "This is my hunky fiancé, Adam. News flash! He frowns a lot when I flirt with anybody but him. But he knows how much I can't resist gorillas." He leaned in close to Trip again and sniffed loudly. "Especially ones that smell deliciously like old leather and wear chains." He wiggled his eyebrows.

Bryson gave Trip's cut a thorough once over. "Got business in town?"

Somebody had a bad attitude. Trip was about to make it worse. "Nope. Just here to steal your man." Anytime he could stick it to the pigs, he would, so Trip leaned in, put his mouth near Teddy's ear and whispered, "Don't swing that way but if I did, I'd bend you over and show you how much bigger my dick is than that cop's."

Teddy's mouth opened wide and so did his eyes.

When Trip pulled away, he made sure a big grin was plastered on his face.

He gave the cop a chin lift and moved toward the driver's door.

Adam grabbed Teddy's elbow. "Get your business done and get out of town. Let's go." The pig grabbed his fiancé's elbow and began to haul the hairdresser behind him.

Teddy's face was flushed, and he wore a wicked smile as Adam dragged him across the parking lot.

After Trip shrugged out of his cut and flipped it inside out before putting it back on, he glanced over his shoulder to see Teddy giving him a finger wave. "Manes on Main," he shouted. "I have a chair with your name on it!"

The cop yanked on Teddy and spun him around, saying something under his breath Trip couldn't catch.

He snorted and climbed into the wrecker.

He had shit to do and it wasn't fucking with the local 5-0.

TRIP JAMMED his boot on the gas and ducked, trying like fuck not to die. But he was getting pissed. His first repo of the day had gone smoothly. He'd snuck in, grabbed the car and towed it back to Dutch's fenced lot behind the garage, where he was storing the cars until the bank decided what to do with them. He and Dutch made a deal to use the lot temporarily until Trip had the time and money to build a secure storage area at the farm.

In the meantime, he needed to make money and a lot of it. So, as soon as he dropped the sedan, he headed toward the second one.

Which happened to be down Copperhead Road and up the mountain.

And up a long fucking dirt road that was a thousand times worse than the lane at the farm. It was hard to navigate the oversized old truck along the narrow path through the thick woods.

He'd passed sign after sign warning his ass not to proceed further. But he had a job to do and green to make. And a Ruger tucked in his waistband at the small of his back.

When he hit the first clearing close to the top of the mountain, he was shocked at what he found. A whole fucking compound of shacks and buildings, junk cars, and just junk in general. It looked like whoever lived there didn't get rid of anything just in case they could use it in the future.

Like doomsday preppers.

Stella had mentioned the people living up on the mountain made moonshine and other shit. While he was there, if he ran into any of them, he planned on negotiating a deal.

But, *for fuck's sake,* when he did run into them—when they heard his wrecker pulling up to the car he was supposed to yank—they all came out of the woodwork like a bunch of angry hornets, not only swarming his truck, but carrying shit like shotguns, AR's, and clubs.

Not only did Trip's asshole pucker at that sight, his brain screamed at him to get the fuck out of there.

He quickly smashed the clutch in, shoved the wrecker in reverse, and, grinding the gears, did a crazy K-turn to head back down the mountain as fast as the fucking truck could handle the ruts and holes.

However, as he was trying to escape, he not only heard the shots, he almost felt them as they struck the wrecker. Stupid thought at the time: he was glad he hadn't spent the money yet on the body work. That relief quickly disappeared when the back window of the cab exploded behind him, covering him with shattered glass.

"Jesus fuckin' Christ!"

If he hadn't needed both hands to not only steer but to shift, he'd be holding onto his balls, so they didn't roll down the mountain faster than the wrecker in their panic to escape.

Fuck them. They weren't going anywhere without him.

In his need to flee, he also hit a rut so deep he bounced off the seat and his head cracked the roof of the cab.

"Fuckin' motherfucker!" he shouted over the pinging of metal upon metal, still staying low, only keeping his head up enough to see where the fuck he was going. It would suck if he wrecked into one of the many trees that closely lined the treacherous mountain road. Then he'd have to abandon ship and hoof it out of the scene from *Deliverance* on foot.

And he certainly didn't want to feel buckshot in his ass, or anywhere else for that matter.

His heart was racing, and his fingers soldered to the steering wheel as he finally hit the bottom of the mountain, the truck's heavy-duty, but ancient, coil springs sounding ready to snap. He lifted his head enough to glance in the rearview mirror.

The lane behind him was empty.

For now.

He swore the wrecker took the left turn back onto Copperhead Road on two wheels and he almost went head-first through the windshield when he slammed on both the brake pedal and the clutch. The tires locked up and the brake drums smoked as he came to a sliding stop. Only a couple feet from a black-and-white.

Leaning against that cruiser was a cop with both his arms and ankles crossed as he shook his head. He uncrossed one arm just to point at Trip through the windshield and then point to the dirt pull-off in front of the pig transporter.

He glanced in the rearview again. His options: deal with gun-totin' hillbillies or deal with a gun-totin' porker.

Oink. Oink.

He sighed, grumbled a "fuck" under his breath and shoved the wrecker into first gear, steering around the cop and parking it in the narrow pull-off.

He slipped his hand under his cut and into his waistband, pulling out his .40 and sliding it under his clipboard and paperwork that sat on the seat next to him. The whole time he'd kept his eyes on the pig using the side mirror. He wasn't allowed to own or carry a gun, and he didn't need the asshole in uniform reminding him of that in a way that might cause a bit of pain. For Trip, not the cop.

The cop remained next to his vehicle, but he'd turned enough to face the truck, his feet now spread wide, his hands on his hips, one way too close to his service weapon.

Great.

Two cops in one day was two too many.

"Any time now," he heard through broken rear window.

Trip set his jaw, shoved the truck's door open, and climbed down.

"Don't forget your license, insurance and registration. As well as your repo license and, while you're grabbing all that, make sure I can see your fucking hands the whole time."

Which would be impossible. "Not askin' for much."

"Not asking for a conversation about it, either."

"Goddamn it," Trip grumbled under his breath. He glanced back at the cop. "Need to reach back into the vehicle to grab some of that."

"Then do it. Just don't be dumb about it, like you were heading up that mountain by yourself."

Trip pinned his lips together to keep his trap shut. Once he gathered what he needed, he slammed the door shut and headed toward the cruiser.

The cop's palm went up immediately. "Don't. Just take a couple steps forward and face the truck. Put the paperwork in one hand, put both palms on the fender and spread your feet."

"Just doin' my job," Trip called out, trying not to let his blood surge.

"Just doing mine," he got back.

"Don't need to harass hard workin' folk."

"That what you are?" Trip heard as the cop approached.

"You don't know me."

"Know about you. Know what you're wearing. Know why you're here today. Just keeping you from making a bigger mistake than the ones you made in your past."

They'd run him.

Fuck.

"What bigger mistake?" Trip asked.

"Ending up dead."

Trip continued to stare at the rusty fender of the wrecker when he asked, "Why do you care if I end up dead?"

"It's a lot of fucking paperwork. And you getting taken out by one or more of the Shirley Clan will attract the FBI."

Trip's simmering blood suddenly went cold.

"Yeah, didn't think you'd want the FBI to come into town. We don't want those pricks here, either." The cop stepped behind him and pulled the paperwork out of Trip's fingers. "Keep your hands there while I pat you down. Got any weapons on you? Anything that might stick me? Like a needle or a knife?"

"Fuck no." Though, if the pig searched the truck's cab, he'd not only find the Ruger, he'd find a buck knife in the glove box.

Then Trip would find himself wearing bracelets again. And he hated wearing jewelry.

Best to cooperate.

The cop kicked Trip's feet out wider and ran his hands over him from his head—pulling his hat off first and tossing it onto the wrecker's bed—all the way to his boots. Making sure to check his waistline, his inside-out cut and his ankles thoroughly.

He picked up Trip's hat next and inspected it. "Got a cuff key hidden anywhere?"

"Am I being cuffed?"

"Not at this time."

"Then I guess it doesn't matter."

Trip heard nothing but his heart in his ears for a few beats before the pig said, "You can relax as long as you promise to cooperate."

"You'd trust a promise from me?" Trip asked, turning around.

Even wearing dark sunglasses, this cop looked eerily

similar to the one this morning, but he was pretty sure it wasn't. Their voices were a touch different, too. But they were definitely related in some way.

"You mentioned the Shirley Clan," Trip said as he read the cop's name tag. "There a Bryson Clan, too?"

"We're working on it," the cop muttered, shook his head and then inspected the blown out back window. He moved to the back of the truck, fingering a few of the bullet holes in the bed that held the wrecker's sling. He glanced down at the paperwork in his hand. "Your insurance company isn't going to be happy."

"You gonna write a report?"

A dark eyebrow lifted above the sunglasses. "You want one?"

Trip pursed his lips. "Nope. I'll pay out of pocket."

"Expensive lesson." He inspected a few more holes then turned to Trip as he pointed to a hand-painted red and white octagon sign at the entrance to the dirt road. "See that no trespassing sign there?"

"You mean the one that says violators will be shot on sight?"

"Yep, that's the one."

"Guess I shoulda took it more seriously."

"You think? If we can't avoid going up there, we take CERT—our county emergency response team—with us, which is our equivalent of SWAT. But we prefer not to go up there at all. They prefer it, too."

"They always like that?"

The cop nodded. "Unless your last name is Shirley, you don't go up that mountain."

"They all inbred?"

"Since their last names are all Shirley, I'll give you one guess."

"How'd you know I was here?"

"You dropped off the repo paperwork at the station. My

brother, who happens to be the chief, radioed me to make sure we didn't have to deal with a murder. You were already hauling ass down the mountain when I arrived. Couldn't miss the scream of that old truck's engine. Or the shots ringing through the woods."

"So, you woulda stopped me?"

"Yep. Better way to deal with that clan."

"Need to repo one of their cars so I can get paid."

Bryson chuckled. "Think you're the first to try to repo one of their cars?"

"Did anyone die tryin'?"

That chuckle died. "Nope and we'd like to keep it that way. Best way to do it is to have someone stake out Walmart. They come into town once a week, but not on the same day or time. They mix it up, so they don't establish a pattern. Eventually they'll come down and you can snag the vehicle right from the parking lot. And if they're not driving that one, they might be driving another one they fucked a sales lot out of the money."

"Appreciate the tip." And he did. Bryson was only being about a three on the one through ten scale of being a dick. On any given day, Trip himself was more like a six. When he was pissed, he was off the chart at a twelve. Trip would take a three all day every day from this guy.

"Expect them to become a regular offender. They consider themselves and their mountain a sovereign nation, which means they don't feel the need to follow any of our laws." The cop tilted his head. "Like some others." Bryson held up Trip's paperwork. "But they wouldn't even have this. No license, no insurance, no registration. They buy cars with fake money orders or stolen checks. You take the one you're after, they'll just go get another. They have to go pretty far now to find a dealer to sell them one. All the used car dealers within a sixty-mile radius have had the pleasure of doing business with them and won't be doing it with them again." He shook the paperwork and headed back toward his black-and-white. "Be right back. Don't be going anywhere."

As he waited, Trip pulled out a hand-rolled, lit it and had over half of it smoked before the cop unfolded from his car and took his time returning.

"See you did a bit of time."

The dick factor just rose to a nine since the fucker already knew that. If he wanted to play games, so could Trip. "Yeah, in the Marines."

Bryson's jaw worked and something changed in his face at the mention of Trip's service. "That's not what I meant."

"Did my time, that's all you gotta know."

"It's also good to know what for."

"You knew that when you ran me, which I doubt you did in the car. Bet that was just for show and you already had that info from your chief brother."

"Right. Does that mean we're going to have that kind of problem with you in the future?"

"Would like to say no but can't guarantee it."

"What can you guarantee?"

"That I'll do my best to stay off your department's radar."

Bryson tipped his head toward Trip's cut. "Probably not going to happen since you're wearing colors."

Trip decided it was best to say nothing.

"Never had to deal with the Fury. But my grandfather and father had to. Best thing that ever happened was that club imploding."

Trip remained silent because he couldn't agree or disagree with that statement.

"Knew your grandfather. Good man. Wasn't caught up in all that bullshit. Always said his son was a disappointment. I'm sure he was hoping his grandson wouldn't be."

Trip didn't correct him with the fact there was more than one. "Thanks for the fuckin' advice."

"Best to give up whatever your plans are for resurrecting that club."

"Again, thanks for the fuckin' advice."

"Just saying."

Trip's dick factor was teetering on that eleven mark. "And I heard you."

"But you aren't going to listen."

"Only time I ever let someone wearin' a uniform rule my life was when I was unwillingly wearin' a jumpsuit that did nothin' for my complexion. If you haven't noticed, ain't wearin' it now, so that means as long as I'm not breakin' the law, don't gotta listen to you."

Bryson slid his sunglasses to the top of his head and his light blue eyes held Trip's. Trip was surprised to find no malice there. More of a quiet concern.

He didn't appreciate that, either.

Or when the cop dug into his pocket and pulled out a business card, holding it out to Trip. He reluctantly took it and read the name. *Corporal Marc Bryson.*

"I was a jarhead, too. So was the chief and some others on the force."

"And what the fuck do you want me to do with that info?"

"Just saying." Bryson shrugged and headed back to his pig mobile. He threw over his shoulder as he walked away, "That brotherhood runs deep, too. Like my brothers in blue. Like your MC. Remember that."

Trip tucked the card into the front pocket of his jeans. If he crumpled it up and threw it on the ground, he was sure he'd get pinched for littering.

"Remember this," Trip called out as the cop opened the driver's door. "Ain't goin' nowhere. Know why?"

Bryson said nothing as he folded himself back into the cruiser.

"Just like the American flag, my colors don't run," he shouted.

Unless he was being shot at.

Chapter Fourteen

TRIP STARED at the sled parked next to him at the curb. It could mean that Stella had a customer, which was a good thing. Or it could mean trouble.

He heeled the kickstand down, twisted the key, and swung his leg over. He pulled two bags of hot food from Dino's Diner out of his black leather saddlebags.

Yanking open the old, paint-peeling wooden door to Crazy Pete's, he went inside.

Yep, just as he thought. Fucking empty.

Except for Stella who was behind the bar talking to a guy on one of the stools with a beer in front of him.

His jaw got tight when that guy leaned in, reached out, ran his fingers down her forearm and she didn't pull away. Or curse him out.

Oh, fuck no.

Both heads pivoted his way as the door closed behind him and he started in that direction, his eyes only for Cage.

Cage sat back, his chest rose and fell under his cut, as his eyes got more wary with each step Trip took toward him. When Trip got to the end of the bar, he put the bags of food down and stepped behind it.

He didn't slow down until his body hit hers and he wrapped his fingers around the back of her neck and under her hair. With a tight grip, he leaned in and demanded, "Gimme your mouth."

When her mouth dropped open, he laid one on her, muffling her complaint.

He kept the kiss brief but left his hand curved around her neck when he ended it and turned to face Cage. "Watcha doin' here?"

Cage tipped his eyes down to the half-empty pint glass. "Havin' a beer. Usually what you do at a fuckin' bar."

Trip dropped his chin and caught Cage's gaze. "That it?"

"Talkin to my girl, here."

"Your girl?" Trip's eyes fell on Stella, who he had pressed to his side. "That right?"

"No," she answered. "Do you want a beer?"

"Want answers first."

"You'll get a beer, instead," she told him and yanked free of his grip.

As Stella moved away, Trip leaned in and said in a low growl, "Let's get somethin' straight from the get-go, brother, so there ain't problems between us. Stella ain't your girl."

"She yours?"

"You gotta ask?"

"You know, Prez, you made me the Road Captain. I sit at that fuckin' table. Didn't hear you claim her durin' that one bullshit meetin' we had."

"Do you think I can't hear you two? Jesus Christ!" Stella snapped as she returned, carrying two fresh beers. "The taps are like five feet away." She slammed one beer down in front of Cage, the foamy head of it spilling over the rim onto the bar top and splashing her hand, as well as Cage. The other, she slammed down in front of Trip. "That's five bucks each."

Cage's head jerked up. "Five? It's usually four."

"It's five for dicks. And you two are being big ones."

Cage shook his head. "He's claimin' you? And you're lettin' him?"

"No and no," Stella said.

Cage grinned, which Trip wanted to wipe off his face. "Good. Still gives me a shot."

"No, it don't," Trip answered.

Stella turned to him with narrowed eyes and said, "Since you're here, you can work the bar the rest of the night." She leaned in. "Just a warning, Cage's tips suck." She turned, and disappeared into the storage area, no doubt heading upstairs.

He'd deal with her later. Right now, he had to get some things straight with Cage.

"You gettin' a piece of her?" the man asked, sounding a bit annoyed. "Been workin' on her for the past year and you come strollin' back to town and she instantly drops her fuckin' panties? What the fuck?"

"She didn't drop nothin'."

"She musta, if you're actin' like she's yours."

"She is mine."

"Again, my ass was at that half-assed meetin', too. Didn't hear you claim her as your ol' lady. And we certainly didn't vote on it."

"Was half-assed 'cause all the spots weren't filled. Now they are. And your vote ain't needed 'cept to fill in when necessary."

If Cage had a thing for Stella, it might be good they wouldn't need his vote. He'd probably vote no when Trip did officially claim her. And when it came to a brother claiming an ol' lady, a no vote was rare. There had to be a good reason for it.

"Who took the secretary's spot?"

"Ozzy."

Cage guzzled down half of his fresh beer. "Have no clue who that is."

"He moved into the bunkhouse today. Was an Original like your pop."

"Yeah, Dutch mentioned somethin' about someone comin' back, didn't say who."

"Well, that's who. Rooms are startin' to fill up, so if you want one, you better grab one. You don't, then you don't. But can tell you, Stella's gonna be movin' into the farm-house with me. That means she's also gonna wear my cut. That also means that shit you did with touchin' her? That ends right here." He poked the bar top with his index finger. "I catch you flirtin', touchin', whatever with her again, you're done. I'm not gonna have that bullshit in my club. Once a woman's claimed, she's totally off-fuckin-limits. You get me?"

"Then you better get to claimin' her. 'Cause until then..." Cage smiled.

"Judge is gonna be dishin' out law and order. I'm sure he won't mind teachin' you a hard lesson if you can't keep your hands to yourself."

"Like you did? Forcin' her to kiss you like that? And you gonna have Judge fight your battles, Prez?"

"Like I said, Judge is the enforcer and will keep law and order. But if I gotta make a statement, I will."

"Sounds like a threat, Prez."

"Not a threat. It's a fuckin' promise."

"Don't think she's on board with your plan."

No, she wasn't, but she would be. Maybe not tonight, but soon. However, Cage didn't need to know that. He just needed to stay out of Trip and Stella's business.

"Not her call." He needed to go upstairs, to not only get Stella to eat something but have a little conversation. He couldn't do that and leave the bar unattended. "Now, since your ass is sittin' in here, need you to watch the bar while I take care of business with Stella. Can you handle that?"

"That an order?"

"Sure the fuck is."

"Do I get free beer?"

"Yeah. But you gotta stay sober enough to serve a customer if they come in."

"Then, I got it covered."

"Good." Trip went down to the end of the bar and snagged the two bags of food, which were probably now cold.

"How long you gonna be?" Cage asked Trip's back as he moved toward the storage room.

"As long as it takes."

"As long as what takes?"

Trip didn't answer him as he pushed through the single swinging door.

STELLA HEARD boots on the stairs before the door handle jiggled.

Then jiggled again.

"Don't make me replace this fuckin' door, Stella," came through it.

She hesitated. She didn't want to let him in, but he wasn't going to simply disappear. He wasn't the type of man to let a locked door stop him from getting what he wanted.

"Gotta keep pushin' me, baby, and I got my limits."

He wasn't the only one who had them. She moved closer and called out, "Who's watching the bar?"

"Open the door." His growl was muffled like he had his head pressed to it.

"Answer me."

He did with a loud, "Fuck," then a grumbled, "Cage."

She hurried to the door, unlocked it and flung it open. As she rushed past him, he hooked her around the waist and forced her back into the apartment, shutting the door behind them with his boot.

"He's not a bartender," she complained.

"Neither am I, but I'm sure as fuck he can figure out how to pour a fuckin' beer."

"Or drink it all himself."

He released her and held up the bags of food. "Right now, we're gonna eat, then we'll go back down and work the bar 'til closing."

She stared at the white paper bags. "Dino's?"

"Yep."

She flared her nostrils and inhaled, wondering what he brought.

He grinned and moved toward the tiny galley kitchen. He answered her unasked question. "Two bison burgers, cheddar cheese, pickles, lettuce, tomato, their special sauce... oh, and double the bacon."

Her mouth watered since she hadn't eaten all day. "Loaded fries?"

He put the bags down and dug out two Styrofoam containers. The burgers. She didn't even care if they weren't hot. He pulled out a large container next. He placed it on the counter and popped open the top.

Loaded fucking fries.

Her stomach growled and her feet moved without her even telling them to.

She snagged a drooping fry covered in melted cheese, sour cream, chives and bacon bits and shoved it into her mouth, closing her eyes as she chewed.

Damn, that was good. She didn't realize how hungry she had been until now.

The sound of Styrofoam sliding over the counter made

her open her eyes again and pop another heavily loaded fry into her mouth.

She opened the square container he'd put in front of her. The burger smelled heavenly, but it was so big she'd never be able to eat the whole thing. But half? She could try.

He removed two more small containers out of the other bag, putting them on the far counter.

"What's that?" she asked around her third fry.

"Two slices of Death by Chocolate cake," he told the interior of the fridge as he pulled out two cans of Sprite, popping them open and depositing them on the counter.

"Damn," she whispered. "That's their specialty."

"No shit," he said, swiping the fourth fry from her fingers and shoving into his own mouth.

He moved around the counter and settled on the second stool, dragging his burger in front of him and the container of fries between them so they could share.

She sank her teeth into the burger and didn't care some of the juice ran down her chin. It was rare she could go to Dino's for a meal, but for a small northern Pennsylvania diner, they had made the best homemade food. The new owners made everything from scratch and most of it was locally sourced.

He didn't say anything for the longest time, which surprised her. So, she took that time to eat in peace, savoring every bite of the burger and fries.

Eventually her stomach cried mercy, since she had eaten not only most of the burger but the fries.

When she was done, Trip finished off her leftover burger and the few surviving fries, then sat back and sighed, patting his stomach. "That shit was good."

"The best."

"Now we need to talk."

Great. "*You* need to talk. Not me," she corrected him.

He grabbed their empty containers, shoved them into

one of the empty bags and tossed them into the garbage, but he didn't settle back next to her. No. He stayed on the other side of the counter, so he was facing her.

She wasn't going to like this talk.

"He buggin' you?"

Oh, Jesus. That was not what she was expecting, but she should've known. While he wasn't the type of guy to let a locked door stop him, he also wasn't a guy who would let another man stop him from getting what he wanted. But that didn't mean she needed to make it easy for him. "Who?"

He cocked a dark eyebrow. "Who you think?"

He was jealous of Cage. Imagine that. "It's nothing new, Trip." Cage always flirted with her, made moves, tried to sweet talk her out of her jeans. While he was admittedly good-looking, he wasn't her type. Plus, he was a few years younger than her and that just wasn't her thing. Not to mention, she was avoiding the bad boy types like the plague. "He's a regular. And I need every regular I can get."

He reached across the counter and grabbed her chin, holding her gaze when he asked, "He get in there?"

Her brow furrowed as she played dumb. He had no right to ask that. "Get in where?"

"*There.*"

She wanted to laugh with how ridiculous that was. Like he should care who all she slept with in her lifetime. It wasn't his business. Just like it wasn't any of hers who he had sex with for the past twenty years. The problem was, she wasn't laughing. She was getting annoyed at his line of questioning. "You mean in my bed?"

"In your fuckin' pussy," he growled.

She stared at him. Was he for real? "Would it matter if he did?"

Trip's head jerked back and he released her chin. "Fuck

yes. No way I'm havin' an ol' lady who's fucked any of my brothers. No fuckin' way."

Trying to keep a lid on her temper, she pushed off the stool and went to the fridge, grabbing a bottle of water. "Well, that won't be a problem."

"Good."

She turned and twisted off the cap. "One, I never slept with Cage. Two, I'm not your ol' lady."

"Yet."

Stella shook her head. "No, Trip. You can't claim me."

"Already did."

"You didn't at the table."

"Not yet."

"Not ever."

"Bullshit," he muttered.

She carefully put her water bottle on the counter and turned toward him. "Thank you for dinner. Now, I need to get back downstairs and make sure Cage isn't shotgunning beer directly from the tap."

"He's fine." Trip reached out to grab her wrist and Stella jerked it away.

He wasn't going to start controlling every aspect of her life. "I have no choice about the bar, Trip. But the rest of my life is my own." She pressed a hand to her chest. "I'm in control, not you."

His lips flattened. He was struggling. She could read it in his face, in his body language. He was trying to keep from saying whatever he wanted to say so he wouldn't piss her off any further.

He was going to fail.

She could see his temper spiking. She could see his frustration.

He wanted her, for whatever reason. So, he believed he could have her. With no question.

He was a man who got what he wanted. By sweat or by force.

But she had learned her lesson about men like him. A lesson she should have learned when she was a girl and watched all that shit go down with the original Fury members and the women who were around them. How they were treated. Not only the sweet butts and hang-arounds but their mothers. Hers. Trip's. All of them.

At the time, she thought that behavior was normal. She later discovered it wasn't. And once she was free of that environment, she should've stayed free.

She didn't.

Bad boy rockers weren't much different than bad boy bikers. Only their toys were different.

"You in control, Stella?"

His voice was so low and gravelly when he asked that, a wave of heat rolled through her. A deeper meaning was behind those words, which shouldn't affect her, but it did.

Her answering, "Yes," sounded shaky. Because it was. The look in his eyes, like his hunger hadn't been sated by the food, made everything inside her quiver.

"You sure?' he asked as he came around the counter and moved to stand behind her.

No. No, she wasn't sure.

She didn't turn to look at him. But with how close he was, how his heat radiated against her back, it sent a shiver through her. Her nipples became points, her breasts began to ache, her skin tingled.

He wasn't touching her, but she wanted him to.

Fuck, did she want him to.

"I need..." What did she need? *Damn it.* She knew what she needed. She didn't want to need it. She cleared her throat and quickly finished, "To go back downstairs."

She was wrong. He didn't fail.

She did.

Once again, she failed to keep him at arm's length. Failed to make it clear that she didn't want him. Because that was untrue. No matter how bad he was for her, she couldn't resist him.

She wasn't mad at him about it, she was mad at herself.

She should insist he leave. To remove the temptation.

She should.

Instead of those words coming out of her mouth, the breath rushed from her lungs as he drew her to him, staying behind her and pulling her back to his front.

She wanted this just as much as she didn't.

Why, why, why did he have to come back to Manning Grove?

Why did she?

She was supposed to be getting her life back in order, not let it spin out of control. Again.

He grabbed a handful of her hair and lifted it, sliding his lips over the back of her neck. His other hand spanned her ribs before sliding across her belly and down. The tip of his fingers skimmed the waistband of her jeans, teasing her.

Her brain was screaming it wasn't a good idea, while her body screamed it was a great one.

Her fingers found his, then the button on her jeans. She released it, lowered the zipper and then she shoved his hand down her panties.

She. Failed.

His breathing became ragged, as did hers, but neither of them said a word as he found her throbbing clit and circled it.

The memory of how he took her, how hard he fucked her in the bar that first time... made her soaked.

It wouldn't take much to tip her over.

She needed it. Craved it.

And, *fuck her*, it was him she needed and craved it from.

His teeth scraped down the side of her throat as he

worked his fingers lower, parting her pussy, slipping inside her. But only barely.

There wasn't enough room for him, and she wanted him there. But not only his fingers.

Shoving her jeans down her thighs, her voice was thick when she demanded, "Condom, then fuck me."

When he obeyed without hesitation, she realized she *was* in control. Though, he would be getting something out of this, too, so he had no reason to fight her.

That didn't matter. What mattered was, he had pulled away to drop his jeans and roll on a condom.

"Palms flat on the counter and keep them there."

"No." She couldn't see him because he stayed behind her. And that made it even more exhilarating. Hearing him, smelling him, feeling him. As he wrapped a hand around the front of her throat, the other using his latex-covered cock to separate her ass cheeks.

Sliding down. Down.

She tipped her hips, giving him better access to find his target.

"Hurry," got caught in her throat.

Again, he listened and didn't waste time, finding where she was open to him, where she welcomed him.

"Fuck me," she demanded in a soft growl. "Hurry up and fuck me."

Still, he said nothing.

But she didn't care. She was doing this for her. Not him. To prove she was in control, not him.

"Trip," she whimpered softly.

"Yeah, baby?"

"Please."

She shuddered when he drove deep with a single thrust. But she was ready for him. Slick and open. She rose to her toes to allow him a better angle since she was shorter than him. Though, as he began to drill her deep, but steady, him having to bend his knees slightly gave him a more powerful thrust.

With both of them standing, he couldn't go any deeper, take her any more fully.

The fingers around her throat tightened and he tipped her head back to his shoulder while he fingered her clit with his other hand.

Being pinned against him as he fucked her thoroughly, his lower belly slapping against her ass, enhanced each thrust.

Closing her eyes, she concentrated on his breathing which skirted across her ear, along with the soft grunt on the very end of each breath, at the very end of each drive up and into her.

She shoved her tank top and bra up, exposing her aching puckered nipples. She cupped one, kneading, thumbing the tip, the wave of pleasure shooting south to meet the waves he sent north. They crashed at her center. She gasped and reached behind him, grabbing a hold of his hair at the back of his head, her fingers twisting and hanging on.

She needed to hold on since she was about to split apart.

It was sex, but it wasn't. It was more.

So much more.

So much she didn't want to see or admit to.

She failed.

But he didn't. He succeeded, grinding deep while thumbing her firm, slick nub, sending all her thoughts, her concerns, her worries about... him, her, them... exploding like a supernova in space. Pieces of matter shooting in all directions, never to be seen again.

His name filled her mind and might have even crossed her lips. He became her center, her focus, as her thoughts gathered and returned.

He wasn't done with her, because he wasn't done.

Both hands took a hold of her breasts, knocking hers out of the way. He was staking claim of them as he kept driving up, his grunts louder but consisted more of breath than sound. The heat of his chest seared her back as he pulled her against him tighter, pinched her nipples harder and quickened his pace.

He was close.

And then he was there. His teeth sank into her neck, his breath pounding against her damp skin, his grunt with his final thrust changing into a long, deep groan as he stayed deep, his cock twitching inside her.

She wanted to lower her feet and stand because her mind was still spinning, and she needed to ground herself. To not rely on him holding her up.

But she couldn't since his cock still speared her deep. And it was one way he could keep control of her. He would pull out when he was ready or when his body forced him to, not a moment before.

Because that was the kind of man he was.

She had wanted to show him she was in control. He turned the tables on her in the end.

She. Had. Failed.

"Baby?"

She closed her eyes for a few seconds, but she knew she'd need to answer because he would only ask again until she did. She knew him and his type too well. "Yeah?"

Releasing one hand from her breast, he dragged his thumb over her mouth, and it got caught on her bottom lip, pulling it down enough so the pad scraped over her bottom teeth. "That's mine."

Christ, she should hate that. She should insist he was wrong.

But she didn't because she didn't hate it. It gave her a feeling she hadn't experienced in a long time.

He slid it over her breast again, his palm skimming one of her now sensitive nipples. "Mine."

He spread his fingers across her belly and then slid them lower until he pressed his middle finger against her clit. Another spot now super sensitive. So much so, she jerked when he touched it and whispered, "Mine."

He kept moving until he found where they were connected and touched her there, too. "Mine," he said softly, lips to her ear. "And that ass will be mine, too."

She needed to shake off the hold he had on her. "What's mine? If you take it all, what's left for me?"

Without even the slightest hesitation, he said, "Me, baby. You got me. You can have all of me."

Holy shit, she wasn't expecting that answer. She also wasn't expecting all those feelings from twenty years ago to rise back to the surface, as much as she'd been fighting them.

She didn't expect to fall for him once again.

She failed.

She fucking failed.

A tear slipped out of the corner of her closed eyes. And she let it. She didn't care if he saw it.

She didn't care if the whole world saw it.

It was real. And it proved she once again felt something. That she was no longer completely empty inside.

Trip had forced his way in, and she failed to keep him out.

She let him in and, though she struggled not to allow it, he was starting to take root in what was barren soil.

Her Tree of Life was beginning to thrive again.

Now she just needed to keep it from losing any more leaves.

Chapter Fifteen

Trip followed Stella down the steps back into the bar. Something had changed, something had switched.

He wasn't sure what.

He also wasn't sure if it would last. But he'd take it. He'd take whatever she'd give him and try to build on it.

As soon as he could, he was getting her moved into his house. He wanted her in his bed every night. He didn't want to have to come find her here. He had too much on his plate to do that. But he also couldn't leave her alone.

He couldn't.

He'd seen the struggle on her face after he'd released her, went into the bathroom to clean up and get rid of the wrap. He didn't think he misread her.

It was finally hitting her, even though it was a lot later than he'd like. Because it had hit him almost immediately, like a sledgehammer to the chest.

While he didn't like fighting for what he wanted, for what was his, he also didn't mind working for it.

Working to build something was one thing. Fighting for it was another.

He was tired.

He had started all of this with too many expectations. He hadn't planned on Stella being one of them.

He held the storage room's swinging door open for her and she moved through it and immediately behind the bar.

Cage was still sitting on the stool where they'd left him. Though, now he had an empty shot glass, as well as a filled to the rim pint glass of beer in front of him. Along with an open bag of chips and an empty plastic barrel that used to hold those round cheese puffs.

Trip also noticed Cage's eyes following Stella as she approached him, grabbing the trash and the empty glass. Cleaning up after him.

While that was the bartender's job, Trip expected Cage, as a BFMC member, to clean the fuck up after himself.

"Legs broken?" Trip asked.

That drew Cage's attention to him. "What?"

"Pretty sure your legs fuckin' worked to help yourself to snacks and a fuckin' shot. Or most likely a few shots. Surprised there ain't a fuckin' empty bottle sittin' next to you."

Cage shrugged. "Told me not to get drunk."

Trip shook his head. "Coulda cleaned the fuck up after yourself since you were in charge."

At least the man wasn't drunk, and the bar was still standing, even though there wasn't one fucking customer in the whole place. The man could've called a few friends in to help support the bar. Trip would have a talk with all his brothers about making sure to encourage people to drink there.

Even though it wasn't that late, they were going to close the bar early because he was ready to drop.

With a long day where he almost got shot, and now with food in his belly and his balls drained dry, he was running on fumes. Even one beer might have him falling asleep on his ride home.

And he couldn't have that since he planned on Stella being on the back of his sled.

"Took you a long time to eat," Cage said, giving Trip a knowing look.

"Didn't just eat," Trip answered. From the corner of his eye, he saw Stella stop dead and turn her head toward him.

"Yeah?" Cage asked, his eyes slicing from Trip to Stella and back.

"Yeah." Trip leaned in closer. "Remember that."

Cage's jaw shifted and he slipped from the stool. "Headin' home. Dutch will club me with a wrench if I show up at the garage late tomorrow mornin'."

"Then get home. We got it from here."

When Cage moved toward the entrance, Trip followed and caught up with him at the door. He pushed his palm against it to keep the man from opening it. Under his breath he asked, "We gonna have a problem?

Cage glanced back to where Stella was watching them closely with a frown etching her face. "You good, babe?"

"Yeah, Cage, I'm good," she answered with a nod and then went back to cleaning dirty glasses, though still holding onto that frown.

Cage turned back to Trip and nodded. "We're good, too, Prez."

They eyeballed each other for a few seconds, then Cage held out his hand. Trip slapped his palm into Cage's and they bumped shoulders.

"Careful gettin' home, brother" Trip mumbled. When Cage opened the door, Trip stopped him with a, "Hey."

Cage hesitated.

"Judge and I are headin' to County tomorrow to talk to your brother. Offerin' Rook a place to land at the barn. Like I said, you wanna room, need to grab one soon."

Cage nodded. "I'll think about it."

"Do that."

He slipped out the door.

Trip took a deep breath, stared at the door for a minute, listening to the rumble of Cage's sled as he rode away, then pulled his cell phone out to check the time.

Still too early to close up.

Fuck.

He needed to get some guys in here to help with the bar and soon. How she was doing this six days a week on her own...? The thought made him even more exhausted.

But he'd see to it she wouldn't be working the bar alone anymore. Or working late, either.

He headed back to her, where she was now wiping down the bar top. "Next liquor order buy double. Need to start stockin' the bar at the barn."

"We can't afford it."

We.

The first part sounded fucking good. The last? Not so much.

"We'll figure it out. Order double."

Her hand stilled for a second, then she continued to scrub the scratched bar top in circles with the damp rag. "Okay."

Trip wasn't sure whether to smile or frown. "No fight?"

"No fight."

Thank fuck.

She tossed the rag into a bucket of dirty ones under the bar, then leaned her ass against the back bar counter, crossing her arms. He studied her studying him. He liked that her expression was soft while she did it.

"You look tired," she said softly.

He wasn't the only one. She had dark circles under her eyes. Regular sleep and food would remedy that.

"Had a long fuckin' day," he finally admitted. But she had no clue just how long it was.

"You can go. I got the bar."

Maybe it wasn't concern after all, but a way to get rid of him. "*We* got the bar."

"I've been doing this on my own for a while now, Trip."

"Not anymore."

"Another night isn't going to kill me."

"Now you wanna fight," he muttered.

"No fight," she said. "Just fact."

"Here's a fact. You're in my bed tonight."

"All I have to do is climb the stairs to go to bed, not drive across town and out into the country just to sleep."

"Wasn't askin', Stella." He lifted a hand to stop her next argument. "You don't gotta drive anywhere; you'll be on the back of my sled."

Her jaw shifted. *Now* she was working up for a fight.

"And I'll drop you back off here in the mornin' on my way to meet with Judge."

"You told Cage you're heading to Lycoming to meet with Rook."

"Yeah?" He tilted his head.

She stopped him before he could ask. "Don't even fucking go there, Trip. Don't even. If you start questioning whether I've slept with every fucking guy in this town, we're going to have a big problem."

"You heard what I said."

"Right. And not only am I not your ol' lady, but I haven't seen Rook since we were kids. When I got back to town, he had already started this last stint in prison. But I'm telling you now, stop asking."

"Just—"

"Stop. I shouldn't have to tell you this because it isn't any of your fucking business, but I swear..." She blew out a breath. "I'm only telling you this so I don't beat you over the head with a whiskey bottle. Understood?"

He grinned. "Yeah."

"Wipe that grin off your face, Trip. Or you can go the fuck home without me."

"That mean you're comin' with me without a fight?"

"Right now, I'm on the fence. Don't push me off it."

He pinned his lips together to hide his smirk. "Okay. Hit me. Just not with the bottle."

"I'm going to tell you this one time and one time only, so make sure you've got your listening ears on."

Fuck, she was making it hard for him not to smile. "Got 'em on."

She stared at him for a moment, annoyance making her eyes two light blue flames. Her next words out of her mouth came slowly, like she was talking to some two-year-old who just got his ass in a sling. "I haven't slept with anyone since my husband."

He covered his smile with his hand. He'd already survived getting shot at once today, he wasn't risking a second time.

She gave him a frown. "I can see your eyes crinkling at the corners. I know you're smiling... Asshole." She sighed and pushed away from the counter.

He body-blocked her and cupped her face, dropping a brief kiss on her pinned and flattened lips. "Thank you, baby."

He hated to admit it but her confession was a huge goddamn relief. He didn't want to be eyeing up every man who walked into Crazy Pete's or every brother in his club, wondering.

He couldn't help he was a suspicious fuck. His ex's bull-shit had planted that seed of doubt inside him.

Which reminded him, once again, they needed to have that talk. He needed to come clean about his prison time and why he landed there.

"Now," she started, hands on her hips, "when's the last time you slept with someone other than me?"

Oh fuck.

His breath was her breath. And hers his.

Their fingers were intertwined tightly, their clasped hands pinned to the mattress, sweat beaded on both of their foreheads, which were pressed together.

On his insistence, their eyes remained open and locked.

And that got him all the way deep down into his very soul.

He rocked his hips slowly, gliding in and out of her tight, wet heat. Hot silk that squeezed him every time he drove it home.

Home.

She was in his bed, in his home, and she felt like home to him.

Coming home couldn't get any sweeter than being inside Stella. There was no place he'd rather be.

Especially having her whimpers and her cries filling his ears. Having her nails dig into his back and ass. Having her lips and tongue sweep along his skin. Having her thighs sandwiching his hips as hers tilted and met him thrust for thrust.

Goddamn perfection.

If he could, he'd never leave that bed, never let her leave it, either.

Last night he expected a fight when he told her to pack a bag as they closed up Crazy Pete's. She didn't even pause, didn't argue. She went upstairs, grabbed a bag, came back down and, again without an argument, climbed on the back of his sled and wrapped her arms around him as he took her home.

Home.

She belonged on the back of his bike, too.

It was the first time she was pressed against him as they rode through town back to the farm, but it wouldn't be the last.

"Trip," she breathed.

"Yeah, baby?"

"You going to take all day?"

He snorted and stilled deep inside her. Tilting his hips sharply, he reminded her who was on top. "Goin' too slow for you?"

"I'd like to come before I have to open the bar. Or I grow cobwebs."

"You came when I ate your pussy and fingered your ass."

"And?"

"And you got yours the way you like it, lemme get mine now."

He was only fucking with her because he damn well planned on making her come again. This woman got as slick as shit, and when she came...?

Fuck.

Trip just about lost it immediately every damn time. He struggled to hang on, to give her one more. If he could give her a dozen, he would. Unfortunately, he couldn't because she drove him to the brink way too easily with the way she responded.

Fucking her certainly wasn't an effort on his part.

Though, last night they had crashed as soon as they got to the house. Both of them just about unconscious when they hit the mattress.

He never fucking slept so well than being curled around her, holding her tight.

Holding on to what was his.

He grinned.

"Should I worry about why you're grinning?"

"Nope. 'Cause I'm about to make you come again."

"Big words, little results."

"Damn," he whispered.

She grinned. "See? Now *I'm* grinning."

"I'll take care of that."

She released a loud dramatic sigh. "Good."

He chuckled, making her breath hitch with the way his body shook, causing his dick to vibrate inside her. "So fuckin' hard for you, baby, you feel it?"

"Yes," she hissed.

"You make me that hard."

"Less talk, more action."

"Just like in the Marines."

Her brow furrowed. "How much sex did you have while in the Marines?"

"I meant... Never mind. Jesus fuck, woman."

"Jesus isn't fucking me, Trip, you are. So, let's *go*."

"Christ," he muttered.

"Kiss me, fuck me and make me come," she demanded.

That he could do. And that's what he did.

Twice.

THE WHISPER of the bedroom door opening had Stella opening her eyes and rolling over to see Trip walking in wearing nothing but a worn pair of jeans.

Just the way she liked him.

He was carrying a huge tray with what looked like two plates of food and two steaming mugs of what she hoped was coffee.

As he got closer to the bed, she smelled it.

Bacon and coffee.

Best morning ever.

He slid the tray onto the antique nightstand and then dropped his jeans to the floor.

Yep. Best morning ever.

At least in the last year.

There had been plenty of early mornings when Kade had snuck into bed with her and cuddled. She'd smell his hair and stroke his back until he'd fallen back asleep clinging to her.

She missed that.

She missed him.

Her heart had been ripped out that day.

Trip was trying his best to shove it back into that empty cavity. Great sex and breakfast in bed was a good start. Him throwing her a life preserver ring to keep her from going under the surface and never coming back up also helped.

She sat up against the headboard as he slid in beside her, then carefully placed the heavily burdened tray between them.

"You're trying to make me fat," she said. Her plate was piled with three pancakes smothered in maple syrup and two thick pats of butter. There had to be a half dozen strips of bacon on the side. And her coffee was just the color she liked it.

Damn.

He snagged a slice of bacon off his own plate and crunched on it.

"I could've come down to the kitchen."

"Yep." Just "yep."

"Are you trying to seduce me, Trip Davis?"

He lifted his mug, blowing the steam off the surface. "It workin'?" He took a long sip before putting it back down.

Yes. "Maybe."

"Remember what I said about liars?"

She shoved a large piece of syrup-soaked pancake into her mouth and only shrugged.

"You drip syrup on your tits, and we might not make it through breakfast."

She shrugged again. "Okay."

He chuckled and she smiled around a bite of bacon.

Once his chuckle died, his face got serious. "Need to explain some shit. Been meanin' to, but other shit keeps happenin'."

"Shit happens," she agreed, because that was only too true.

"But I need to get it out. You haven't asked but you need to know."

"About the charges you caught."

"Yeah."

She looked at her plate and then at Trip, who was shoving a pancake-packed fork into his mouth. "Is it going to ruin my breakfast?"

"Maybe," he said as he chewed.

"Maybe I should eat more bacon first." She lifted a crispy piece and studied it. "This come from the Amish?"

"Yeah."

"The syrup?"

"Yep."

"Are you going to be buying from them on the regular?"

"Plan on it. For us and for the barn."

Us.

"Maybe even some stuff for Crazy Pete's."

That drew her attention away from the "us" part. "Like what?"

"Thinking about getting a kitchen installed. Serving bar food. Potato skins, wings, whatever. Something other than pretzels, chips and those shitty orange balls. It'll help draw in more people."

"We don't have the money to install a kitchen or hire cooks."

"We will. Gotta start slow, refurb the bar, get a team working it. Run specials. Run pool and dart leagues, like I told you. A regular night of fuckin' Karaoke," he winced, "even if it's goddamn country music. Whatever does it."

"That's a lot of work."

"Yep."

"They're good ideas, though."

He smiled as he shoved more bacon into his mouth. "Yep."

"Again, it all takes marketing and money."

"We'll get it done. That bar and The Grove Inn's gonna be a good source of income. Just gotta get it workin' for us."

Us.

He continued. "Bring money into the club coffers, put money in the brothers' pockets, put money in our pockets. Invest back into the businesses."

Our pockets. "You want to build an empire."

He nodded. "A fuckin' empire. With you and me at the head of it. That make you wet? Because it sure as fuck gives me a hard-on."

She stared at him, ignoring the food on her plate. He had his hair up in a ponytail, probably to keep it out of his face while he made breakfast. But the back of his neck had a few small scratches on it.

She reached out and ran her thumb over them. "Lean forward."

His brow rose but he leaned a bit forward. He had scratches on his upper back near his neck, too. "Damn. Did I do that, or did you get into a fight with a cat?" She looked closer. "No, they're not fresh. I'm guessing a cat."

"Somethin' like that."

She pulled her hand away just in time as he pressed his back into the antique wood headboard which matched the nightstands.

"Gettin' off track again."

"You were the one who mentioned empires and hard-ons."

"Right. Need to get this shit out, Stel."

She frowned, lifted a *wait-a-minute* finger, quickly gobbled down her last two slices of bacon, chugged a mouthful of coffee, said, "Okay," before bracing.

"There's gonna come a day where I'm not gonna wear a wrap and will come inside you. That day's gonna be soon. So, do whatcha gotta do to prepare for that."

What? That was the big talk? "Trip, are you serious?"

He lifted a *let-me-explain* hand while holding a strip of bacon between his fingers, then he shoved it into his mouth. "No. I mean, yes, about that. But that's not what I need to tell you. Just wanted to get that out while you were payin' attention."

She whacked his arm and rolled her eyes.

"Seriously, though," he continued. "Whatever you need to do."

"And what about you?"

"I'll get it done."

"I don't have health insurance."

"Whatever you need done, get it done, baby. Got it covered."

"Trip, you can't pay everything for me."

"You bust your ass in that bar, you stick by my side, I got your back."

"But—"

He held up his hand again to stop her, this time without the bacon. "Off track again."

"Go," she said, then shut her mouth and waited.

He ran his finger through the syrup on his plate, then stuck it in his mouth, sucking it clean.

"Well, fuck, Trip..."

"Sorry. Know I'm hot and irresistible. Didn't mean to distract you."

"Christ," she whispered. "You're going to cause me eye strain from how hard I'm rolling them."

He grinned, leaned over, gave her a maple-flavored kiss, then settled back against the headboard.

He put his massacred plate back on the tray and grabbed his mug, wrapping his long fingers—the ones he was so skillful with—around it. She placed her plate of half-eaten pancakes next to his and did the same with her coffee.

She waited.

And waited.

His body jerked next to her, like somebody had pushed his start button. He blew out a long breath, sucked in air, then began. "Was seein' a girl when I enlisted at eighteen. Once I was done with boot camp and found out I was headin' overseas, she begged me to marry her before I left."

Stella didn't like the direction this tale was going already. A woman should never have to beg a man to marry her. To her, it always seemed like a bad start to a relationship.

"I did."

Fuck.

"Was over playin' in the sandbox when she told me she was pregnant. Didn't think much of it since I'd been home on leave just a few months before. She was on birth control, but that's no guarantee..." He shook his head. "Never thought I'd want a kid 'til I heard those words."

Ice slithered through Stella's veins.

"My original plan was to reenlist, but that news changed everything. Wanted to be there to raise my kid right. Be a real father. So, when my time was up, I headed home. My time wearin' fatigues, combat boots, gettin' shot at, and eatin' MRE's came to an end." His fingers tightened up on his coffee mug to the point his knuckles turned pale. "Wanted to surprise her. To do that, told her the wrong date for when I was hittin' American soil." He was staring straight ahead, his jaw tight, but his expression blank. "You already know the ending to this story. It's a common one. Mine's no different... Came home. Caught 'im in the house

I paid rent for every fuckin' month, drinkin' my mother-fuckin' beer. Eatin' the food I paid for. Fuckin' my goddamn wife. I'd put my life on the line every fuckin' day over there. Every fuckin' day to provide for her. Saw red and wanted to kill her. Was close to it, too. Took it out on him instead, even though she also lied to him. Never told 'im she was married. Was a liar all the way around. Lived off the sweat of my brow, ate sand while she ate fuckin' steaks, paid for her A/C while I lived in a goddamn sweat box of a tent for months. Had to fist it while she was home gettin' fucked."

Then he just stopped talking. His chest rose and fell several times, his muscles were tight. He was struggling to hold his temper. And it seemed as if he was failing.

She quickly pried the half-empty coffee mug from his fingers before it went flying across the room. She set it on the tray, then slid the tray onto the nightstand on her side of the bed, out of reach and safe from him making a mess.

"Trip," she whispered, and he only blinked in response.

He was back there, standing in his bedroom of a house he paid for, seeing another man fucking his pregnant wife.

He was reliving it for Stella, when he didn't want to.

He was reliving it for her, when he just wanted her to understand.

He was reliving it for her, so there were no secrets between them.

But she felt his pain, his fury, his disappointment.

He hated liars because he'd been told some big lies. And she waited for him to tell the rest of the story. But like he said, she already knew where this was going. It was an old tale no one wanted to live.

When the silence continued, she prompted, "What happened with the baby?"

He turned his head to look at her. "What do you think?"

"Wasn't yours," she murmured, already knowing the answer.

His jaw worked and his fingers curled into fists against his bare thighs. Another sign he was struggling to keep from exploding. "Right. Wasn't mine. Wasn't his, either. Don't know whose it was. Don't fuckin' care. Caught a four-year stint in the joint for agg assault with a deadly weapon. While inside, caught two more years 'cause of my temper."

She closed her eyes and whispered, "What did you do to him?"

"Pistol-whipped that motherfucker. Totally fuckin' lost it. Broke his eye socket, a few ribs, broke every one of his fingers for touchin' my wife. He's lucky I didn't cut off his fuckin' dick."

"You had a gun but didn't shoot him." Thank fuck he didn't because his term would've been a lot longer than the initial four years. It would've been a very long time, or even life.

"It was close but wanted him to live with what he did. Know what he did was wrong, even though she lied to him, too. Shoulda known somethin' was up when she was livin' large without a fuckin' job. Shoulda asked how she was payin' the bills, feeding her fuckin' ass, drivin' around town in a decent cage. He didn't give a fuck. Why? 'Cause he was all about the easy pussy. Now he'll think twice before stickin' his dick where it don't belong."

Unfortunately, this was too much of a similar story to Trip's father. In that nightmare, it was Buck doing a woman he shouldn't have for years. It was Buck who was stupid enough to fuck a woman when he knew the consequences if he got caught.

He got caught.

He paid the price.

The rest of them in the Fury also paid the price.

Only Razor got shot dead for doing what he did to Buck. Unlike Trip, who ended up in prison for losing his shit. Similar scenarios, which ended up destroying families, but with two different consequences.

Trip probably didn't want to hear it, but Stella was glad he ended up in prison instead of six feet under. There was an end to a prison sentence, there wasn't an end to being dead.

"After catching that extra time, I got smart. Began to work on myself. Body and mind. Do my best to control the temper I got from my fuckin' father. Swore to myself I'd never land behind bars again."

"Did she have the baby?"

"Don't know. Don't care. The fuckin' greedy bitch used me. She begged me to marry her and I did so, thinkin' she..." He shook his head. "Now I know it was just for her to collect the death benefits if somethin' happened to me over there. She was hopin' I wouldn't come home unless I was in a box. Even told me so to my fuckin' face durin' my fuckin' trial, where she also served me the divorce papers. Death bennies are a hundred grand. That's how much my life was worth to her."

Stella reached out, grabbed his clenched fist and squeezed it. He uncurled his fingers and, turning his hand over, intertwined them with hers.

"Don't ever lie to me, baby. Don't care how fuckin' hard the truth is. Don't care how much it'll fuckin' hurt. Just don't lie. Won't tolerate that shit for a second. I'll lose my shit and it won't be good for either one of us."

That last part made her chest tighten. "I'm asking you to do the same."

His brown eyes met hers as he lifted their clasped hands to his mouth and he kissed her knuckles. "Promise you here and now, I'll be brutally honest. I'll give what I get. Remember that."

"I promise, too. Kellan lied to me about his sobriety. The result just about destroyed me. If he'd only been honest..."

"If he'd been honest, your son would still be with you."

"Yeah," she breathed.

"Make you a deal. You ever have to tell me somethin' you think will flip me the fuck out, then you do it with Judge at your side. I'd rather that man kick my fuckin' ass than me hurt you 'cause I lost my shit." He reached out and slid his fingers into the back of her hair, finding her scar and tracing it with his fingertip. "Never wanna fuckin' hurt you again. Hear me?"

"I hear you." She should be worried about being with a man with a temper like his. But he recognized his problem, dealt with it as best as he could and was openly honest about it. He wasn't hiding his faults.

It was something he inherited from his father, a man who had an extremely short temper and used violence to rule the club. Stella remembered always being afraid of Buck. The man could be loud and brash, and quick to punish someone without hearing both sides. That punishment was usually pretty harsh.

She wondered how Buck's ol' lady, Trip's mother, dealt with it for all those years. "Did Buck hurt your mother?"

"If he did, she hid it well. Know she miscarried two babies after me. Not sure if he was the cause of it. Because after we left and landed in Wisconsin, she married another man, had two more kids without a problem."

Jesus. She wasn't expecting that. Trip had two more half-siblings beside Sig.

"Did you ever ask her?"

"Yeah. But once we left Manning Grove, she wanted to forget that life. Wanted to live her new one and put the old one behind her. Never wanted to talk about what happened. Had a good relationship with her 'til I told her about resurrectin' the Fury. She had warned me about Deb, and I didn't listen. She used that against me about not only doin' time but rebuildin' the MC. Said I'd end up just like Buck."

"Maybe she was worried you'd end up dead."

"Maybe."

"So, you don't talk to her at all?" *God*, just like her mother, who stopped talking to her after Kade's death since she blamed Stella.

"Ended up dead to her anyway."

Stella's heart squeezed and so did her fingers around his. "Is bringing back the club worth it?"

He answered without a hesitation. "It's gonna be."

She hoped he was right.

Chapter Sixteen

TRIP KNEW the second she saw it because of her body going stiff and her sharp intake of breath. Now he was kicking himself for not parking the wrecker in the shed yesterday. He had left it at the house because he'd been anxious to shower, change, and pick up dinner before heading to Crazy Pete's and Stella.

He hadn't thought with his head, but with his dick.

Now he was going to pay for it.

Last night when he brought Stella home, it had been dark, so she'd missed it. This morning, the light didn't hide anything.

"Jesus, Trip. That was the cat?"

He didn't answer, because apparently, none was needed. He gritted his teeth as she rushed over to the tow truck, inspecting the blown out back window and the bullet holes.

She spun toward him, her face pale, her eyes holding worry. "How the fuck did that happen?"

They promised not to lie to each other, so he wasn't going to lie. "Tryin' to repo a car."

"Someone fucking shot at you?" she shouted.

Her getting upset wasn't going to help him remain calm.

But he needed to. He sucked in a deep breath and released it after a slow count of five. When he was done, he answered, "Bunch of hillbillies."

She froze in place, her eyes wide. "You didn't."

Fuck. "Didn't what?"

"Go up that mountain trying to repo one of the Shirley's cars."

Christ. "A job's a job."

"Is the money worth dying for?"

Good point. Yeah, he needed the money, they both did. But it wouldn't do either of them any good if he was dead. "Would you miss me if I was dead?"

While he made it sound like he was teasing, he wasn't. He really wanted to know.

"Shut up, Trip! That's not even funny!" She strode back to him, her body tight, her lips curled into a frown, her fists clenched and pinned to her thighs.

"Think you would. Damn." The corners of his mouth tipped up slightly at the thought of her actually missing him. Maybe he was making headway with her.

"Don't you fucking smile! You forget what I already lost. I can't do it again."

His smile dropped. Now he felt like a complete ass. He didn't forget. He could never forget. "Fuck, baby," he whispered, reaching out for her.

She stepped back out of his reach. "That just proves why this," she waved her hand between the two of them, "is a bad idea."

Okay, now she was going too far. "Not a bad idea."

"You think it was funny you were shot at."

"Wasn't laughin' at the time."

"You'd be happy if I missed you. To do that I'd have to fucking mourn you, asshole."

"Baby..."

She threw her hands up. "Take me home."

He bit back the urge to tell her she *was* home. His house, his farm, was her goddamn home.

He needed to get her out of that apartment and fill it with someone else so she couldn't use it as an escape.

They needed to deal with this kind of shit head on. Not run from it. "Stella..."

"You could've died."

"Coulda, but I didn't."

"Was that job worth it?"

Not yet since he didn't get the car. But he would. It was just a matter of time. However, what he made on that job wouldn't cover the cost of the damage. But he was getting that motherfucking car no matter what.

"You don't fuck with the Shirleys unless you're giving them something like cash for their moonshine. You can barter with them, buy stuff from them, but taking something from them, like their wheels, will get you killed."

"Learned that the hard way, babe."

"Tell me you won't fuck with them."

He couldn't tell her that, but he also couldn't lie. "Will be more careful in the future."

She shook her head and moved toward his sled. "I have to go open the bar."

She was dismissing him, and he didn't like it, but he'd let it go for now. He needed to get her dropped off and go meet up with Judge at Justice Bail Bonds.

He had work to do, a club to keep building and businesses to run. He'd deal with her later tonight when she was back in his bed.

Because tonight she *would* be back in his bed.

And every other fucking night from now on.

She might be pissed off, but it was because she was worried about him.

And that right there proved to him that she cared about him as much as he did about her.

That was a good thing.

TRIP's skin crawled as they went through the metal detectors at Lycoming County Prison. They had left their guns, as well as Judge's big-ass knife back in the safe at the bail bonds shop.

He had sworn to himself he'd never go back to prison and there he was, standing in a goddamn prison.

He hated the smell, the atmosphere and, most of all, hated the fucking screws who guarded the unwilling occupants.

His upper lip curled as they were escorted by one of the out-of-shape screws down the hall towards the visiting area. The buzzing of the doors and the noisy prisoners who could be heard in the distance put his nerves on edge. He felt naked and vulnerable not having his gun, or even a shank, with him.

His chest was tight, and his breathing strained as he followed the pale, wheezing screw, as well as Judge, deeper into the prison.

Fuck this shit. It was a good reminder to keep his ass out of there.

Never fucking again.

In truth, he'd rather die than go back behind bars.

He'd survived his time in the Marines, he survived his time in prison.

Now he was living for himself. No one else was going to tell him what to do. He wouldn't constantly be on the offensive, worried he might get stabbed, shot at or beaten.

Or even fucked up the ass by a man twice his size.

He'd spent thirty days in the hole after making sure that didn't happen one day in the showers. Those thirty days were worth keeping his asshole a virgin.

He and Judge hadn't talked the whole way to Williamsport since they were on their sleds. But as they settled at one of the tables, and after the screw reminded them not to touch Rook or try to give him anything, the man waddled away to stand along the wall with a few more of those uniformed motherfuckers.

Fuck, he hated this place and he hadn't even been incarcerated here.

"What do you know about the Shirleys?"

Judge's head pivoted toward him and he cocked a brow. "More than I wanna. Did you—" His booming laugh filled the large room where a shitload of family and friends waited at round tables with hard plastic chairs for the prisoners to arrive. "D'you hafta change your fuckin' pants after dealin' with 'em?

"No, but it was damn close. They shot up my wrecker."

"That'll teach ya."

"Wasn't a lesson I wanted to learn. 'Specially since I had one of the local pigs waitin' for me at the bottom of the mountain, also waitin' to teach me a lesson."

Judge shook his head. "The current herd of pigs won't fuck with you unless you fuck with them."

"Not plannin' on fuckin' with 'em."

"You are if you're goin' up that damn mountain."

"One of those Brysons gave me a tip 'bout snaggin' the car at Walmart."

"Yeah. They come down that mountain every once in a while. When it suits them. And when they gotta visit me."

Trip's ears perked. "You?"

"Deke and me deal with 'em on a regular basis. Every time they get pinched and need bail money."

"They pay their bond?"

"Yeah, but with them, I only deal in the green shit and I check to make sure it's real. They're good at fakin' checks and money orders."

"The reason they get their vehicles repo'd."

"Right. One of the many reasons they end up arrested, too. They also love to sue and tie up the courts. They sue everyone. The town, the PD, whoever and whenever. Just to be a pain in the fuckin' ass."

"They sue you?"

"Fuck no. Nobody else will bond their inbred asses out." Judge tapped his temple. "Learned my lesson about 'em real quick and now know how to handle 'em. They make me a fuckton of scratch." He sat back in the plastic chair, causing it to complain as he crossed his thick, tattooed arms over his chest and stretched out his long legs under the table. "We all call them the Shirley Clan. Clan should probably start with a K instead of a C, but doubt they got a sheet up in that compound white enough to make a hood out of. But you can't always tell the supremacists anymore since some are no longer hidin'. Bold motherfuckers. Those fools call themselves the Guardians of Freedom." Judge snorted and shook his head. "Guardians of fuckin' freedom. Guardians of their sister-cousins and brother-uncles more like it. Surprised some of 'em don't have three legs and one eye. Though, maybe some of 'em do and they just don't let 'em off the mountain. Probably keep 'em in cages and feed 'em raw meat."

"Are you fuckin' serious?"

Judge's booming laughter filled the room again and everyone's head swiveled toward him, including the screws who wore frowns. *Fuck 'em.*

"Hope not. But anything's possible with those fuckers. Plan on 'em suin' your ass if you successfully repo any of their wheels. Might wanna think about puttin' a lawyer on retainer. Couldn't hurt between the Fury and the repo business."

"And the bar."

Judge tipped his head and his green eyes narrowed.

"Yeah. And the bar. Speakin' of, what's goin' on with you and Stella?"

A buzz sounded, the door opened, and a line of inmates walked in, interrupting their conversation. He had no idea what Rook looked like since he hadn't seen him since the guy was about twelve. He was three years younger than Trip, but he'd still hung around Sig, Judge and him whenever he got a chance.

It didn't take long to identify him, though, since he was the last man standing. All the other inmates had found their family or friends and had settled into seats.

"Jesus fuck," Rook muttered, shaking his head, as he moved towards them. "Was hoping to see some pretty pussy sittin' at my table, not your ugly mugs. How's that gonna help my wet dreams?"

Trip watched Rook carefully as he settled in the chair across from him and Judge. He took the same stance as Judge. Leaning back in his chair with his arms crossed and his legs stretched out.

"It's been a while," Rook said to Judge. "I'd shake your fuckin' hand but don't wanna get my knuckles rapped with a ruler by the line of ugly nuns against the wall. They frown when it comes to contact. Even when you try to hug it out with 'em."

Trip dropped his head and laughed. When he lifted it, he said, "Never tried to hug it out with any of those assholes. If I did, they wouldn't have been breathin' afterward."

Rook grinned. "Besides fantasizin' about pussy in here, I dream about chokin' some of those rude motherfuckers out, too. Gettin' out soon, so need to be an angel 'til that happens." He turned to Judge. "So, what's up with you, fucker? Don't owe you shit on my bond, right?"

"No," Judge answered. "We're square."

Rook nodded. "Good. Then why you here?"

"You know why we're here," Trip answered him. Rook had to add him and Judge to his visitor's list, so he knew exactly why they were there.

Rook scraped a hand down his bearded jaw. "Yeah. Talked to Cage. He mentioned you were back in town and raisin' the Fury. Also said Dad's takin' the VP spot 'til Sig rolls back into town."

Judge snorted and shook his head. "Trip might be waitin' a while for that and doubt Dutch wants to wait that long."

Rook tipped his head to the side and met Trip's eyes. "Right. So, you're here to offer it to me."

Fuck. "Here to offer you a place to land when you get out."

Rook cocked an eyebrow. "Got a place with Dutch. Job, roof over my head, my sled. What more do I need besides booze and babes?"

"Got a room for you if you want it. And a cut."

"Yeah, heard you moved the Fury's church to the barn on your granddad's place. But when I said babes, didn't mean the pig named Babe in the barnyard. I don't fuck animals. I mean real pussy."

"We'll order you one of those fake pussies. Feels like the real thing," Judge said.

"Speakin' from experience, big guy?" Rook asked with a smirk.

Judge's heavy shoulders lifted and dropped. "Lot less hassle, less bitchin' and cheaper in the end."

"A-fuckin-men," Rook said, then turned to Trip. "Ended up here after tryin' to buy some bitch weed just to get down her fuckin' pants. No pussy's worth prison."

A-fuckin-men to that, too.

"Got time because you fled, made those fat fuckers run, and then fought 'em, Rook," Judge reminded him. "Shoulda taken the slap on the wrist instead of creatin' a cluster-fuck.

Then you wouldn't have been here for months with no pussy, fake or real. Though, an asshole might do in a pinch."

"Not if it's fuckin' hairy," Rook muttered.

"All right," Trip interrupted. He was not there to talk about fucking another man's ass. He wasn't there to talk about pussy, either. "So, you in?"

"What's in it for me?"

"Like I said, a cheap place to lay your head that's not under your pop's roof, stocked kitchen, stocked bar. Most importantly, a brotherhood."

"Yeah, I remember how that all worked out. Also remember my mother up and fuckin' leavin' us after all that shit went down. Not enough good memories to wanna be a part of somethin' like that."

"Buildin' somethin' worthwhile."

"For who? You? Or for all of us?"

Rook saying "us" was a step in the right direction. It meant he'd been considering it. Especially since Dutch and Cage were now wearing BFMC cuts.

"Know you got blood to watch your back. Some of us don't. How the Fury was before that whole disaster... while it wasn't perfect, we were all family, blood or not."

"Buck was a bastard."

Trip wasn't going to argue that fact about his own father. "Yeah."

"You gonna preside at the head of the table like he did?"

"Might be prez now but that doesn't mean I'll still be prez next year. You know how it works; the patched members vote. My ass could be voted out if I suck as prez."

"Cage said he's not prospectin' and I wouldn't have to, either. That right?"

"Right. Fury blood is Blood Fury. Now and always. You'd get your rockers, your cut and a vote the second you walk out these fuckin' doors. Fact, we'll even give you a fuckin' escort on the way home."

Rook twisted some of the wiry hairs of his beard between two fingers as he considered everything Trip said. And Trip let him work it out on his own.

"Sig out?" Rook finally asked.

Last he checked. One stupid move and that could change. "Yeah."

"But he's not in."

"Not yet."

"I'll think about it."

"All I can ask."

"What's the pussy situation? 'Cause if there are no club whores, who's gonna suck my dick?" His hand dropped below the table to grab his crotch.

"Word spreads the Fury has risen again, sure it'll be no time before the sweet butts are swarmin'," Trip assured him.

"Yeah," Rook said on a sigh. "Need 'em to take care of me and my shit. One thing I always envied about the patched members when we were kids. You wanna fuck, you fuck. They never said no. They'd bring your ass a beer, suck your cock, then go do your fuckin' laundry."

Trip remembered one female hang-around, not even a sweet butt yet, told to strip naked, get on her hands and knees and lick the brother's boots clean. She did.

Nothing like seeing a naked woman willingly licking a man's dirty fucking boots. Trip had to have been six or seven at the time and he never forgot it. First time he recalled seeing pussy, too. In fact, Trip remembered the brother's road name was Tin Man, or Tinny. Tinny had called him, Sig and Judge over and...

Fuck.

Trip squeezed his eyes shut trying to wipe out not only that scene, but one where if Pete's ol' lady had stayed, kept Stella as part of the club...

His temperature began to rise as he couldn't stop his mind from replacing Stella with that woman.

If any of his brothers did that shit, he'd end up back in prison for sure. He was going to have to draw a line and make that line clear when it came to any hang-arounds and sweet butts.

He could see Stella squeezing his nuts until they popped if he encouraged that shit or even allowed it.

"Long as they keep clean—meanin' not bringin' in drugs, not sellin' themselves, anything that'll bring the law down on us—they're welcome. But the moment one of 'em brings trouble, she's out."

"Fair enough. You want 'em sweet and innocent."

Judge snorted again. "Even if they walked in sweet and innocent, they certainly wouldn't be walkin' out that way. There's a certain type of woman who can deal with a bunch of bikers. From what I remember, it ain't easy and I got no fuckin' clue why they'd want to put up with all that bullshit in the first place."

Judge was right. Trip remembered the sweet butts not only getting fucked whenever and wherever by whoever, he remembered them getting knocked around and knocked up. Though if the last happened, that problem was swiftly taken care of or the woman was never seen again.

If she insisted on keeping a baby that a brother didn't want or didn't know who the baby daddy was? She was banned from the club. And she was going to raise that kid all on her own. She knew that coming in and knew that when she was kicked back out.

None of those brothers wanted to claim a kid by a patch whore.

Fuck.

That brought back a memory Trip had tried hard to forget. He might have been about five at the time.

A sweet butt had lied about being on the Pill and got knocked up on purpose, trying to become an ol' lady. Three brothers cornered her inside the warehouse and kicked the shit out of her until she miscarried.

Trip remembered her screaming, crying, begging and then afterward, the fucking blood... All that fucking blood...

Jesus fuck.

Yeah, he was drawing that line and nobody—none of them—better cross it. He would not tolerate that shit.

Trip rapped his knuckles on the table and stood. He needed to get the fuck out of there. His throat was closing, and his heart was beginning to race. "Think about it," he told Rook again.

Judge was slower getting up. When the tall man was on his feet, he planted both fists on the table and leaned toward Rook. "Like he said, think about it. But you're either in or out, Rook. We ain't doin' shit half-assed."

We.

Damn, that sounded good.

"When you gettin' sprung?" Trip asked Rook as he rose to his feet, too.

"Got another twenty-eight days."

"Let Cage or Dutch know ASAP. Only gonna hold a room for you so long."

Rook nodded, then said, "Might have a prospect for you."

"More the better," Judge said.

Not necessarily. Trip was hoping for quality over quantity, but he wanted to hear Rook out first. "Who?"

"One of my cellies, Dodge. Gettin' out a few days before me."

"How'd he get the name Dodge?"

"Born in the back seat of one."

Made sense. "What's he in for?"

"It matter?"

"Depends. Think he can keep his shit clean or at least under the radar? Need members who aren't spendin' months or years at a shot in shitholes like these. Need bodies, need hands, need numbers, but all of those need to be worthwhile. Get me?"

"Yeah, I get you. Thinkin' he'll fit good. Got a sled, needs a bit of work, but that's all he's got. Nothin' else. No place to land. If he got that, he should be able to stay outta places like this. Father and uncle were Shadow Warriors. They disappeared a couple years ago. He hasn't heard from either since. Two years ago, his mother was found raped, beaten and dead in a crack house. He's got no one."

"He got issues?" Trip asked.

"We all got issues," Rook muttered.

That was too damn true.

Rook continued, "He had my back in here, would like to return the favor. You give 'im a place to belong and I'll fix up his sled as soon as I get out. Think he'll be loyal and he's a good one to have at your back."

"If he's willin' to prospect for six months, then let me know when he's out. I'll get someone to come pick up his ass and get 'im settled."

Rook nodded. "You take him in, you got me."

Trip nodded. "Deal, brother."

Trip held out his palm and Rook slapped his in it and they bumped shoulders over the table making the screws shit their pants.

Trip and Rook quickly parted before one of the guards manhandled them. If one of them touched him, it might make Trip flip the fuck out, turning a productive meeting into a shit show.

Grinning, Rook turned to Judge. "I'd give you a kiss, big boy, but pepper spray makes me cry. So, I'll blow you one instead." He made kissy faces at Judge then laughed when Judge gave him the bird. "See you on the outside," he yelled as he got escorted out of the visitor center.

Chapter Seventeen

TRIP's nose nuzzled the hair by her ear. "Baby?"

She pretty much knew what was coming next. Every morning for the last three weeks, this was how he woke her up.

With sex. Then he followed it up by making her breakfast.

She had to admit, the breakfast was great. But the sex was even better.

Also, every night for the past three weeks, except for Sundays, he brought dinner to Crazy Pete's and he stayed with her until they closed the bar.

He promised to get her help soon. He also had the Amish working on the bar during the early morning hours. It was slow but it was steady.

So was the money. She had put flyers around town about the new pool and dart leagues and that alone had caused business to pick up. They also scrounged enough cash to get a used professional Karaoke machine. Once the Amish built a small stage in one corner of the bar, they'd get that up and running, too. Maybe even invite some local bands once the bar was renovated.

Also, once they got some help, he was planning on opening the bar on Sundays, getting a few large screen TVs and signing up for the sports packages. She didn't give a fuck about sports, but apparently other people did.

Imagine that.

He had some good ideas.

But she shouldn't be surprised since he'd already done so much to raise the Fury again. The man had vision and drive. No doubt about it.

"Baby?"

However, Trip waking her up this early on a Sunday, her only day off, was not one of his good ideas. "Yeah?"

"Know what today is?"

"Sunday," she moaned into the pillow. She just wanted a little more sleep. They hadn't crawled into bed until three.

Though, once she hit the mattress and his arms, she was out.

"Not just Sunday. It's Sunday Run Day."

What?

"Baby?"

He really wanted to be smothered with a pillow. "Yeah," she groaned.

"You hear me?"

"How can I not? You're talking right into my ear."

"Then you heard me."

She flopped onto her back with a sigh. "I heard you, Trip. It's Run Day Fun Day."

"That's not what I said."

"Mmm 'kay." She yawned and ran a hand over her bare breasts—he insisted they both sleep naked, not a hardship with him by her side—and down her belly. Her ribs didn't show anymore, nor did her hip bones, but she was still thinner than he wanted.

She was fine with her weight. He was not. She had

reminded him a thousand and one times, it wasn't up to him.

He disagreed.

They did not agree to disagree.

As she stretched and yawned a second time, he tugged the sheet off her. "Wanna fuck you."

She blinked and murmured, "Nothing new."

"Don't have time, though."

"Why?"

"Need to get you fed and get ready for the run."

The run.

The haze in her brain cleared and she shot up to a seated position in bed. "The run?"

He was on his side, his head propped up in his hand. "Yeah. Said you heard me."

"You're doing a club run today?"

"*We're* doin' a club run today."

She'd been on a run twice in her life. Both times as a kid with her father. Usually he had ridden alone, not even wanting Stella's mother with him.

When none of the ol' ladies were allowed on a run, that usually meant trouble. They were either going to get into it or make it. And the type of trouble just depended on where they were headed.

She couldn't imagine her father had been faithful to her mother. Stella pretty much figured out none of them had been.

But still...

Those two rides...

She could still feel the wind on her face, the air whipping her hair, the freedom she felt on the back of Pete's bike. She'd put her arms straight out on either side of her and pretend she was a bird with outstretched wings, gliding on an air stream.

Sometimes one of the other brothers would ride up next

to them really close and tease her by grabbing her fingers or tickling her palms, making her giggle.

Any problems and stress in the club seemed to disappear during those runs. Or at least it seemed that way on the two she'd been on.

"You with me?"

She turned to meet his brown eyes. "Yeah. I'm with you."

"Not just right now in bed, Stel, on my sled."

"Yes," she breathed. "I'm with you."

"You got a brain bucket?"

"No."

"You want one?"

She only thought about it for a split second. "No."

Trip grinned. "Got an extra bandanna or two if you need it. Cover your hair, your mouth. Whatever."

She had her own bandanas, just back at her apartment. "Do we have time for you to drop me off at Pete's so I can get ready? I'll head back here for breakfast as soon as I am. That'll give you time to make it and also get ready."

Most of the times, he hauled her back and forth on his sled as long as the weather was good. He didn't want her driving her Jeep.

Stella was beginning to think it was so he had control of her coming and going. If she didn't have her vehicle, she couldn't leave the farm until he decided it was time. She didn't like it and told him so.

This was the perfect excuse to bring her Jeep back with her.

"Don't like you drivin' that piece of shit."

"It's fine."

"When I can, will get you somethin' better."

"I won't need anything better if you insist on hauling my ass around all the time."

"You belong on the back of my sled, and I like haulin' your ass around."

"I don't." She lifted her palm when he began to argue. "I like being your backpack. I don't like relying on you to get me around. There's a difference. I'm not helpless."

"No one said you're helpless, baby."

"Then don't treat me like I am."

He told her time after time he wanted her in his bed every night and by picking her up at the bar and bringing her back to the farm, he got his way. If he didn't do that, he was afraid she wouldn't come out to the farm on her own. He didn't voice that, but she heard it by his actions.

He was right to worry.

She loved being in his bed, and she was beginning to love being with him, but there were times she needed to be alone. Sometimes the only alone time she got was in the middle of the day when the bar was empty.

Using the tip of his finger, he circled one of her nipples then the other, waking them up. "Still wanna fuck you, though," he whispered.

"Do we have time?" she asked, knowing they didn't.

He twisted his head to look at the ancient clock radio on his side of the bed. "Fuck."

"The sooner you drop me off, the sooner I can get back here."

"I can wait for you."

She froze mid-roll as she was getting out of bed. "I told you the plan, let's stick to it. When is everyone meeting?"

"Eleven."

"Here?"

"Yeah."

"It's nine-thirty now. It'll give me enough time to shower, pack a bag and then head back over here so we can eat before the run." She added the next to sweeten the deal. "And I'll be able to pack a bigger bag if I have my Jeep.

Clothes to change into after the run. More stuff to stash in the bathroom."

She finished getting out of bed, slipped on the clothes she had discarded in the middle of the night and faced him. He was now out of bed, completely naked and staring at her with his hands on his bare hips. And his jaw was working.

She waited for him to argue, but he didn't. He bent over, swiped his jeans off the floor and tugged them on.

He was not liking her plan. In fact, he was struggling with it.

She was not his property to control and this was a good reminder for him.

It was one thing to sleep with him, or spend time together, it was another for him to try to rule her life.

She wasn't going to have it. And if he insisted on it, this wasn't going to work.

"Trip," she said as she sat on the edge of the bed and yanked on her boots. When she was done, she glanced over her shoulder. He was still just standing there only wearing jeans. "You've got something to say?"

It probably took everything he had for him to say, "No."

Even though they promised not to lie to each other, he just told her one. Because she was damn sure he had plenty to say.

HER CHEEKS WERE WIND BURNED, maybe even a little red by the early June sun, and her ass even hurt, but she didn't care. It was to be expected after a four-hour long ride when she hadn't been on a club run in a couple of decades.

As they rode through the mountains and countryside of northern PA, that wind, that sun, the vibration of the Harley, holding onto Trip, being in a formation of roaring bikes, had lifted the weight of the world off her shoulders.

The only word for it was freeing. Totally fucking freeing.

Just like she remembered when she had ridden with her father.

She didn't catch one of the club brothers not wearing a smile or a grin. Not Dutch, who whooped and hollered for the first hour of the run. Cage. Ozzy. Judge. Deacon. Even Whip, who everyone was calling Sparky now that he wore a cut with a "prospect" rocker on the back. Mouse, aka Mickey, was another one of Dutch's mechanics sporting a prospect cut. And Dodge, a new prospect, who Deacon had picked up at prison just a couple days ago, wore the biggest smile of all.

She didn't blame him.

She also hoped Rook's release from County wasn't delayed and he got to join them on the next one. She knew of one old man who was riding at the front of the pack who would be damn happy about having his son home.

Now Rook just needed to stay out of trouble and so did Dodge. *Hell*, all of them did. Trip was right when he told her late one night that having members behind bars weakened the whole club.

With the way Trip was, Stella was sure he'd be giving his brothers a constant reminder of that. Especially if they were being stupid. That man was working too hard to have everything come crashing down around him.

But the club wasn't the only thing he was working hard on, he was working hard on her.

And he was winning.

They just needed to get some things settled between them. If they did, they'd be good.

After the last month or so, she was reminded time and time again of why she had been drawn to him in the first place when they were younger. It had been not only his confidence but the way he carried himself.

And it didn't hurt he had always been hot as fuck. Even

a young Stella had recognized it and had become totally enamored with Trip as a boy.

He was no longer a boy, though. He was definitely all man. And that confidence had only grown and matured.

Though, he fought to keep his temper under control.

It didn't worry her as much as maybe it should. He'd promised not to hurt her, and his promise was sincere. Even when he was rough with her in bed, he still constantly checked to make sure she was okay.

She always would be and encouraged him to continue because she never felt more alive than when they connected during sex.

Except for today. On the back of his bike. On this ride.

That deep, dark hole inside her was filling quickly.

And all it took was one man walking into her bar one night.

The boy who never wanted her turned into a man who did.

The formation of sleds pulled off the road into a lot in town designated for public parking. One by one, the bikes were crab-walked back into a long line, filling up multiple spots, and their rumbling engines silenced.

Trip did the same with his, backing in next to Dutch. Then Cage, as Road Captain, was the last, so he parked on the end, first in the long line.

It was a beautiful sight to see in the early evening sun. The sleds, the men, and the colors they all wore proudly.

Suddenly, Stella was overwhelmed with a sense of home. She had forgotten what this felt like. And it wasn't because the MC was back up and running, it was because of who was in that MC. The only one she didn't know was Dodge. The rest? She knew them growing up or, more recently, from around town.

Trip was relaxed and loose as he surveyed the lineup and

was turning his head to say something to her or Dutch when he went tight.

He wasn't the only one when a Ford Explorer pulled up to the end of the line where Dutch, Cage and Trip were parked, blocking them. Even though it wasn't marked like a typical police vehicle, it was easy to recognize what it was. Especially when the tinted window powered down and Chief Max Bryson's head became visible, as well as his elbow as he propped his arm on the bottom edge of the opening.

The man wasn't in uniform but his demeanor and his dark sunglasses, which hid his beautiful crystal blue eyes, had cop written all over both.

This did not make any of the guys smile.

"Max," Dutch greeted gruffly with a chin lift.

"Dutch." Max gave him an answering nod. "What's going on?"

"Just out for a ride to enjoy the beautiful spring weather."

Max's head turned, taking in the line of bikes, which Stella noted would only get longer in the future as the club grew. "Yeah?"

"Yeah," Dutch answered, still sitting on his fully-dressed Road King. "Ain't doin' nothin' that needs your attention."

"Hope not." Max aimed his sunglasses at Trip. "You're the one who decided to start all this shit up again?"

Stella was pretty sure the Chief knew that info already. She didn't know Max to be a dick, even though he policed Manning Grove with a pretty tight fist.

Since she was still plastered to Trip's back—now on purpose to help keep his temper in check—she knew the second he went from tense to wired. "Not illegal."

"Didn't say it was. Knew your granddaddy well. Good man. But my grandfather and my pop both had to deal with your father and his kind. They passed down some stories—"

Dutch cut him off. "We've shared some of those stories, Max. I've also made peace with Ron."

Max turned his sights on Dutch. "You think my pop won't have a problem with the Fury being resurrected?"

"Ron's retired. He should just be enjoyin' his grandbabies."

"Ever think having the Fury active again might worry him because of those very grandbabies?"

When Trip said, "Tell 'im he's got nothin' to worry about," it pulled Max's attention back to him.

And her, apparently. The deep frown Max was wearing loosened. "Hey, Stella."

"Chief."

Max's lip twitched but not enough for a smile. "You know you don't have to call me that."

No, she didn't and normally wouldn't, but she was making a point. He might not be in uniform but as chief, he was on-call twenty-four-seven and this could be harassment if anyone pushed it. Even so, she kept her answer in a light, teasing tone, "You make Marc and Matt call you that."

Max laughed dryly. "Just to bust their balls."

She liked all the Brysons. They were decent people. And she couldn't imagine they'd judge Trip or the rest of the BFMC unfairly. They occasionally came into the bar and they used to hang out there all the time when her father was alive and before the three Bryson brothers had wives and children.

They never had a problem with Pete, and they knew he was former BFMC. But then, he had no longer been wearing colors by the time Max, Matt and Marc were not only old enough to drink but had come home from the Marines.

"What are you all doing in town?" Max asked.

Before Trip could answer, Stella did. "We went on a long

run to enjoy the day. Now we're all hungry so we're hitting up Dino's."

Trip answered anyway, which Stella was hoping to avoid. "Can't come into town? When tax time rolls around, I'll be payin' my fair share. And since I will be, means we got every right to come into town."

"Like I said, your granddaddy was a good man. Hope you took after him more than your father."

Stella gave Trip a squeeze when he took a deep breath. He was winding up to let loose, and they needed to stay on Max's good side.

If they kept shit cool, Max would eventually see the Fury wasn't there to make trouble. That Trip was building a brotherhood, not a gang of heathens.

And Stella hoped to hell that was true. He needed to be careful on who he accepted amongst their ranks because it could get ugly really quick. And they did not need a repeat of history.

"You should bring Amanda out to Pete's for a beer, Max. First round on me. Haven't seen you in ages."

"Heard you're making changes."

"Sure am. For the better."

"Good to hear." Max's jaw worked a couple of times as he stared at her and Trip, which Stella pretty much figured was him sizing up Trip and also wondering why Stella was on the back of Trip's bike. But in the end, he only gave them a nod and put the Explorer into Drive.

"We good?" Dutch asked the chief.

"We're good," Max answered, "as long as I don't hear about any trouble."

"If you do, it won't be from us," Dutch assured him.

Stella hoped to hell that remained true, too.

"I'll hold you to that," Max said as he gave Dutch a nod and drove away.

Once the Explorer pulled out of the lot and down Main

Street in the opposite direction of Dino's Diner, everyone began to breathe a bit easier.

"Ready for grub?" Ozzy yelled.

"Fuck yeah," came from the guys as they dismounted from their sleds and headed toward the diner.

It was time to grub, and Stella was surprisingly hungry.

Must be all that fresh air, sunlight and having her arms wrapped around Trip.

Chapter Eighteen

Trip's fingers flexed in Stella's long, loose hair as her mouth pistoned his dick.

Jesus Fuck. He was going to lose it and he wanted to fuck her yet.

Hell, he'd wanted to fuck her all day. From the moment they'd woken up this morning to the whole time she was plastered to him on his sled during the run, and even watching her eat a huge slice of Dino's famous Death by Chocolate cake.

He'd been drawn to her mouth every time she lifted her fork, opened it, and slid that moist cake between her lips, before licking off any remaining icing caught in the corners.

Those same lips currently circled his cock and were about to suck him dry.

He did not want to nut in her mouth. At least not this time. No, he'd been waiting all fucking day to fuck her and that's what he was going to do.

But, *fuck*, could she suck.

His fingers twitched and his hips bucked a little when she squeezed the root so hard, the veins bulged. But when she began to stroke him with her tight hand as well as her wet, hot mouth, he had to cry mercy.

"Baby," he groaned, tugging at her hair.

All she did was tip her light blue eyes up to him in response.

"Baby," he groaned again, a little louder this time. "Not blowin' in your mouth. Need to stop."

With one last slide down and back up, she released the head of his dick with a wet pop.

Her face was flushed, her lips shiny, and her eyes held a promise that his nuts would be empty soon anyway as she went to her hands and knees.

Her tits were fuller now than when he first saw them and there was enough to not only catch his attention, but swing as she moved up his body, stopping when her knees were lined up with his hips.

It was then when he knew exactly what he wanted. Without unlocking their gazes, he reached out, slapped his hand blindly around the nightstand until he found a wrap, tucked it between his teeth and tore it open.

As he brought it down to roll it on, she snagged it from his fingers, and did it for him. Even better, she did it slowly while caressing him, even palming his heavy, aching balls for a few seconds.

"Stella," he pushed from his throat. "Baby."

She said nothing. Her lips were parted, her breathing ragged. And he knew she wouldn't be quiet for long. The noises she made when he fucked her drove him nuts. Loud. Soft. Whimpers. Cries. Screams. Curses. He loved it all.

But there was nothing like driving into and having her buck beneath him as she called out his name. To feel her nails digging deep, her lips along his skin, her teeth leaving marks.

Best fucking thing in the world.

But as she grabbed his dick and held it still, rose to her

knees and positioned herself, he had a feeling her riding his cock where he could watch her every move, every expression, would come in at a close second.

Though, he hadn't had her ass yet.

Not yet.

That could end up being one of his top three.

However, he wasn't in a rush and could wait until she was ready. They had plenty of time for that. If it was up to him, they'd have forever.

Not to take her ass, but for the two of them.

He was ready to claim her at the table. He wanted no other woman in his bed. No other woman to be standing by his side. He didn't want to make breakfast for anyone else but her.

She was his.

He was hers.

He just needed to settle a few things with her before he took it to the executive committee.

The biggest one being her cooperation.

The next being, getting things clear about what the two of them expected from each other for the future.

One thing he wanted, she'd already had and lost.

And if she said no to his request, he wasn't sure if that would be a breaking point for him. It might be, but he couldn't imagine having kids with anyone else.

That meant Stella needed to agree or he might not get everything he wanted. He wouldn't get everything in the vision he'd created for himself.

He'd need to make sure he could live with that. So, they would have to have that conversation.

But not right now.

Right now, Stella was pumping his dick with her hand while she tucked the throbbing head between those plump, slick lips of hers and began lowering herself down.

Again, way too fucking slowly.

But when that warm, smooth glove surrounded him, squeezed him, rippled around him, he didn't care that she was taking her time, going slow. He was just happy it was her.

The woman who got under his skin the moment he saw her in Crazy Pete's.

It had never been like that with anybody else. Just Stella.

If any other woman had resisted him like she did, he would've just shrugged and walked away. To him, snatch was snatch.

But Stella was in no way just snatch.

Never would be.

"Trip," she breathed, her hands planted on his chest. "You with me?"

He almost laughed because it was something he normally asked her. But what she was doing to him made laughing impossible.

She was riding his dick slow and steady. Every time she hit bottom, she rocked forward and back, her body bowing, her expression showing nothing but ecstasy. His might be showing the same.

But he didn't care, he wanted her to see how he was with her. How much he enjoyed being inside her, with her, around her.

The weight she was giving him from her palms planted on his chest lifted, and she brushed them over his nipples, making the tips harden like hers.

Crazy but true, women hardly ever paid attention to his nipples. Also crazy but true, when they did, he found he liked that attention.

But he never asked for it. Just like he didn't now.

Instead, every play she did with his, he mirrored on hers. Even though her mouth was slack as she continued to ride him slowly, he caught when her eyes flared and the corners of her lips tipped up slightly.

Whatever she gave him, he'd give it right back.

Whether it was the lightest touch or the most painful twist. A hard pinch or her fingers feathering along his skin.

The game quickly stopped when she fell to his chest, sucking one of his nipples into her mouth.

His chest rose and a groan rolled deep from his belly before he could stop it.

His fingers buried into her hair as she worked one nipple and then the other. Flicking and then scoring each one with her teeth.

Fuck.

Fuck.

Fuck.

His balls were pulled tight and it wouldn't take much more for him to blow. And he wanted her to come at least once more before he did.

Because he couldn't get enough of her.

And if he came now, he wouldn't have had enough. Not yet.

But he also couldn't tell her to stop since he was having a hard time forming his thoughts into words. So, he yanked roughly on her hair and when she gasped, he broke her mouth free from his now sensitive flesh.

Using her hair, he jerked her up, her hands grasping his arms for balance as she continued to rise and fall, not once breaking her rhythm. He kept pulling until her head dropped back far enough to arch both her back and her neck, exposing the delicate line of her throat and those tits he was about to worship.

Curling up from his waist, he kept his hands tightly fisted in her long black hair, as he sank his teeth at the side of her throat, scraping them down her pounding pulse, pausing only for a second to suck at the hollow before using his teeth to score each nipple. One. The other. Tucking one hard tip between his teeth, causing her breathing to stop as well as her movement.

With her hair still held prisoner and that delicate, vulnerable tip held hostage, he gently scissored his teeth back and forth, feeling her whole body begin to tremble. Her pussy squeezed and released, squeezed and released, as she circled her hips only enough to grind down on his dick. Her subtle attempt at taking back control.

But he was done with that.

He had let her have what he wanted her to have. Now he would take them both where he wanted them to be.

He unlocked his jaw, releasing the tip, then sucked as much of her into his mouth as he could. Keeping one hand buried in her hair, he dropped his other arm to wrap it around her hips, then began to thrust up.

He moved his mouth up from her swollen, wet nipple back to her throat, burying his face there, sucking her skin as she moved faster, slamming herself down on him every time he powered up.

Her whimpers filled his ears.

"Come, baby. Let me feel you soak me," he grunted against her neck, using her hips to jerk her down as he drove up even harder.

So fucking deep.

So fucking wet.

He couldn't wait until there was nothing between them. Until when he came, he filled her. So when he pulled out, something of him would remain. A reminder of who she belonged to.

Of who he belonged to.

Because she might not know it yet, but she held him just as tightly as he did her.

"Give me you," he demanded, pulling a whimper and a shudder from her. "Give me everything."

"Trip," came out on a shaky breath.

Her body tightened and arced as she drove down one more time and he met her there at the bottom.

She convulsed intensely around him, making him lose his fucking mind.

Because that's what he was, lost.

Inside of her.

But he was also found.

The pressure inside him exploded as he latched onto her neck, coming deep, his dick twitching, his breathing labored.

And even though he stilled as he rode that high, she slowly and gracefully continued to rise and fall. Her pussy squeezing, milking every last drop from him.

She not only gave him everything, she took everything from him, too.

He was okay with that.

No. More than okay. Everything finally seemed right in his world.

His future set.

Now more determined than ever to remain on the path which was clear to him.

With the club, the businesses and Stella.

He needed to stake his claim on his woman at the next meeting because he was never fucking letting her go.

Never.

At fifteen he was too young and clueless to see it.

At thirty-five, he saw it as plain as day.

His woman.

His ol' lady.

His partner.

The mother of his children.

His. Queen.

"Today was a good fuckin' day."

It was late, she was half asleep, but he was right. It was the best fucking day. She couldn't deny it.

"The ride was nice," she murmured, her eyes still closed. Her ass was sore from the long ride. Her nipples were a bit tender from his teeth and mouth, and her pussy a little worn out, but satisfied, from all the pounding. Not only from when she was on top, but from when he was ready to hit it again twenty minutes later.

Trip might be in his mid-thirties, but she swore he had a libido of an eighteen-year-old.

She voiced no complaints about that. Thirties were sexual prime time for a woman. She just never expected to find someone to explore that time with. Nor had she been looking.

But *he* found *her*.

"Havin' you on my sled, bein' surrounded by my brothers, was more than nice."

"I was surprised you wanted me to come along." And that was true since she was the only female on the ride. She figured the club's first run together would be used as bonding time for the guys, to solidify their new brotherhood.

"Was makin' a statement."

She didn't need to ask it because she already knew the answer, but she asked it anyway. "Which was?"

"Who you belong to."

She pursed her lips. Her being on the back of his bike was definitely a statement, she couldn't deny it. She knew it when she climbed on and wrapped her arms around him. But still... "I wasn't wearing your cut."

"Not yet."

That was a line she wasn't sure she wanted to cross. Because the minute she slipped on a "Property of Trip" cut that's exactly what she became. Property. However, she saw the way things were headed, especially when she knew he'd claim her in front of the rest of the committee, that was the direction this was going anyway.

She had tried to ignore it. But it was getting to the point where she couldn't ignore it anymore. Trip would want to push on, claiming her and making her untouchable to the rest of his brothers.

Hell, to any other man.

Or at least that was supposed to be how it worked. Though, that was one of the reasons the Fury imploded in the first place. The biggest reason. Not only because Trip's father cheated on his ol' lady, which was common amongst the Originals, but because he slept with Sig's mother. And not just once, either. When the truth was discovered, it had been going on for years. *Years*. Like a dozen or so. Stella had no idea how they got away with it for so long.

It always seemed that when a brother claimed an ol' lady, it meant she was to remain loyal to her ol' man. But her ol' man? He didn't follow the same rules. The problem only came about between Buck and Razor because Silvia was Razor's ol' lady. And while bikers didn't care if another brother cheated on his ol' lady, they had a huge problem if he cheated with one of theirs.

Total fucking hypocrites.

But that was the way of the MC. She also did not want to live that. Where Trip was her one and only and she had to watch him getting whatever whenever from whoever.

She refused to live that life. She was also not going to let him rule her life, either.

If she ever committed to a man again, it would be fifty-fifty. She was not a doormat for a man to wipe his dirty boots on.

Not now. Not ever.

"Are you going to push this? Because if you are, I'm going to push back."

He rolled into her, crowding her with his presence. "Not

gonna push shit. Want you there. But want you to wanna be there. Hopin' you see it's where you belong."

Being on the back of Trip's sled felt right. Once again, that warm feeling of home swept through her like it had earlier during the run.

Born into the Fury, maybe it *was* where she belonged. Had fate brought her full circle?

That warmth in her belly suddenly mixed with uncertainty because it wouldn't take much for things to go badly. Like it had when their fathers were wearing those same cuts the guys wore today.

That unsureness and worry pushed away that warmth. But her gut turned to a block of ice with his next question.

"Would you have another one?"

Shit. She could hardly inhale enough air to ask, "One what?"

His palm slid from where it was settled possessively over the *S* pendant lying between her breasts to her belly. Right where her scars were. Right where her stretch marks were. Right where she nurtured her own baby while he grew inside her.

"Kid."

Her heart began to pound in her ears. Why was he doing this now? They'd had a good day. A perfect day full of sun, smiles and laughter. Why was he bringing the darkness into the night? "I... don't know."

"Want a son."

Stella moved her hand to settle next to his, not touching, but close, as she remembered her stretched belly, the moment Kade was placed on her chest with his umbilical cord still attached. The first time he latched on and nursed. When he ate his first solid food. When he said his first word. When he first said, "Momma." When he first stood, first walked. First rode a bike without training wheels. His first skinned knee she kissed. The tears—both hers and his—on the first day of kindergarten.

When he caught his first fish with his father on the shore of the Susquehanna River. A Sunny. But she would have thought it was a fifty-pound tuna with how big his smile was. How big his father's smile was.

All of those memories so precious. Priceless.

While she was glad she had those, she was also sad she no longer had new ones to store away. And never would. That opportunity had been ripped from her.

Even so, she never wanted to replace Kade. Never. He'd always own her heart. And not just a piece of it, either.

"I'm not sure I can give you that."

"Truth is, want more than one. And I need to put that out there, baby. You need to think about that."

Her chest was becoming tight, the pressure beginning to crush her. He was asking too much, too soon.

"I don't know if I can wear your cut, Trip. I don't know if I can give you sons. I don't know if I can give you what you want. And if I can't and you still claim me, anyway... And then you go elsewhere to get what I can't give you..." She rubbed at the crushing weight in her chest which had turned into an ache.

He rolled enough to put his own weight on her, which made her feel even more suffocated. In the dark, his fingers found her jawline and spread along her cheek. And when he talked, his breath meshed with hers. "Sons or no sons, Stella, I'm not goin' anywhere else. It's somethin' I want. Somethin' I've always wanted. But..." Air rushed over her cheek. "But that's not gonna change the way I feel about you."

Until later. Months, maybe years, when he realized he sacrificed something he wanted, something important to him, just to have her.

When he realized she hadn't been worth giving up that dream.

When he became bitter and blamed her.

When another woman showed up with a son who looked just like Trip.

That would destroy her.

Totally fucking destroy her.

She wanted to ask how he felt about her. No, not ask. Demand an answer.

Because she needed to know.

She also didn't want to know.

He had broken her heart all those years ago, the day he split open her head.

She wasn't sure she had a piece of her heart left to give him.

She was worried the little she did have, it wouldn't take much to rip it right back out of her chest.

He'd been the one filling her darkness with some light. But he could also be the one to extinguish it.

And she wasn't ready to give him all that power.

She wasn't sure she could give him everything he wanted.

So, while yes, today had been a great day, now she knew this night would not be the same.

"You can't do this, Stella, fuckin' tell me now. Because I am not goin' to catch your ass in bed with another man. Fuckin' tellin' you right now, you're either with me or you're not. I need to know."

He just said nothing would change the way he felt about her, but maybe what he felt wasn't what she thought.

She could hear the heat in his words when he growled, "Need a solid answer, Stel. Either with me or you're not. Told Rook he's either in or he's out. Nothin' half-assed. Tellin' you the same thing. Don't have the fuckin' time or patience for games."

And she did? She wasn't playing games. She just

couldn't make a decision like that. Not now, not yet. "Why can't we continue as we are?"

What was wrong with what they currently had? Why did he have to push her?

He jerked against her, his fingertips digging into her cheek. Not enough to be painful, but enough to make her very aware his temper was rising. "Continue what? Us fuckin'? Me gettin' your ass out of a jam? That all you want? To use me?"

Use him. That was the last thing she wanted to do. But she also didn't want to feel used.

She needed to shut this down because her own blood was now at a simmer and it wouldn't take much to bring it to a boil. And that would get neither of them anywhere. Any major decisions needed to be made with a clear head. "I'm done talking about this, Trip. I can't give you an answer right now. And if you can't accept that..." She let that hang.

He released her and rolled away, giving her his back. "Then you sleep on it. But I need an answer soon."

She stared at that back and even in the dark her eyes could see the club's colors permanently inked into his skin, permanently a part of him.

She reached out to trace them with her fingers, but before she made contact, she balled those fingers into a fist and dropped her hand to the bed instead.

The Tree of Life had meaning for her, it's why she had it done, just like those colors had meaning for him.

But did they mean the same to her?

Being with Trip would mean being a part of the club. And she wasn't sure she was willing to be a part of it, too, especially with what she knew was involved. Being BFMC as a girl had not been the best experience, and not only did he want her to be involved, he wanted her to have his children and involve them, too.

He wanted her to sleep on it.
But for her, sleep became impossible to find.

Chapter Nineteen

Trip used his key to get into the rear door of Crazy Pete's. He locked it behind him, took long, *fuck-this-shit* strides down the short, dark hallway, slammed the swinging door to the store room with both palms, making it crash into the wall behind it. He was through it and at the bottom of the stairway before it violently swung the other direction with a loud whoosh.

He took the stairs two at a time, the muscles in his jaw so tight, they were popping.

The second he woke up. The second he rolled over. The goddamn second he noticed the bed was empty.

The second he knew somehow her piece of shit Jeep traveling down the rough lane hadn't woken him up.

That *very fucking second* he knew he'd lost her.

He had pushed the kid thing before he should have. But he'd needed to know. He needed to know where she stood on it.

He should have let it lie. He didn't and now he was going to pay for his impatience.

He should have waited until after the meeting, until after

the vote on making Stella his ol' lady. Until after she was permanently moved into his house.

Until she was a solid part of his life. Of *their* life.

Then he could have gradually worked on her. Showed her life could be good again. Life could be complete.

Showed her that he'd have plenty to offer her and their kids, if they had them.

Once she saw the businesses, both the bar and the motel, as well as the repo business, were successful, so that she and their kids would want for nothing.

Once he proved his fucking loyalty to her.

Once the club was crawling with sweet butts and female hang-arounds and she'd see he only had eyes for her.

But fuck no.

He had fucked up.

And now he had to pay.

Those steps they'd taken forward in the last month? He'd undone it all in a matter of minutes and now he'd stumbled twice as many steps backward.

She had scars.

Not just the one on her scalp he'd given her.

Not just the one on her belly her pregnancy had caused.

But the loss of her son had scarred her deeply. And irrevocably.

So deeply, Trip didn't know how to handle such pain. Because no matter how much he tried to imagine that pain, he knew he couldn't.

He wanted to hand her the fucking world. Even if it was their own small world. But instead he had handed her some hurt.

He didn't mean to. But he wasn't sure how to deal with it.

Because as much as she hurt, she also needed to live her life. He needed to live his. And he was trying to build *their* world together.

However, her fucking sneaking out of the house in the middle of the night, or the early morning, while he was zonked out, pissed him the fuck off.

That was not how they were going to deal with shit.

Not by running away.

Not by hiding.

Not by curling into a ball in the corner.

Or putting their arms over their heads, hoping it all went away.

Because it wouldn't. It simply wouldn't go away.

It was something they needed to deal with head on.

At the top of the steps, he paused at the door and pressed his forehead to it, his breath beating violently against the wood. After a moment, he closed his eyes, sucked in a deep breath, held it as his pulse pounded in his ears, and counted to five. While he did so, memories assaulted him.

One.

Him so pissed and shoving Stella so hard she split her head open on a wall. But it was the look in her eyes after it happened... The surprise. The betrayal. The disappointment. *Fuck.*

Two.

Buck and Pete kicking his ass so badly, he couldn't walk for a couple days. He didn't beg them to stop because of that look she gave him... He knew he deserved what they did to him.

Three.

His father splayed on his stomach naked on the bed, bleeding out from being shot point-blank in the back. He had broken everyone's trust. And trust was huge in a brotherhood.

Four.

His mother quickly packing their bags and taking off in

the middle of the night, not only leaving his best friend behind but also everything and everyone he'd ever known.

Five.

Finding out too late his best friend was actually his brother. When he finally tried to get a hold of Sig, he was gone.

Trip slowly released his held breath, his boiling blood now at a simmer.

It wasn't their choice to scatter. They all were forced into it.

All Trip wanted to do was take the broken pieces of the club and make it whole again. To repair what had been shattered.

It had been his burning desire. To have something that was his.

To build something worthwhile.

To give him a reason to continue. A reason to stay out of jail. A reason to rise up and move forward.

He was doing what he set out to do.

He hadn't started this journey with the intent to have a woman by his side. He could still do it without her.

He could.

But he didn't want to.

He refused to.

Everything had gone full circle.

Which, to him, meant it was meant to be.

So, he was not going to let her run away from him, from the club, from the only people left who she could call family.

She needed them as much as they needed her.

Maybe she needed them all a little more right now. For support. But eventually they may need to lean on her. That was what family was for.

That was what a *real* family, not necessarily made up of blood, was for.

A give and take.

Those who stuck around through the highs and the lows.

Those who could fight one minute, then laugh the next.

This wasn't Buck's club anymore. This wasn't Buck's family, either.

It was fucking Trip's.

And, *goddamn it*, Stella was a part of it.

His fingers curled around the doorknob. But before he could turn it, before he could see if she'd locked him out, it turned.

He straightened as it opened.

The apartment wasn't lit. The limited light came from the couple windows that faced the back alley. But it was bright enough for him to read her expression.

Which made him want to puke.

He had lost her.

He had done something stupid again.

And now he was going to pay.

The dark circles under her eyes, her drawn face, her pale skin.

She hadn't slept.

She probably hadn't eaten, either.

She was retreating. Escaping to that dark place that had consumed her in the past and cutting him out.

That was not going to work for Trip.

If she couldn't do this with him, if she couldn't do this for them, then she needed to tell him that to his face. Not run away, refusing to deal with it.

"Tell me to fuck off, Stella. Tell me to my face. Tell me how I'm not good enough for you. Or how I'm not good *for* you. Tell me how much I remind you of your first husband. How you think I'll be just like him and let you the fuck down. Tell me how you're worried that I'll fuck up your life and make it impossible for you to live it. Tell me how I'll destroy everything for you. Need you to tell me all that to my face. Need to hear it from you, not just read it in your face."

His stomach was so twisted, his chest in pain. And the need to puke was only getting stronger.

This was killing him.

If she told him to fuck off, he would respect that and walk away. They would remain partners in the bar, but that would be it. But if that happened, he knew it would be harder than him doing six years in the joint.

Giving up on Stella would be harder than doing goddamn time. And doing time sucked ass.

It took everything he had not to fall to his knees when he whispered, "Talk to me."

Her expression twisted and she turned away from him to hide it, which gave him the opportunity to move past her and into the apartment. He shut the door with his boot, keeping his eyes on her.

He stayed by the door, watching as her shoulders rounded forward, as her head dropped, as she kept her back to him.

Hiding.

"Perseverance." He let that single, but powerful, word fill the quiet apartment. Let it engulf them for a moment. "That word means to not give up. You're givin' up. You should have that tattoo fuckin' covered up, Stella. You don't deserve it."

It was harsh. He knew it. It cut him deep, too. But he needed her to talk to him. And if he had to push her to do it, he would. Because without talking, they'd never move forward. Not together. Not apart. They'd remain in limbo.

And that was not a good place to be, for either one of them.

"I don't know if I can do this." Her strained answer tore through him.

Fuck. He dug deep to ask, "Do what?" She needed to say it. He needed to hear it no matter how painful it would be.

"This... Us."

Bile bubbled up from his gut, but he kept his mouth shut and, as difficult as it was, gave her time to say her piece.

She turned toward him, and even in the limited light he could see her eyes were shiny, her expression tortured. He probably looked the same. Because he sure as fuck felt like it.

She threw a hand out. "It's been three weeks since you went up that mountain and I still can't stop thinking about the tow truck and how it looked. The cuts on your back and neck, Trip. Not only how dangerous that job is, but how dangerous being in an MC can be. Look what happened to your father. He was fucking shot in the back." Her words caught on a sob.

Her being upset gave him a sliver of hope. That meant she felt something for him. That she worried about him. The same as he did for her.

He hadn't said it out loud because he wanted to make sure she felt the same before he did. There was no fucking way he was telling her how much he loved her without her not returning that love. There was no fucking way he was going to rip himself open and sacrifice himself if she wasn't willing to do the same.

But he needed to assure her of one thing. His loyalty. "Don't plan on gettin' caught with my dick in someone else's ol' lady. Or, hell, any other woman. Stella, it would be you and you only. Trust me on that."

He remembered what it felt like to find another man fucking his wife. He'd never want her to feel that betrayal. That disappointment. That fury.

"You know it's more than that. There always is with an MC. This isn't some tennis club or bowling league, Trip. This. Is. A. Fucking. Motorcycle. Club. This is serious shit."

She wrapped her arms around her stomach, squeezing, like she was feeling just as sick as him.

Like her stomach had also been carved out with a spoon.

"I know what the fuck it is. But it's a family first and foremost, Stella. Family. Got that?"

"Family that can turn on each other in a blink of an eye. Family who likes to party, get drunk, carry guns and knives. A group of alpha males who beat their chest thinking they're invincible and can get triggered easily into violence. One wrong word. One wrong move. We've seen it. You. Me. Sig. Judge. Rook. All of us. We witnessed what can happen. We were a part of it. We were the fallout. There's no guarantee that won't happen again. No guarantee you won't end up dead. I just can't... I can't..."

She was right, he couldn't give her that guarantee. "We all die eventually."

She squeezed her eyes shut and shuddered. "You did not just say that."

"Yeah, I did, baby, because it's true. We can't live our lives worried what *may* happen, because then we're not livin' it. You get that?"

"I can't lose any more, Trip. As fucked up as he was, I lost my husband. Twice. I lost my father. Even though she's still alive, I lost my mother." She sucked in a shaky breath. "I lost *my son.* My blood. The boy I carried for nine months inside me. The boy I loved the second I saw those two little red lines on the test stick. The boy I protected and loved for eight years." She lifted her head and a tear rolled unchecked down her cheek. But she met his eyes and held fast this time. "I lost him. I can't bear to lose any more... Including you."

Including you.

Holy fuck, those two words...

They stood only six feet apart, but it seemed like a mile. With a couple long strides, he closed the gap and didn't stop until his body hit hers and he wrapped his arms around her, holding her tight, wanting to absorb her, to absorb her pain. To protect her from the past. Protect her from the future.

He realized he couldn't do that for her. She had to do that on her own. But he'd damn well help as much as he could.

"I can't give you everything I have left to only lose you. Whether it's by burying you or watching you end up with another woman when you finally realize I can't give you everything you want or need."

His throat was tight when he said into her hair, "Can't lose you, either, baby. That's why I'm here. Will give you everything I have, everything I am, just to make you happy. But you have to want it, too. Have to reach for it, not push it away. If you ain't ready, then you ain't ready. Just tell me to fuck off, Stella." *Goddamn it.* "Just say it. I'll walk out that fuckin' door behind me because I'm movin' my life forward, not gonna get stuck in place, not gonna go backward. Movin' forward and want you to be there with me. You can't, you can't." He swallowed hard, trying to rid the lump stuck in his throat. "Tell me to fuck off."

Every second that ticked by seemed like an eternity. Every second she said nothing killed him a little more.

"Tell me to fuck off, Stel," he whispered.

For fuck's sake, just do it and let me go.

Her arms snaked under his cut and wrapped tightly around his waist. "I can't do it," came smothered from his shirt.

He closed his eyes and went solid. She was letting him go.

"I can't tell you to fuck off."

Oh Christ. Thank fuck.

She lifted her face from his shirt and said again, louder this time, "I can't tell you to fuck off."

He combed his fingers through her hair, moving it out of her face, so he could see her clearly. "Why, baby?"

Her hands twisted tightly in his T-shirt at the small of his back. "Because I don't want you to walk out that door. I can't let you go."

His voice caught as he asked again, "Why, baby?"

Her light blue eyes hit his and held. "Because somehow I fell in love with you. No..." She shook her head.

Trip's heart pounded in his chest. But as hard as it was, he waited.

"No. I've always been in love with you. Even when I didn't understand it. Even after you pushed me away. Back then, I knew you were mine. That you'd always be mine. You couldn't see it. And after that day... *that day*... I thought I was wrong. I'd made a mistake. I was just a stupid young girl with a foolish dream."

"No, baby, it was my mistake. And now I see what you saw back then. That you belonged to me. That you'd always be mine. You're right, I didn't see it then. Took me twenty fuckin' years to find you again, to prove you were right and I was wrong. And here we are. If you're not gonna tell me to fuck off, what are you tellin' me? 'Cause it's all or nothin', Stella. I want it all. Hopin' you want it all, too."

"I don't know if I can give you it all. But I can try."

Fuck, that sounded good. "Perseverance, baby. That's all I can ask for."

"Perseverance. I'll promise to give you that."

He closed his eyes and pulled her against him even tighter. "We can build from there."

Suddenly he felt whole. Not only had he made his father's cut his by making Buck's club his, but his woman was tucked against him, that very cut wrapped around her just like his arms. Those colors would represent and protect them. Those colors would be their future. Their kids' future.

Even so, this wasn't over. They couldn't live easy yet.

They had a lot of hard work in front of them. All of them did.

But in the end, that hard work would pay off.

In the end, they'd have something so solid no one could rip it apart. Not from the inside, not from the outside.

Those thoughts weren't just about the club, they were also about him and Stella.

"We'll take it day by day, baby. But every night need you to lay your head next to mine, every mornin' need you to wake up by my side. You walk beside me and support me and I swear to fuck I'll do the same for you. But need one more thing..."

She tipped her face up to him. "What's that? To wear your cut? To let you claim me?"

"More important than any of that."

When her brow furrowed, he realized she thought he was going to bring up his desire to have sons again. That wasn't what this was about. He smoothed a thumb over it, then he ripped himself open. "Need you to love me as much as I love you. Might not tell you on a regular basis, but you'll know it if you let yourself feel it. Know I'm askin' a lot from you—"

One of her hands slipped from under his cut to wrap around the back of his head as she tugged his face closer to hers. "You aren't asking for anything more than what I'd ask from you. I do love you, Trip, that's why I worried—"

"No worries," he said before sliding his lips over hers, stopping her words. "Takin' it day by day."

"Okay," she whispered against his lips. "Day by day. Some days will be worse than others."

"Yeah. And I'll be there for those, too. Just don't shut me out."

"Okay."

"Okay," he echoed, relieved, and smiled against her lips. "Love you, baby."

"Love you, too, Trip."

Best words he'd ever heard in his fucking life.

Best feeling he ever had, right after feeling the sun on his face the second he stepped out of prison.

Today, the sun was shining on his face and he would do his best to keep it there.

Epilogue

SUN ON HIS FACE

Stella headed his way, carrying two beers, her narrow hips swinging and a relaxed expression on her face.

They were sort of celebrating.

Not that his brothers needed a reason to party.

They'd just had their second club run this afternoon, someone had gotten a pig from one of the local Amish farms, and now there wasn't much left of it in the smoker that sat right outside the newly built pavilion.

The pig had literally been torn to shreds. One of the picnic tables that sat under the metal roof of that pavilion was overflowing with a whole bunch of food, plasticware, and the rest of the shit needed to eat, drink and fucking be merry.

Not every day was a good fucking day, but this one was and he'd take every good day they could get.

The early July weather cooperated. The club was growing. Even if slowly.

And, best of all, today Stella donned her "Property of Trip" cut for the first time. He'd given it to her a couple weeks ago after the last executive meeting where there had been no opposition to the vote on making her his ol' lady.

She said she'd only wear it for the runs and he was fine with that.

But as she approached, she still wore it, which made him smile.

Even if the reason she kept it on was most likely to make it clear to the other women around the courtyard Trip belonged to her.

Because that was how it was. *He* belonged to *her*. Every fucking cell in his body was Stella's.

He was leaning against one of the pavilion's posts, smoking a hand-rolled and surveying the whole courtyard. Right now, it just included the pavilion with mismatched old and new picnic tables and chairs, the smoker, and a half dozen fifty-five-gallon drums scattered around the area, all burning high, creating pockets of light amongst the dark.

Maybe one day they'll build a stage and dig a large pit for a bonfire just like the Dirty Angels had at theirs.

Baby steps. He needed to remind himself of that because there were days that went to total shit for him.

Complete and total shit.

There was so much pressure on his shoulders that sometimes it got overwhelming and swallowed him up before spitting him out. Sometimes it was Stella who had to pick him back up, brush him off and encourage him to continue with a hard kick to the ass.

One of those times, she'd insisted, "You've helped me. Let me help you."

Another time she said, "If you need to lean on me, I'm here."

"You don't know how much hearin' that means to me, baby," he told her. Because it was so damn true.

She saw his vision. She was helping make it come to being.

They all were. Rook, Judge, Ozzy, Dutch, Cage, Deacon,

Sparky, Mouse, and Dodge. And now the newest prospect, Shady.

Word was spreading about the Fury's resurrection and just last week, the man showed up on his doorstep wanting to be part of something that made them much greater as a whole than as an individual.

Judge had given Shady his nickname because the man didn't say much and was a bit withdrawn. Most of the time, he only spoke when spoken to.

Trip didn't have a problem with it, but it spooked Judge. Especially since they didn't know his whole story. Not yet anyway. But then they all had their secrets. As long as it didn't fuck with the club or shake the brotherhood, Shady was welcome to keep them.

But the man already was proving to be a hard worker and immediately set out in helping Ozzy renovate The Grove Inn. Again, like Crazy Pete's, another vision that was slow to come to fruition—because it took scratch to make scratch—but would be worth it in the end.

While everybody tonight was chasing the pussy that had shown up—all except for Dutch, though the old man was certainly not keeping his eyes or thoughts to himself—Shady was just observing. If any of the women approached him—and he had certainly grabbed their attention—he'd simply give them a chin lift but didn't encourage contact.

For a moment it made Trip wonder if Shady wasn't into women and if that might cause a problem with the rest of the brothers. But if the prospect proved himself, Trip didn't give a fuck who the man liked to stick his dick into. That was between Shady, his dick and whoever was taking it.

But Trip wasn't sure that was it—

"Hey," Stella whispered, interrupting his thoughts and holding out his beer.

"Hey, baby," he murmured, pinching the end of his

partially smoked hand-rolled and tucking it away. She didn't like him smoking around her, so he tried to avoid it.

He accepted the beer and took a long pull before hooking her around the waist and pulling her against him, her back to his chest, her legs sandwiched between his. "I tell you you look fuckin' hot in that cut?"

She grinned up at him. "Heard it a few times."

"I tell you you'll be wearin' that cut and only that fuckin' cut when I'm makin' you come with my name on your lips later?"

"I might have heard that, too."

"Might need to fuck you doggy-style so I can read that cut while you take my dick."

"Sounds super romantic, Trip."

He grinned, tipping the bottle to his lips. "Figured you'd think so." He took another long pull of beer.

Stella drank from her own beer, then sighed and a moment later lifted her bottle, arcing it in front of her, indicating the courtyard and its occupants. "You've built all this."

Yeah, shit was coming together. "Only the beginnin', baby."

"It's a good, solid start." She pulled away to face him. He pushed away from the post and once again smiled as she slipped her arms under his cut and around his waist. She planted her chin on his chest. "Putting Dodge in charge of the bar was a good move."

His brows raised as he tipped his beer to his lips once more. "So, you're finally admittin' it?"

"He's doing well."

"The bar's doin' better because of both of you," he corrected her.

"Like you, he had some good ideas."

"You had 'em, too."

"But I didn't have the money to implement them."

He simply answered, "Now you do," because this shit had been talked to death and while they weren't buried in cash, they weren't hurting, either. The more the businesses grew, the more the club grew, the bigger the bank accounts would grow.

If he had his way, not one of them would be hurting for money. Not just him and Stella. But all of them.

"Because of you."

"'Cause of us," he corrected her. "Partners, remember?"

He frowned because her eyes were no longer on him, but instead focused elsewhere. The hairs on the back of his neck prickled as she went stiff in his arms. Was she winding up for a fight?

"Partners in life, Stel," he repeated more firmly, expecting a response.

"Trip," she said under her breath, still staring past him.

His heart skipped a beat when he heard a deep, "Heard it once somewhere... If you build it, they will come," from over his shoulder.

Trip spun toward the voice, shoving Stella behind him, his hand automatically finding the butt of his gun at the small of his back. Before he had a chance to free it from his cut, the man standing before him in the shadows raised both palms up in surrender.

"Jesus. Didn't mean to fuckin' startle you."

He tucked the gun back in place. "Didn't," Trip lied. "Just can't be too careful."

"Imagine so," the man murmured, eyeing up Stella as she moved to Trip's side.

She fisted the back of his cut and tilted her head, giving the new arrival the same amount of eyeball he was giving her. "Sig," slipped past her lips.

It took Sig a few moments and Trip let him work it out on his own. "Goddamn," Sig murmured. "All grown up, Stella."

"So are you," she answered, but Trip could hear it in her voice: the question asking if the man actually acted as mature as he looked.

His mile-long rap sheet said otherwise.

But unless he was on the run and looking for a place to lie low, Trip had hope his half-brother was keeping his shit clean.

And by him showing up at the farm, Trip hoped Sig planned to keep his ass out of cuffs and off the pigs' radar.

"Just ridin' through?" Trip asked, dropping an arm around Stella's shoulders, making it clear to Sig that it was time for him to shift his eyes elsewhere.

Sig took in the arm that staked Trip's claim and finally turned his attention back to him. "Thinkin' I'd settle for a while."

A while. "Not lookin' for drifters. This ain't a motel," Trip said. "Lookin' for men wantin' to put down some roots."

Sig studied him for a long moment, his mouth tight, then he nodded. "I hear ya. Only time I've stuck in one place was when I was forced to." His whole adult life, Sig had spent more time in jail than out of it.

"Kept an apartment open for you, even though I ate a lotta shit about doin' so."

"From who?"

"Anyone who knows you or knows of you, Sig."

Sig cocked an eyebrow. "You figured I'd show."

No, brother, but I hoped you would. "Eventually. Long as your ass didn't land back behind bars," Trip said honestly. "Ain't gonna be easy, brother. This ain't some place you eat grub all day, eat pussy all night, and not pull your fuckin' weight. Ain't a resort."

Sig's chest rose and fell as his gaze slid from Trip to circle the courtyard. His eyes caught on something in the distance and stuck there while he asked, "Still need a fuckin' VP?"

He did, especially since Dutch bitched about being temporary VP at every meeting. *Hell*, every time he talked to the old man. But Trip now had second thoughts about handing over that spot to Sig. It was a powerful position to hand over to a possible loose cannon.

But he also wanted to mend fences with the man, rebuild what they used to have. And to do that, he'd need to trust Sig.

To a point, anyway. At least until Trip had more confidence that Sig wasn't going to self-combust, end up on some kind of crazy spree and drag the rest of them into it, destroying what Trip had been busting his ass so hard to build.

Again with a tight feeling in his gut, he said, "Yeah, brother, I do. But like I said, ain't gonna be an easy ride."

Sig's gaze finally hit his again and stuck. "Nothin' worth havin' is easy, brother."

No shit. Trip knew that only too well. But he wondered what was behind Sig's dark eyes when he said that. They'd been apart way too long and he could no longer read the man who turned out to be his real brother.

Half-brother. Same shit to him. Though, he wasn't sure if it meant the same to Sig.

With a chin lift, Trip extended his hand, hoping he wasn't making a mistake. If down the road, Sig bit the hand that was offered, Trip would kill his brother himself.

Sig slapped his palm into his and they bumped shoulders. "Welcome home," Trip murmured as he did so. "Welcome home," he repeated again, as he patted his brother on the back and glanced over Sig's shoulder at his woman.

He may not be able to read Sig any longer, but he could now read Stella like a fucking crystal ball and she looked as uncertain as Trip felt.

Time would tell whether this move would be one of Trip's fuck ups.

He hoped like hell it wasn't.

If it turned out to be, he'd rise up from those ashes again and start the fuck over.

Because stubborn fuck that he was, he refused to let the Blood Fury remain buried in those ashes.

And the Fury was in his blood and always would be.

Turn the page to read a sneak peek from
Blood & Bones: Sig
Blood Fury MC, book 2

Sneak peek of Blood & Bones: Sig

Turn the page for a sneak peek of
Blood & Bones: Sig
Blood Fury MC, book 2

Blood & Bones: Sig

Prologue

Awakening

SIG GROUND HIS TEETH, hoping it would help drown out the noise. The bed squeaking. The thumping of the headboard against the wall. The deep, loud grunts of the man between his mother's legs.

Years.

He'd heard it for years. Ever since he could remember.

He'd peeked in on them a few times when he was too young to know better. Not understanding what was going on.

Curious.

He'd quietly open the door just a crack and put his eye to the sliver of space.

Watching.

Wondering why the man was on top of his mother. Why they were both making those noises.

Why this happened so often.

But it did. A lot.

Anytime his father wasn't around.

Which was also a lot.

But he knew his father would come home later, usually after Sig was in bed, and do the same thing to his mother, too.

Only there wasn't as much noise. At least on his mother's part.

He'd also watched them a couple times.

Then one day he realized what they were doing.

What it all meant.

And for a while, he had a hard time looking his mother in the face.

A long time.

Eventually, he learned what they were doing because he'd watch the same type of thing happen in front of everyone at the warehouse, which was the Blood Fury's church, the clubhouse for his father's MC.

Other women. Other men. Lots of them.

He'd even seen his father do it right out in the open to women who weren't his mother.

Right there.

In front of everyone.

He wasn't the only one. In fact, sometimes there was a line-up. All his father's club brothers. Sticking their dicks into the same woman as she was held down on a table or over a barrel. And she'd be smiling and encouraging them.

At least most of them. Not all.

Some were awake, some weren't.

Some would leave after that and never return.

Others came back for more.

When he'd gotten older, his body began to react when watching it. And he wanted to stand in line, too.

Hell, he'd even watched his best friend get his cherry popped by one of those sweet butts. What he thought, at the time, was a nicer name for what he learned later was a club whore.

He'd been in the crowd that circled Trip and the sweet butt as Buck ordered the woman to spread her legs and let Trip nut inside her.

Trip did. And he'd only been fourteen.

Sig had been eleven at the time and hoped his father, Razor, would order the sweet butt to do the same for his own son.

He hadn't.

So, when his body would react, he would have to hide for a while until his painful erection went back down, or he'd end up making a mess in his underwear because he couldn't control it.

Once, one of the other women in the warehouse had noticed his discomfort and blown him a kiss, saying, "Whenever your daddy says it's okay."

Razor never did.

Because Razor didn't give a shit about his boy.

Not one shit.

Not like Buck did for Trip.

While Trip was his best friend, he also never told him that his father was coming over and screwing his mother.

Because he couldn't.

Buck had always warned him to keep his "fuckin' mouth shut." To keep the Blood Fury's president's visits to his mother a secret.

"You tell anyone, I'll fuckin' kill her, boy. You hear me? She wants it. Begs for my dick. That's the only reason I'm here. You say somethin' an' if I don't kill her first, your pop will." He had grabbed Sig's long hair, fisted it painfully and ripped his head back. "You fuckin' hear me?"

Sig had struggled not to cry out or show his fear. Because that was what Buck wanted. Buck liked people to be afraid of him. "Y-yeah."

"Not a goddamn word, boy."

In truth, Sig was afraid of Buck. Most everyone was.

Except for Sig's mother, Silvia. And maybe Trip's mother, Tammy.

Buck had a nasty temper and you didn't want it focused on you. Otherwise, you'd be hurting and that hurt would last a while.

Like the time Buck caught Sig watching a couple weeks ago. He'd rolled off his mother and within a couple strides, had a frozen Sig by his throat and thrown to the floor at the foot of the bed.

Sig was just glad the man wasn't wearing his boots. Otherwise, he might have ended up dead.

Instead, a naked Buck stomped on him a few times. In places Razor would never see. Sig's back, his stomach, his ribs, even his junk.

Sig had curled into a tight ball, trying to protect himself. When that didn't work, he struggled to crawl back out the door, clawing his way across the dirty, worn carpet.

Luckily, Buck let him go, still kicking Sig as he did his best to escape. And once he got near the open door, Buck kicked his ass right out of it, slamming it behind him and just missing Sig's foot.

Sig had laid in the hallway for the longest time, simply trying to breathe, trying to think, trying not to cry out loud.

But then he'd heard it again. The bed squeaking, his mother moaning, Buck calling her really dirty names between his grunts.

His mother had said nothing while Buck had kicked him. Never begged Buck to stop.

She just let him do it.

Later on, when asked, she'd answered, "You did wrong, you deserved what you got."

That was it.

Sig was so mad about that, he'd done something stupid.

Last time Buck was screwing his mother, he'd snuck into the room while they were busy, took the knife the club prez kept in his boot and hid it under his dad's jeans that had been left in a pile on the floor.

That was a week ago. And he was disappointed nothing came of it.

Razor never confronted Silvia. Or Buck. Not that he knew of, anyway.

If his dad had found the knife, he must not have thought anything of it. Or only thought it was his own.

But either way, eventually Sig would give Buck what he deserved. Even if he had to wait until he was older.

He wouldn't always be twelve. One day he'd be big enough, strong enough, to teach Buck a damn lesson he wouldn't be able to forget.

And then he'd take the club's top spot from him.

But that would be years from now, so he had to wait.

He had to suffer through listening to the bastard screwing his mother.

He had to suffer through hearing that bed make noise, as well as the two occupants.

He grimaced and covered his ears.

He could still hear them.

Buck screwing his mother. His mother letting the bastard do it. Encouraging him to give "it" to her harder. Faster.

He squeezed his eyes shut, took a deep breath and rolled off his bed. He needed to get out of the house. Needed to get away from them.

That bastard got what he wanted, whenever he wanted.

It was like Buck was king of the club.

He ruled them all.

And no one was going to stop him.

Sig vowed it would be him someday. Buck would pay.

He tagged his jeans from the floor and yanked them up his legs, pulling on the first shirt he came across. He snagged his sneakers as he went and threw open his door, trying to ignore those noises as he passed his mother's bedroom door.

"Asshole," he muttered under his breath as he kept rolling.

His feet stopped moving as the front door of their tiny house was flung open and his father came barreling through.

Finally!

Finally, his dad was going to stop Buck. Take him down a peg or two.

Before Sig could say anything, his dad shoved him out of the way and into the wall, not saying a word to him.

Like he wasn't even there.

Like Sig didn't even exist.

Like he was only in the way.

His mouth dropped open as he saw his father pull his Sig Sauer from under the back of his cut, lift his boot up and kick in the bedroom door, even though it wasn't locked.

It wasn't locked. Why did he have to kick it in?

Sig's feet unfroze and he quickly followed his father, now scared to death for his mother. "Ma!"

All that got him was a big hand to his chest and a painful shove backward. "Get outta here, kid," Razor yelled, raising the gun.

"But—"

The room was so small the sound exploded around him. He squeezed his eyes shut and fell to the floor, hearing nothing for the longest time.

Nothing but the ringing in his ears.

The acrid burn in his nostrils.

His heart escaping out of his chest.

He was afraid to open his eyes.

His father had killed his mother.

That was what he'd done.

That wasn't what was supposed to happen.

He forced his eyes open and all he could see was his mother's open mouth and her wide eyes as she screamed.

But Sig couldn't hear it.

He couldn't hear anything.

But he could see it.

Razor's .40 pointed to Silvia's head. And his beet red face, the angriest Sig ever saw him. His father's finger twitching dangerously on the trigger.

His mother wasn't dead, but she was about to die.

Just like the lifeless man lying naked on top of her. A hole dead center in his back. A dark red puddle spreading quickly over the dirty sheets beneath them both.

Sig's throat was raw because he was screaming. He just couldn't hear it.

He still couldn't hear shit.

But he could see it.

He could see his father raise that gun and strike her in the head with it.

Not once.

Not twice.

Too many times to count.

That wasn't supposed to happen.

He could barely hear his father bellowing, "Knew you were a fuckin' whore! Never shoulda made a whore like you my ol' lady."

Razor was only supposed to kick Buck's ass. Teach the bastard a lesson.

That was it.

Nothing more.

"See your fuckin' whore mother?" The shouted question sounded muffled over the loud ringing still in his ears.

But he heard it.

And, yeah, Sig saw her. He'd never be able to un-see her.

Naked and bloody, her distorted face swollen and split. Sig wasn't sure if she was still breathing.

"Ain't nothin' but filthy snatch. Here's a lesson for ya, don't make a cunt like that your ol' lady, kid."

His father spun on his boot and Sig never saw him again.

It wasn't until a few days later, he discovered he had witnessed the man he thought was his father shoot the man who turned out to be his real father point-blank. That was also when he agreed with Razor's opinion his mother was no better than a lying, cheating whore.

It wasn't until a few days later, the whole club imploded. Just like his family.

Ox, the club's enforcer, shot Razor dead right between the eyes. Then another member tried to take out Ox and failed.

When they thought things couldn't get worse, they did.

Brothers became enemies. Family became strangers.

And his best friend became blood.

Only by then, once he found out Trip was his half-brother, his best friend was long gone.

Get Sig's story here:
mybook.to/BFMC-Sig

If You Enjoyed This Book

Thank you for reading Blood & Bones: Trip. If you enjoyed Trip and Stella's story, please consider leaving a review at your favorite retailer and/or Goodreads to let other readers know. Reviews are always appreciated and just a few words can help an independent author like me tremendously!

Want to read a sample of my work? Download a sampler book here: BookHip.com/MTQQKK

Also by Jeanne St. James

*** Available in Audiobook**

Made Maleen: A Modern Twist on a Fairy Tale *

Damaged *

Rip Cord: The Complete Trilogy *

Brothers in Blue Series:

(Can be read as standalones)

Brothers in Blue: Max *

Brothers in Blue: Marc *

Brothers in Blue: Matt *

Teddy: A Brothers in Blue Novelette *

Brothers in Blue: A Bryson Family Christmas

The Dare Ménage Series:

(Can be read as standalones)

Double Dare *

Daring Proposal *

Dare to Be Three *

A Daring Desire *

Dare to Surrender *

A Daring Journey *

The Obsessed Novellas:

(All the novellas in this series are standalones)

Forever Him *

Only Him *

Needing Him *

Loving Her *

Temping Him *

Down & Dirty: Dirty Angels MC Series™:

Down & Dirty: Zak *

Down & Dirty: Jag *

Down & Dirty: Hawk *

Down & Dirty: Diesel *

Down & Dirty: Axel *

Down & Dirty: Slade *

Down & Dirty: Dawg *

Down & Dirty: Dex *

Down & Dirty: Linc *

Down & Dirty: Crow *

Crossing the Line (A DAMC/Blue Avengers Crossover) *

Magnum: A Dark Knights MC/Dirty Angels MC Crossover

Guts & Glory Series

(In the Shadows Security)

Guts & Glory: Mercy *

Guts & Glory: Ryder *

Guts & Glory: Hunter *

Guts & Glory: Walker *

Guts & Glory: Steel *

Guts & Glory: Brick *

Blood & Bones: Blood Fury MC™

Blood & Bones: Trip

Blood & Bones: Sig

Blood & Bones: Judge

Blood & Bones: Deacon

Blood & Bones: Cage

Blood & Bones: Shade

Blood & Bones: Rook

Blood & Bones: Rev

Blood & Bones: Ozzy

Blood & Bones: Dodge

Blood & Bones: Whip

Blood & Bones: Easy

COMING SOON!

Blue Avengers MC™

Everything About You (A Second Chance Gay Romance)

About the Author

JEANNE ST. JAMES is a USA Today bestselling romance author who loves an alpha male (or two). She was only thirteen when she started writing and her first paid published piece was an erotic story in Playgirl magazine. Her first erotic romance novel, Banged Up, was published in 2009. She is happily owned by farting French bulldogs. She writes M/F, M/M, and M/M/F ménages.

Want to read a sample of her work? Download a sampler book here: BookHip.com/MTQQKK

To keep up with her busy release schedule check her website at www.jeannestjames.com or sign up for her newsletter: http://www.jeannestjames.com/newslettersignup

www.jeannestjames.com
jeanne@jeannestjames.com

Blog: http://jeannestjames.blogspot.com
Newsletter: http://www.jeannestjames.com/newslettersignup
Jeanne's Down & Dirty Book Crew: https://www.facebook.com/groups/JeannesReviewCrew/

facebook.com/JeanneStJamesAuthor
twitter.com/JeanneStJames
amazon.com/author/jeannestjames
instagram.com/JeanneStJames
bookbub.com/authors/jeanne-st-james
goodreads.com/JeanneStJames
pinterest.com/JeanneStJames

Get a FREE Romance Sampler Book

This book contains the first chapter of a variety of my books. This will give you a taste of the type of books I write and if you enjoy the first chapter, I hope you'll be interested in reading the rest of the book.

Each book I list in the sampler will include the description of the book, the genre, and the first chapter, along with links to find out more. I hope you find a book you will enjoy curling up with!

Get it here: BookHip.com/MTQQKK

CPSIA information can be obtained
at www.ICGtesting.com
Printed in the USA
LVHW090417080621
689678LV00011B/66